CULMFIELD CUCKOO

Celia Moore

'...not easy to put down – so many twists and turns...'
Other Books by Celia Moore
Fox Halt Farm and A Hare's Footprint

Celia Moore

Copyright

Copyright © 2019 by Celia Moore. All Rights reserved. No portion of this book may be reproduced, stored in a retrieval system, or transmitted in any form or at any time or by any means, electronic, mechanical, photocopying, recording or otherwise, without the prior written permission of the publisher. The right of Celia Moore to be identified as the author of this work has been asserted by her in accordance with the Copyright, Designs and Patents Act 1988.

Contact Celia

Website Celiascosmos.com
Facebook Celia Moore Books

Dedication

Culmfield Cuckoo *is dedicated to my mother for her endless encouragement with all my endeavours and is also in memory of Crinkle.*

I want to recognise the support of Kate, Tracey (still championing my writing with the same thoughtfulness and generosity she has from the start) Peter and Jenny too.

My books wouldn't be written without the love, patience and understanding from my incredible husband – he has so much to put up with.

This book is for all my family, my friends, all those I have worked with and everyone who reads my books. Without each of these special people this sequel to Fox Halt Farm *would never have been written.*

Celia Moore

Prologue

CHARING CROSS POLICE STATION, ENGLAND
MONDAY 11 AUGUST 2008
BILLY MAY

My thoughts are so chaotic, I struggle to breathe. *If I'm sent to jail, will Fox Halt Farm need to be sold?*

'Richard, I'm sorry,' I whisper to the stark walls of this police interview room.

But inside, I'm *not* sorry about Michael, I won't regret the death of the man who has cast a shadow over my world for so long.

I think back over the events that brought me here, and a song starts to resonate through my mind.

Celia Moore

PART ONE

Celia Moore

Chapter 1

FOX HALT FARM, DEVON, ENGLAND
SATURDAY 26 JULY (16 DAYS BEFORE)
BILLY

'*My undying, death-defying love for you.*' These song lyrics still evoke the man who stole my breath away when I was just eighteen. A naive girl who believed she couldn't survive without him, but I did.

Twenty-two years later, and this anthem has a new place in my heart. 'The Power of Love' blasts through Richard's new home. It's our song now. The whole village must know there is a party tonight; the music is far too loud. Freddy insisted it was fine but how can anyone talk?

People squash into every nook of the cottage pushing us closer together in the pocket-sized entrance hall; '*Love with tongues of fire–*'

'Billy, will you be my wife?' Richard asks, but it is hard to hear. I frown at him, while delight crackles through my body. A tinge of annoyance too – *after all this time, he asks me here? Surely, he could have chosen somewhere romantic?*

I will let the song finish before I accept. I want to be certain he hears my answer. I'll lead my wonderful man outside into the farmyard first; I will say *yes* under the stars on this balmy hot night.

The front door swings against my back, making me turn from Richard's expectant face to see who has shoved it so hard.

The two latecomers hold hands. One is a striking young girl with long red curls but it's her mother who blasts away the joy I felt just seconds ago.

'Jessie!'

Jessica O'Rowde's dull eyes well up but there is no greeting, not even a smile. Instead, her fragile frame looks like it will give way. Instinctively I step forward to hold her, and Jessie's familiar smell of jasmine and roses catches in my throat.

I see the contrast of my toned and tanned arms against her snow-white skin. She is wrapped head to toe in magenta; her silk shirt contours each protruding rib and her matching bell-bottomed trousers emphasise her stick waist.

'Auntie Billy, can we stay tonight, please?' The girl lets go of Jessie's hand to grab my wrist. I remember Mary snatching at me like this when she was a toddler, and I picture her round freckled face looking up at me. I was her honorary aunt; her mother's best friend. Tonight though, our eyes are level; Mary is as tall as me, she must be thirteen years old.

'Darling girl, of course you can stay,' I reply. I feel Jessie's body tense up so Richard's contradictory words don't register at first. 'You need to go,' he says. His stern response conjures up Jessie's husband, Michael, into my mind, and this new thought runs a shiver along my spine.

Jessie turns to leave. 'No. Please, Jessie, stay,' I say, pulling her back.

'Billy, I don't want to be here.' Her response is icy. 'This was Mary's idea. We should never have come.'

'I wanted to see you, Auntie, and Fox Halt Farm wasn't far to come.' Mary hesitates, her cheeks colouring to match her mother's clothes. 'We didn't have enough money to go any further or enough to pay for somewhere to stay.'

I stare at Jessie but all she does is shrug at me. 'Come on,' I say, making my voice upbeat. 'I'll take you over to the farmhouse, we can talk there. You can tell me what's happened. And why you're here.'

Jessie nods but her eyes are focused on the floor. She continues to examine the ground as I shepherd her across the yard towards my home. Mary follows us.

'They must go first thing in the morning,' Richard calls out. He turns to Jessie. 'Where's your car?'

'What does it matter?' I snap back at him because I want him to be caring, he is usually so kind.

'I suspect Michael doesn't know where his wife and daughter are. Am I right, Jessie?' Richard asks, his words full of disdain.

'He doesn't know.' She hasn't looked up and her stance makes me think of a swan bending her graceful neck downwards to avoid the attention of a predator.

Richard is beside us now. 'If Michael turns up, I don't want Jessie's car confirming her whereabouts.' His eyes are slits, like a fox.

'It's okay, we came by taxi; Mum never drives,' Mary reassures him.

In the quiet and messy kitchen, I sit my reluctant visitor down, and I drop onto a mismatched chair beside her. I want to ask a hundred questions. I can't believe the way she looks, this is not the beautiful and self-assured woman I remember. 'What's happened, Jessie?' I ask.

She doesn't answer. Her gaze is now transfixed on our fat, orange cat who has just jumped onto her lap and is kneading her bones.

Eventually, she looks up. 'Billy, I'm tired. We'll talk in the morning.'

I touch her arm. 'I'm so sorry,' I tell her. I am not sorry that she is here, nor am I concerned about the reasons that might have brought her and her daughter to Fox Halt Farm tonight. I am full of remorse about what I did in the past, terrified that Jessie will never forgive my foolish affair with her husband.

RICHARD MARCFENN

The party started breaking up after Billy left with Jessie and Mary. It's a few minutes to midnight, Freddy and I are alone in our cottage, clearing up. *'I'll protect you from the hooded claw, Keep the vampires from your door–'*

'Turn that song off, please,' I call out. My son ignores me, acting like a stereotypical teenager; sulking because I messed up my marriage proposal to his potential new mum. This is not like him at all, often Freddy feels like the grown up in our relationship. Seemingly wise beyond his fifteen years. He was the one who insisted on changing schools at this crucial time, finding solutions to each of my concerns about moving to Devon.

My son just wanted us to live at the farm, so I could be close to Billy. He gets on well with her, and desperately wants me to be happy.

'Dad, you're an idiot. You've ruined everything.' This was the last thing he said to me tonight. Freddy asked why I was set against Jessie and Mary staying, but I couldn't tell him. My son and I usually talk through everything, but I can't explain. No good will come from dredging up the past.

Our housewarming was meant to be a surprise but I knew weeks ago. Billy tried to keep all her organising hush-hush; while she ironed out niggles with her new farm shop, promoted its grand opening, looked after the cows and ran her new dairy. However, I was wholly aware of her racing around making sure the celebration would be a success.

I don't think I would have realised what she was up to, but Billy's mother accidently told me about the plan; I assured Daniella that I wouldn't let on, and Freddy and I did our best to look surprised. But as the first guest arrived, Billy said, 'You knew, didn't you?'

'No,' I protested.

'Mum told you, didn't she?'

'Yes, Daniella…'

Billy smiled. 'My dear mum is hopeless at keeping secrets,' she said, starting to giggle, an infectious laugh that is a bit too loud. I couldn't help joining in, and laughter filled the cottage until Jessie and Mary arrived.

If only I had stuck to my plan to ask Billy to marry me next week. It is all sorted so we can be away for a few days; a paradise break for us. My late mother's sapphire ring hidden in my luggage, ready for my romantic proposal on a faraway beach. Asking for Billy's hand in marriage is all I've been thinking about for weeks, and I couldn't resist popping the question sooner. It was such a happy moment, with all our friends around us and our song playing. Everything seemed perfect, but how I wish I had waited.

Billy and I are supposed to leave for our holiday in the morning, but now as I stop the music, apprehension fills my stomach.

Fox Halt Farm
Sunday 27 July
Billy

It is a relief to get up, even though it is just four in the morning and I have hardly slept. As I dress, I think how hard it will be to leave the farm to go on holiday. Normally, my home, the shop, the animals and the dairy consume every moment of my life, it is hard to let go.

To begin with, I was cross with Richard for booking a special holiday for us both; I didn't see how I could leave the farm, but everyone has been incredible; with family and friends volunteering to take on extra work and responsibilities.

I have mixed feelings still – worrying about leaving everyone to look after things here, contradicting my excitement about going away with Richard.

I check the instructions I have written to ensure everything runs smoothly with the cows and cheese-making while I am away. Then I make a new to-do list for the farm shop. My new venture has only been open for a month, so I am going to have to rely on my manager, as well as my mother, to make sure everything stays on track for the next few days. The shop took nearly three years to set up and Richard helped me every step of the way; my sounding board with honest feedback always at the ready.

Richard provided half the start-up cost too; giving me a loan from some of the funds from the sale of his own company. He said he didn't want the money back, but I insisted on a proper business contract, guaranteeing to repay every penny within six years. The cows weren't making enough money to sustain Fox Halt Farm, so we built a new dairy too. Thankfully, making cheese from our milk is proving profitable.

Mum discovered an old Devon cheese recipe that we adapted slightly because today's milk is creamier than the milk cows produced years ago. Our Foxy Lady cheese won a major competition last month which boosted sales further. We have also developed a yoghurt with locally sourced, in-season fruit, and we are finding it hard to keep up with demand at the moment.

On top of all this, two weeks ago I started developing a new soft cheese, but Mum and I are struggling to agree on the texture and taste our customers will like the most. Experimenting and recording each little variation is taking hours but we are following the same processes we used to create the cheese and yoghurt, and that method worked out well before. We keep on sampling and agree that there must be worse jobs.

I haven't spent time away from Fox Halt for years, so milking the cows this morning takes ages. I give each of my ninety-eight black and white animals special attention. I lecture William Westcott about all the crucial things he must remember while I'm on holiday. This is wholly unnecessary because William stands in for me once a week already. He lives on the farm next door and has been coming here since he was small, when his father used to help me.

William politely agrees to remember everything I remind him about. He's keen to help, and he understands I am nervous about leaving everything to him. It is the school summer holidays too, so I am sure he will be pleased to have the extra money.

When I am not badgering my stand-in, I chitter to all the animals, trying to keep my mind off Jessie, but it's not working. Richard is right; she and Mary should not be here, but I felt quite unable to turn them away last night.

I have longed to see my friend again, to explain my reasons for betraying her trust.

Jessie is exactly the same age as me, born on the same day and also in Devon, but we didn't meet until we were twenty-five. That was just before she married Michael. We said we felt like twins, saying we were the other half of each other, but that was before I messed it all up between us.

We both had our fortieth birthdays last month, but last night, the way Jessie looked was as much of a shock for me as seeing her again; she's aged and was so subdued. Her daughter too; she was a real daredevil like her mother. I used to call her Mad Mary... always a chatterbox but last night, the firebrand was muted. The pair felt like strangers.

As I walk towards the farmhouse, Jessie watches me from the kitchen window. Her blank expression gives no indication that she is aware of my approach. I avoid staring at her, looking down at my feet. I sniff the arid air, the acidic smell of the cows stings at my nostrils a little.

Just inside the door, I kick off my wellington boots. 'Morning,' I say, trying to sound sociable and happy, as if Jessie waits for me every morning.

There is no reply. I try to follow my normal routine because I don't know what else to say. I am desperate for a mug of tea and some breakfast. Usually at this time of day, as I slam the front door, Mum is ready to put a drink and a bacon sandwich in front of me. But this isn't a normal morning, and there is no sign of my mother or my breakfast.

'Would you like a drink, Jessie?' She shakes her head. It was like this last night; Jessie helped me in silence to make up a bed, then I showed them the bathroom and left.

There were no explanations, other than they were both tired and we could talk this morning.

'I found her in her bedroom yesterday, packing a suitcase.' Jessie's bottom lip quivers so much, I struggle to hear.

'Sorry?' I ask.

'Mary, she'd booked a taxi and she was about to run away from home, so I made her agree I could go with her. She won't tell me what's wrong.' Jessie stops and looks away. Minutes seem to pass.

Our Border terrier, Crinkle, is sitting by Jessie's feet and the dog starts scratching under her chin, so violently and noisily, that I wonder if she is feeling uncomfortable too.

'What about your sons, Jessie? What about Arthur, Mikey and little Max?' I ask.

She looks up at me, fixing her eyes on mine. 'I couldn't let Mary go on her own. She was mad as hell.'

'But she won't tell you why she wanted to leave?'

'No.'

'Where was Michael when you left?' I check quickly, reluctant to mention his name, assuming he must be on a business trip, but then I reconsider. *Was he out riding?* I know he is a man of routine; when I lived at Culmfield, he and I used to ride every Saturday morning, taking our horses around the boundary of the six-thousand-acre estate, always the same route.

For a moment, the memory makes me feel peaceful; I used to look forward to our rides. Back then there was nothing between us, just friendly companions relishing the ever-changing seasons and the beauty of the place; the fallow deer herd and the River Culm that meandered through the grounds.

'Paintball,' she coughs.

'Paintball?'

'Yes.' Jessie scoops up Wallace, the fat ginger cat, holding on to him like a comfort cushion. 'Michael and the boys were at a paintball birthday party, so I left a note, saying we will be back tomorrow night.'

I picture him screwing up the paper in his fist. 'Jessie, did you say where you were going?'

She shakes her head.

'Do you want to ring him?' I ask.

'No, he'll fetch us back!' Her eyes widen.

'Okay, okay.' I try to sound soothing.

Jessie doesn't seem reassured. She tells me, 'I have to find out why Mary was running away. I am worried it's something he's done.'

'He would never hurt Mary?' I frown.

'No, I don't think he would either.' Jessie stares into my eyes. 'Mary says he hasn't hurt her, but I'm unsure about it. Michael may have caused her to leave.'

I reach out to touch her hand, and when she doesn't pull away, a tiny spark ignites inside me; a small hope that we might be friends again one day.

Richard comes into the kitchen, he looks worn out. His lightly tanned skin looks sallow. His blond hair – sprinkled with grey around his ears – has not been brushed. 'I have booked a taxi for Jessie and Mary. They have half an hour to leave,' he says, walking across the room to sit at the table.

'Mary isn't even up yet,' I reply sharply, enraged that he is continuing to be unpleasant. I don't kiss him good morning, nor do I check if he's slept. I don't ask if he enjoyed his party or tell him how much I want to marry him.

'Fetch her then.' His tone softens, but I still hear agitation. 'Billy, are you going to be ready to leave at ten?'

'I am not going on holiday,' I reply. 'Jessie and her daughter are staying right here. They are not leaving Fox Halt Farm. I'm not either.' I feel tense too, unaccustomed to Richard disagreeing with me. He always lets me have my own way. I want to make him realise how important it is to me that Jessie is here. I am also a little agitated that he walked in on us just as I thought, my former best friend was beginning to open up to me. 'They need me. They are staying,' I tell him, taking it for granted that Richard will accept my demand.

I see him flinch. Suddenly, I feel guilty about how much we have been looking forward to our holiday; precious time together in the place where we first met twenty-two years ago.

'What's going on, Jessie?' he asks. Richard is sitting directly opposite her and I watch as he leans towards her.

'Why don't you want us here?' Jessie replies quickly.

I don't want him to tell her the truth so I quickly reply instead. 'Richard thinks this is one of the first places Michael will come looking for you. He doesn't think Fox Halt Farm is the best hide-out.'

'Yes,' Richard agrees, 'Think of somewhere else to go, Jessie. Somewhere your husband doesn't know about. The taxi can take you anywhere you like, I'll pay, and I'll pay for somewhere nice for you to stay. Stay there as long as you like, but you *have* to go.' He doesn't take his eyes off Jessie. 'Billy, please get Mary.'

'Alright,' I say, deciding that it is exhaustion, and how upset Richard is about me not going on holiday that is making him so hostile. I find Mary at the bottom of the stairs.

'Don't let Mum take me back. I never want to be at Culmfield again.' Her voice cracks and her eyes are pleading. I feel like the auntie I used to be.

'Darling, can you tell me what's wrong?' I say, hugging her.

Mary wraps an arm around me, squeezing tight, but she doesn't say a word. It is as though neither of us wants to let go. It is my mother who finally separates us. I am not sure where Mum was before. 'Mary, you and your mum can stay here as long as you like,' she says, smiling. 'It will be good to have company while Auntie Billy and Richard are away on their holiday.'

'Thank you.' Mary looks like she might cry.

My mother scans me up and down. I am still wearing my grubby milking clothes. I know what she is going to say before she says it. 'Billy, go and get ready to leave.' Her instructions remind me of all the times I was late for the school bus because I spent too much time with my horses. She was always nagging me to hurry up.

'It's okay, Mum, I am not going anywhere, I'm staying here with Jessie and Mary. I'm going to make sure they're alright.'

'Is that your final decision, Billy? No holiday?' Richard calls out from the kitchen.

'Yes,' I am close to shouting. 'No holiday.' When he doesn't respond I assume my ever supportive and wonderful Richard, the man I am going to marry, has accepted my decision, finally understanding that I want to have this one chance to mend my relationship with Jessie. I feel sure his love for me is unwavering, and he realises that we can go on holiday some other time. We have the rest of our lives to be together.

I see through the window that a taxi has arrived in the farmyard. Jessie and Mary spot the car too, and they rush to the front door. I suspect they are unnerved by Richard and me arguing, both keen to scarper.

'Thank you all,' Jessie says.

'Thank you, Auntie, and er…Mrs…' Mary looks at my mother, she is not sure what to call her.

'Daniella,' Mum tells her.

'Thank you.' Mary pauses and in a little voice, conveying discomfort about using my mother's first name, she says, 'Daniella.'

'No, Jessie,' I say, blocking the door. 'You can't go. I'm not going to abandon you again. Richard doesn't really mind.' I glance at him, then I turn to Mary. 'Maybe you will talk to me, or Richard, perhaps? He's a very good listener.'

'Billy. You mustn't get involved. Let them go.' Richard shakes his head.

We have been through so much together, and if anyone asked, we would say we never argue and constantly help each other. He is always there for me, ready to discuss anything. We laugh and we love each other. Disagreeing with him is tearing me up, but I owe Jessie.

'Please send the taxi away,' I say, feeling confident I will win Richard over.

'You're not coming to Paros?' he checks again.

'No,' I reply, yearning for Jessie to forgive me; years ago, I chose Michael over our close friendship, but now, I hope Jessie sees I am opting for her over Richard. In truth, I am not choosing her, because I know he will come around. But now, the man, who I believe I know better than myself shakes his head. 'In that case, Billy,' he says, 'I'll spend this week with Marcus in Cornwall. He's been badgering me to look at a new housing scheme, and it will be good to see him. I'll come back when Jessie and Mary are gone.'

It is as though he has hit me. I rethink everything: Richard was awake all night, just like me. We were both guessing at reasons why Jessie came to the farm, both haunted by a terrible secret, knowing her presence could endanger us all. Richard must have planned his options too, but he has made a different choice.

He may be right, mine could be a dangerous decision, but I won't send Jessie and Mary away, it's too late for that.

I watch him hand the taxi driver some cash, and then the vehicle leaves empty of passengers. Then Richard drives away too. Not even a smile, or a goodbye.

Chapter 2

FOX HALT FARM

BILLY

Mum heads to the dairy, but not to work, I'm sure she is escaping the uneasy atmosphere in the kitchen.

We don't make anything from our milk at weekends, instead the milk is stored in a huge refrigerated tank until Monday. There are two reasons for the weekly shutdown: firstly, we need a break, and secondly, most Saturdays and Sundays we sell our products at local shows and farmers' markets. These outlets have proved to be a great way to find new customers, and a chance to chat to potential new buyers and explain what we do.

There are other factors too; the Foxy Lady cheese takes six months at least to mature, so anything we make now will be ready for the quietest time of our year; just after Christmas, when our customers have fridges still stuffed with special goodies they bought for a festive indulgence. Also, January and February are the months when everyone's New Year resolution is a diet, and unfortunately, so far, no-one has come up with a study finding that cheese helps weight loss, but I live in hope.

My holiday is another reason we cut back production. Mum is eighty-one years old, and even though she seems as fit as a fiddle, I want to avoid putting too much pressure on her while I am away.

There are two ladies from the village who come in on weekdays to help in the dairy, but Mum loves the cheese-making, so she finds lots of jobs to do which aren't too strenuous for her. The 'Hamsgate Honeys,' as the ladies have nicknamed themselves, are always chatting while they work, so that makes it enjoyable for Mum too. The moment Richard drove away, she went to hide, and I don't blame her one bit.

Indoors, none of us are talking, all too scared to start a conversation for fear of opening wounds.

I decide to break the phoney quiet because to me, the silence is worse than a potential quarrel. 'I'm having a cup of tea. Do you want one, Jessie? Mary, what would you like?' I ask.

Wallace is flat out on Mary's lap and Crinkle is annoying the cat with a tennis ball, which she has dribbled out of her mouth onto Wallace's outstretched legs. The terrier hopes to provoke a game, but the cat is resolute; he is not going to move, ignoring both the dog and its ball. Mary is engrossed in the animal antics, so she doesn't look at me. 'A cup of tea please, Auntie,' she replies. Crinkle seems to understand, she turns her pretty brown and black head to me, licking her top lip. It's as though the dog wants tea too.

I am surprised at Mary. *Do thirteen-year-old girls drink tea?* But then, what do I know about her? I haven't had anything to do with her for years. From the moment she was born, and for the first five years of Mary's young life, I felt like her second mother. I couldn't have children, so she became my beautiful surrogate daughter. Back then I lived at Culmfield, and her mum and I were inseparable. That's was before I double-crossed my way out of their lives.

'Nothing for me, thank you,' Jessie says, cutting through my thoughts. 'I'm going to ring Michael and ask him to pick us up.'

'Can't you leave it for a while?' I ask. 'As soon as he knows where you are, he'll come. Why don't you let Mary have some time to talk things through with you?' I look at the girl. 'She might talk to me?' I say.

Mary keeps her head down; just like Wallace, who is still paying no attention to the dog.

Jessie follows my lead. 'It's always good to talk, don't you think?' she asks me, speaking loudly.

'Definitely,' I agree but Mary still doesn't react.

'Okay, Billy, I won't ring him yet,' Jessie says, her eyes fixed on her daughter.

'May I go and see how the cheese is made?' Mary asks, and I realise this is the best idea yet, my mother can get anyone to confide in her. 'Yes, sweetheart, of course you can,' I reply.

'Thank you, Auntie. I'll have the drink later.' Mary transfers the cat to her mother's knees.

'Come on then,' I say.

Inside the dairy, I kit Mary out with wellington boots, my protective white coat, hat and hairnet. My mother is thrilled to see her visitor and immediately steers her away. 'I'll show you everything,' she tells Mary. 'I have a little job you can help me with.'

The white coats walk away without another word. My mother is as mad with me, as Richard is; not because I wanted Jessie and Mary to stay. Mum's anger is rooted in me not going on holiday. She adores her would-be-son-in-law. She was as excited as I was when Richard said he would move into one of our holiday cottages. In her diplomatic way, she didn't say how she would have preferred him and Freddy to live with us in the farmhouse. My mother always stays on the side-lines of our relationship, she's been our cheerleader for years, never a referee.

Mum has seen our tears and witnessed much of our winding parallel lives, which sometimes crossed paths, but never quite merged. That was until three years ago, when Richard and I finally got together. My mum has been our steadfast supporter and confidante. She is my rock and Richard's too, especially when his mother died, and through his divorce, ready to listen whenever needed.

My mother says Richard is always more open than I am. It's true, I hold on to secrets, varnishing over anything bad, shielding her from my disastrous choices and in doing so, I usually cause her more grief.

•

It's a triangle of love and support. Richard was there for me when I was hiding away from my first love disaster. He was there for Mum when I was taking my misery out on my family. During the foot and mouth crisis, he kept in touch with my parents. He was instrumental in making our beloved Fox Halt Farm viable too.

The farm has been in my mother's family for generations, and Richard is a major reason why we still have the Friesian cows, whose bloodlines were established by my great-great-grandfather. We do all love each other, and I understand why Mum is mad at me for letting Richard leave on his own.

My empty stomach rumbles as I walk back into the kitchen, and I wonder if Jessie will have some breakfast with me, but then my mind starts thinking about what might be happening at her home.

'Jessie, your boys, can Michael look after them? Can he even get them a meal?' I ask her.

'You should know if my husband can cook,' Jessie spits her reply, 'you were with him long enough. When he was away during the week; while he was working in London, I know he was with you every night.' Her fury subsides as quickly as it fired up. Her tone is quieter now. She pinches at her arm. 'The boys will be fine; Nala will look after them all.'

'Nala? Your chauffeur's wife? She and Amir are still at Culmfield?' My words catch in my throat as I try to avoid further mention of Michael and me. My actions were devious; I want to explain how it happened, but I can't think how to start.

'Yes, they are still in The Gatehouse,' Jessie replies.

'Nala helps you a lot?' I ask. I have been trying to work out how this fragile woman was coping. Mary and Arthur were always full of mischief, and I am sure Mikey and Max are equally hard to manage.

'What about Charlotte, does she help too?'

'Not really, Charlotte sticks to looking after the ponies and horses. She'd help if I asked but you know she was never really that fond of children.'

'Yes, she said she never wanted them,' I agree.

'Nala is my rock.' Jessie breathes in a deep sigh. 'I don't know what I'd do without her. She'll be fussing around them all now.'

'Jessie ...' I stop. I want to tell her how sorry I am for what I did, but no words seem big enough to express my remorse.

'What?' Jessie's hollow black eyes bore into me, making me feel even more of a traitor.

'Do you have pictures of the boys on your phone?' I say, changing the subject because I have lost my nerve. 'I'd love to see them. I expect you have one of these smart new iPhones that Richard keeps telling me I need. He says they are great for photos.'

'No, Billy, I don't have a mobile phone. I don't need one.'

I am not sure what to say next; the way Jessie confronted me about my affair with Michael makes me wish I had sent her away. I have wanted her forgiveness for so long, but now I feel I'll never win her trust back.

I should be heading for Gatwick with my fiancé to fly away on the most romantic holiday. *How many years have I dreamt about being with Richard?* Yet I chose a selfish desire for forgiveness over my future husband. I must make this up to him. I press my pocket to check my mobile phone is inside.

'I have to make a quick call,' I tell Jessie as I open the door to go outside.

'Okay,' she says.

Richard does not answer, I try again and then again. Eventually, I leave a voice message. And now a text. *'Darling, I'm so, so sorry – I've made a stupid and heartless mistake. I'll get J and M to go – I love you so much. I'll come and find you and we'll spend the rest of the holiday time together – I just want to be with you. I'm sorry with all my heart xxxxxx.'*

I wait five minutes for an answer, telling myself he is driving, so he can't reply straightaway.

More minutes go by.

I want to give him time to reply, and I don't want to go back inside the house – my confidence about explaining to Jessie why I had an affair with her husband, and telling her how much I regret it, has evaporated.

I expected Jessie and I would argue, and then talk about what happened. I imagined us both crying and clearing the air. I felt we were so close before that I could sort this out, but now, I see that things are different.

Mary is on the steps of the dairy, and I walk across to her. I see she is smoking.

'My mother is a wreck,' Mary tells me, before exhaling some of the smoke towards me, keeping her lips purposefully apart to maximise the time the smoke rolls out of her mouth. 'Dad has destroyed her – You shouldn't have left us, Auntie,' she says. I find myself analysing her behaviour; it's a throwback from my university days and endless discussions about psychology. I watch people for the unconscious signs they give away about their feelings. I look at Mary and the smoky trail in the air. I notice her jerky movements, and as I recognise her turmoil, my heart goes out to her.

'Sorry, Mary, I wasn't there for you and your mum,' I say, and the guilt about how I messed things up for her too makes my insides churn over. I selfishly deserted them both. I want to ask Mary what happened to make her decide to run away from Culmfield, but at the same time, I don't want to push her.

'You shouldn't be smoking,' I say, hoping it will start a conversation between us.

She smiles but it doesn't reach her eyes. I can't help wondering if something I did years ago has led to her being so upset; so distraught that she felt she had no choice but to leave her beautiful home.

I am losing control – I haven't slept, and the distress I have caused with Richard, Mum and Jessie spills out into the single question I know I shouldn't ask. 'Why were you running away, Mary?'

She pins her emerald eyes on mine. She doesn't blink. 'Not saying,' she replies, dropping her cigarette and squashing it with the toe of her boot, before heading back inside the dairy. I watch her and Mum through the window, wishing Mary would come back to talk to me, but she doesn't.

I check my phone again. Richard heading to Cornwall is a shock. He has been there for me for such a long time, I am not sure how I will manage without him. I tell myself he has no signal at the moment, and I turn to go indoors again.

Jessie meets me at the front door, she is wearing the same outfit from yesterday, but she has stuffed the flared trousers inside a pair of wellies. They are my boots, stained with cow muck. Jessie looks so out of place that I try not to laugh. I imagine she is not wearing socks and I dread to think how slimy her feet must feel. 'I fancy a walk. It's a shame to be inside,' she tells me.

'Can I come with you?' I ask, fixing my eyes on a large bottle of cider she is clutching, which she must have taken from the fridge.

'If you want,' she shrugs.

'Yes,' I say, not commenting on the bottle. It's just before eleven, and too early for alcohol, but I wonder if drinking is a crutch for her now. It's so hot that the sanctuary of the cool kitchen seems more appealing than a walk, but Jessie has never been to Fox Halt Farm, so I can show her around.

In the past, I spent hours trying to describe the place where I grew up to Jessie. She can see all the animals and we can talk. I have a little hope that while we are walking, I might be able to explain my affair. I know Michael will have lied to his wife, just like he deceived me. He will have told her I seduced him, and he ended it because he realised how much he loved her. Facing up to what I did is so hard, but I can't hide from it anymore.

'Jessie,' I say. 'Can I suggest you lose the wellington boots? I'm sure you'll have painful blisters on your heels within minutes. I'll give you some trainers to wear instead.'

Jessie doesn't say anything as she kicks off my boots.

'Wait here, and I'll fetch the shoes,' I tell her.

I kit Jessie out with trainers, socks and shorts. We used to be the same size and same height, as well as the same age but now my shorts are much too big for her, and I have to find her a belt as well, which nearly wraps around her twice.

As we set off, I don't know how to start to explain. There are many times when I think of an opening line but then dismiss it, so we walk without words, side by side across the fields. The only noise is our feet crunching parched grass, and sloshing cider.

Most of the sheep ignore us but a few of the curious ones stop eating, look up for a moment, and then start munching again. The cows are lying down in the shade of three oak trees, chewing their cud. They are not really bothered by anything, except an occasional horsefly. We climb to the top of a small rounded hill, the highest place on the whole of the farm.

We sit on the bare earth at the top, thankful that the single tree there provides a little shade.

'This is my favourite place on the farm,' I say, and then I keep talking, relieved to have at last broken the silence. 'You get the best view of Dartmoor, Yes Tor and High Willhays from here. In the spring, we'd be surrounded by primroses – hence its name, Primrose Mound.' I dry up, not knowing what to say next.

My companion screws off the top of the cider and lets the fizzy yellow liquid spill into her mouth before handing me the bottle.

'How could you?' she asks.

I take the bottle and start to glug the cool drink, delaying the answer. But then, some of the excuses I had been considering start to bubble up like the cider.

'Michael was there for me when Saffi committed suicide. My darling Ed had just deserted me too, and Michael really seemed to care. He looked after me. He was thoughtful, in the same way he was when I lost Richard's baby.'

'Right.'

'He understood what I was going through. I believed that Michael's mother had killed herself too, so he could really empathise with my loss, when Saffi died.'

Jessie's stern look, makes me feel I need more reasons, but she doesn't let me speak again. 'You had me too,' she says, 'you could have come home to Culmfield when Saffi died. I would have been there for you too. You always said I knew you better than anyone. I would have–'

'But I hated you, Jessie. You didn't tell me about Grégoire and Charlotte, and if I had known about those two, I might have talked to Saffi. I might have stopped him killing himself and my wonderful friend would still be alive.'

'I wish I had told you, Billy.'

'And I wish I hadn't turned to Michael, but I was devastated; I can still see Saffi lying in that bloody water.'

I swig more cider. Tiredness and lack of breakfast add to its potency, I already feel its dulling effect.

'Do you still love him?'

'I'll always love Saffi; he was a brilliant friend…'

'I mean Michael,' she says.

'No, no,' I tell her, horrified that she thinks I might still love her husband, but then I realise Jessie is unaware of Michael's actions. I can't tell her what he did, so I spin the truth. 'I don't think I ever truly loved him. I always knew he was your husband. He was there for me and he cared. I've only ever loved Richard, but Richard was determined to save his marriage – he wanted to be with his children. Richard was unattainable. Michael was not, your husband was always generous, and I loved all the attention he gave me.'

Jessie ploughs her manicured fingernails into her thighs, pressing so hard that I expect her to draw blood. 'Michael told me you went crazy when he ended it.'

'Michael told you that *he* ended the affair?' I emphasise 'he', like a hissing cat; *'heeeee ended the affair?'* 'That's wrong, Jessie, *I* ended the relationship.' I look into her eyes hoping she will believe me.

Jessie turns away. 'That's why you came to Culmfield that day; you wanted to make sure I knew, and you begged Michael to leave me. I saw you, Billy. I saw you both, don't you remember?'

I am determined to make her listen. 'No, Jessie. I hated him. He deceived me, and I was confronting him about all his lies. I wanted to destroy his seemingly perfect life with you. It's true, I did want you to know about us, but it was for revenge, not to beg him to leave you. I hate Michael; he's evil. I wish he was dead, not Tom–' I stop, I have made a mistake.

Remembering the row with Michael has stoked up anger inside me. It is just like the mania that consumed my whole body when I went to Culmfield to confront him; all the hatred I felt about the way he had manipulated me.

'*You* finished it?' Jessie stares into my eyes, trying to ascertain I'm telling her the truth.

I nod.

'So, Billy, what has Tom Westcott's death got to do with your affair? Your friend Tom, that's who you meant, didn't you?'

I ignore her questions, I need to lead her away from this direction. 'Yes, I finished it,' I say. 'You have to believe me, Jessie. I am truly, truly sorry about the affair.'

'You suddenly felt guilty, did you? Cheating with your best friend's husband?'

'I wish it was like that, but it wasn't. Something happened that made me see that Michael is a control freak. He wielded power over everything I did. He is doing the same to you. Don't you see?'

'What happened?' Jessie asks quickly. 'Something with Tom? Tell me.'

She is backing me into a corner, so I try another tack to avoid telling her about my friend.

'Before our affair started, I was seeing a man called Ed Mackintosh, but Michael was jealous of him, and he secretly threatened my lover out of my life. He told Ed he must never see me, or talk to me again, or there would be serious consequences for him and me.'

'So how did you find out Michael sent him away?'

'Because two years later, I saw Ed again, and I started seeing him behind your husband's back.'

'Two-timing Michael, that was dangerous.'

'It was platonic, I just loved my time with Ed, we went on long walks together twice a month, while Michael was home with you at weekends.'

'Did Michael find out – did he hurt him?'

'No, he didn't find out about us, but he did kill him.' My voice breaks up, remembering my wonderful vibrant Ed dying in front of me.

Jessie shakes her head. 'Explain, Billy,' she says.

'Your husband found Ed a job with one of his companies in Dubai – he made him take on the role, leaving straightaway. Michael even took him to the airport to make sure he left.'

'Did the plane crash?' she asks.

'No, Jessie. It was heroin and cocaine which slowly killed Ed. Michael forcing him to break up with me triggered his addiction. Five years later the drugs had completely wrecked his body, he was paranoid at times and no-one, not me, his family, or friends could stop him. He died in the most horrible way. That's why I came to Culmfield that day, that's why I ended the affair. Ed died as I held his hand but just before, he told me how Michael had sent him away. I realised the truth and Michael's ruthlessness. Do you understand what I'm talking about?'

'Yes, I think so,' she says.

'Why do you let him take control?' I ask. 'Look, he's killing you too. Where's the vibrant woman I used to know?'

Jessie hunches over, pressing her nails into her thighs again. She rocks back and forth. 'I see it now, Billy. I am seeing it for the first time. I realise what he has done to me. Finding Mary about to leave woke me up to it. I don't want him to drag her back to Culmfield. Not until I know what's wrong with her.'

'Drag her?' I frown.

'Yes, she'll have no choice, and Michael won't be pleased about my disappearance either. He has to know where I am all the time. I hardly leave the house these days.'

'Jessie, I was blind, selfish and thoughtless. I regret what I did with all my heart.'

'All your heart?'

'Every bit of it, and I regret not coming to see you and telling you the truth about our affair. I should have saved you from that murderer.'

'That *what*?'

I think quickly. 'It's the cider, sorry, I meant manipulator.'

'Billy, you meant what you said. Tell me.'

'Michael manipulates everyone, that's what I meant.'

'Murderer.' She shakes her head. '*That's* what you said.'

She knows I am lying. 'Just believe me, Jessie, I intended to say manipulator.'

'If Michael killed someone you have to tell me. I have seen how angry he can get. For Christ's sake, Billy, we have four children and they wind him up sometimes, he could hurt them too. You have to tell me. Tom Westcott? Did Michael murder him? Was Tom's death not an accident?'

I trying to work out why Jessie is so convinced that Michael might have been responsible for Tom's death. Everything feels unclear, the alcohol and everything that's happened since Jessie came to Fox Halt Farm is muddling me. I look up at Jessie. 'Please stop, I can't say anything more. Please, Jessie,' I say. 'Please stop asking.'

'So, you will let me go back to Michael, knowing it's not safe.'

The woman I remember is confronting me now. I recognise the determination in Jessie I knew from years before. My relief at seeing her like this gives me faith in the return of our old friendship. I am desperate to have her back, and I think maybe desperation makes me tell Jessie the secret I have kept for so long. In a way, it is a relief to say it out loud. 'You're right,' I say. 'Tom's death was not an accident, I don't know if he meant to kill him, or if it happened when they were arguing, but I'm sure Tom Westcott's death was caused by Michael.'

There is silence now. I stare out across the yellow field and notice how the sheep have moved into the only shade they can find; the animals have formed a thin white line tight against the distant hedge.

'Why would Michael have hurt Tom?' Jessie asks.

'Did you know Tom and his wife separated?'

'No.'

'After the foot and mouth crisis.'

'No, I didn't know, but what has that got to do with Michael?'

'I need to start at the beginning if you're to understand.'

'Okay.'

'Tom's wife, Martha, was a vet, and she couldn't come to terms with everything she'd seen and done during the foot and mouth crisis. I am sure you can imagine how the cull affected everyone, can't you?'

Jessie nods at me.

'When the outbreak was over, Martha said she wanted to be on her own for a while; a temporary split from Tom. He did what she asked – he moved out and their children lived with him half the time. When Michael went home to you at weekends, I used to come back to Hamsgate to see Mum, and sometimes I helped Tom with the cows. We were friends. That's all we were.'

'Alright, Billy,' Jessie says. 'Tom and you were just friends. Go on.'

'*Good* friends. Just like we had been all our lives, growing up together on our neighbouring farms. But when Michael found out that I was spending time with Tom, his jealousy got the better of him yet again.'

I touch her hand. 'You know how Michael always makes things go his way. I think he planned to frighten Tom, so he wouldn't see me again. I don't believe he meant to kill him. Michael shoved him, and Tom got caught up in the machinery, but he made no attempt to save my friend. Michael left him to die.'

Jessie pulls her hand away. 'Were you there?'

'I wasn't, I didn't realise until much later. I thought like everyone else, it was a terrible farm accident, but I slowly started piecing things together.'

'So what proof do you have, Billy?' Jessie shakes her head. 'Why didn't you tell the police?'

'There was little evidence,' I reply.

'So, you're just pinning this on Michael. You think another person in your life dies, and therefore it must be his fault, is that it?' Jessie stands up.

'Please hear me out,' I say, holding my hands out to her. 'Sit down again.'

She kneels next to me. 'Convince me then,' she says.

'Michael's jealousy was his motive, and his car was seen driving away after the accident. He had no reason to be in Hamsgate. But the real proof for me, was the way he reacted when I told him I suspected he'd killed Tom.'

'Did he confess?' Jessie wipes a strand of hair from her face.

'No, but he threatened that he would hurt my mother or Tom's children if I reported him, and he said he'd make sure their deaths looked like another unfortunate tragedy.'

'So, you did *nothing*?'

'Don't you see, Jessie, I couldn't tell the police.' I push my fingers into my temple and rub upwards. 'Michael said he'd create a new *accident*. He ordered me not to go near you either, he repeated his evil threat to hurt someone I loved if I did.'

'You should have informed the police, Billy. You should have told me. Do you know what I have been through since your affair ended? Do you have any idea?'

'I think I do,' I reply.

'You left him free to keep on hurting and controlling people.' Jessie jumps to her feet again. She looks down on me. 'Michael makes me believe I am useless at everything, everything is *my* fault. He has almost driven me out of my mind. He is possessive, jealous and obsessive.' She kicks the ground, creating a ball of dust. I think she might be doing this to the dry earth rather than me. *Maybe it's a substitute for Michael?*

'I was his puppet,' she says. 'It was only the fear of losing Mary yesterday, that finally woke me up to what he's been doing to me. I was terrified to go with her, but I couldn't lose my daughter. The only reason I am here, is because I was more frightened of losing Mary than of him.'

'I am so glad you're here,' I say.

'As Mary told you last night, we didn't have enough money to go anywhere else. Michael controls everything. Mary took the taxi fare from Nala's handbag.'

'What?' I say, but then I remember how Michael kept a tight rein on the Culmfield budget when I lived there. Jessie had inherited the sprawling estate in an almost derelict state, and Jessie and I worked our guts out to get the place back on its feet. We ran the whole project, but Michael was always looking over our shoulders checking our expenditure. In control, even then, but at the time, we didn't see it. We thought he just wanted to help.

He was running O'Rowdes' during the week from his London home, so Jessie and I were grateful for his attention on the minutia of the renovations when he came home at weekends.

'Yes, Billy, Michael holds every penny. I don't have a bank card. He pays for everything.' Jessie pauses for a second or two. 'I can believe what you're saying about Tom,' she says, 'but you were wrong, you should have told the police.'

'But there was something else, another reason I kept quiet.'

'Sorry. What?'

'I didn't want to stir everything up again.'

'What do you mean, Billy?'

'By the time I realised the truth, Tom's family had been through the funeral and the farm safety investigation. I didn't want them to endure further heartache. As I said, Jessie, we had little evidence and I knew Michael would hire the best defence lawyers, who'd probably save him before the case got to court. And even on bail, I imagined him carrying out his threats.'

I don't say how I was scared that Michael would sue me for accusing him of murder, making me pay for smearing his precious name. He would have hated O'Rowdes' being tainted with the scandal of our affair. Headlines in all the tabloids – his showcase marriage and perfect family life, exposed as a sham. The litigation would have driven me to bankruptcy, and I'd have lost the farm.

'Okay,' Jessie says. 'Maybe I get your decision not to involve the police but, Billy, you should have made sure I knew what Michael had done. You truly have no idea what it's been like living with him.' She pauses, brushing the hair from her face again. 'Billy, you said *we* had little evidence, who else knows about this?'

'No-one.' She stares at me and her knowing glare compels me to tell the truth. I breathe out slowly, and in again. 'Richard was the one who realised what happened, that Tom's death wasn't a terrible farm accident, and he was there when I challenged Michael about what he'd done. He stopped Michael from throttling me.'

'Right, I see,' Jessie says, making me feel like a small child; she is the teacher in kindergarten disciplining me for bad behaviour, and like a scolded toddler, I rope someone else into my excuses. 'It was both of us, Richard and I made a joint decision not to report him.'

Jessie nods.

'We agreed Michael was too dangerous and we must keep it secret. I was scared, and I am still terrified of what your husband might do if he finds you and Mary here. Richard is frightened too; that's why he was so desperate for you to go.'

'Billy, maybe in time I might have forgiven the affair but, girl, you can be certain, I will never forgive you for abandoning me. You knew what Michael was truly like. What the hell has he done to Mary? If I lose my daughter, you will think my husband's cruelty was charity.' Jessie spins around and she is about to stride away, but then she turns to me.

'I will find Mary,' she says, 'and she *will* tell me what's happened. We will go back to Culmfield and then I am going to get out of there for good. *He* can have my house, but I will make sure my children have a new life far away from that evil man.' She starts down the hill.

'Jessie, stop!' I call out.

'What?' She spins around.

'Would you have listened back then? Would you have believed me? Michael made sure you thought it was me who ended our affair. You would have thought I was making it all up, and I was just being vindictive. You would have brushed me off, saying I was just your husband's jilted lover seeking to cause trouble.'

Jessie doesn't answer, she continues to walk away.

Chapter 3

FOX HALT FARM

BILLY

*I*n the late afternoon, Mary and Mum carry containers of fresh milk into the kitchen from the dairy. I watch my mother's helper closely, hardly believing this is the child I used to know. Mary isn't the hothead who would stamp her feet to get everything she wanted. She is being wonderful with Mum; all cool and considerate. Mary hasn't said what's upset her, but she has reluctantly agreed to return to Culmfield with Jessie. 'I'll talk then,' Mary says.

Michael's chauffeur-driven Bentley drives into the yard. His car hardly stops before Mary rushes outside. She yanks open the car door and slides onto the back seat next to her dad, pulling the door closed behind her. Jessie and I watch from the kitchen, so we can't hear the conversation, but it looks like they are arguing. The chauffeur, Amir, must feel awkward so he moves away from the car and heads towards us.

As ever, Mum rushes to the front door to greet the approaching visitor, welcoming him in.

My mum is always the same, everyone is offered hospitality. She has met Amir twice before, both times were years ago; firstly, when he came here to drive Michael and me to London and later, at Jessie and Michael's wedding.

The first time, the chauffeur had Sunday dinner with us. On the second occasion, my mother was chatting to him at the wedding, assuming he was one of the many celebrity guests. For some reason she mistook him for a mid-fielder who played for Manchester United. There were so many prominent people at the posh do that it might well have been true. The chauffeur was exceptionally well-turned out, so I do understand her error – my star-struck mother asked Amir for his autograph for my football-mad cousin.

Mum immediately reminds Amir about their first encounter. 'Do you remember when you first brought Mr O'Rowde to Fox Halt Farm?' she asks him. 'You stayed in this kitchen with my daughter and me for two hours or more, while Mr O'Rowde took my late husband and our neighbour out in the Rolls Royce.'

'I remember,' he replies.

'Yes.' Mum smiles. 'Jack and Pat never forgot how they were both allowed to drive. They used to reminisce about it often.'

'Sorry. Your husband no longer live?' Amir's eyes scan the floor. 'I sorry,' he says without looking up.

'Yes, Jack and Pat have both passed away.' My mother stands still for a moment.

Silence.

Amir shifts his weight from one foot to the other. 'Mr O'Rowde, he still have that car,' he says. 'I drive Bentley sometimes. Sometimes Rolls Royce, but I like that Rolls Royce best. Beautiful car. Shines up new.'

Mum is smiling now. 'Oh, it's a shame you didn't bring the Rolls today, I should love to have seen it again.'

'Yes.' The chauffeur smiles with a grin that fills the whole of his face, his teeth are sugary white against his coffee skin.

'Sit down, Amir,' Mum says, pushing a cat off a chair so he can sit at the kitchen table. From all the fuss my mother makes of our unexpected visitor, any onlooker might guess that Amir was her long-lost relative who had travelled from the other side of the world, overcoming many perils on a treacherous voyage to get to the farm. She offers her guest tea, or coffee, or 'maybe a glass of wine,' while piling a massive wedge of Foxy Lady cheese, cream crackers and green and red grapes onto a plate for him.

'Sorry, Mrs M, I not eat,' Amir says.

Michael always referred to my mother as Mrs M, so the chauffeur has addressed her in the same way.

'Are you sure?' Mum asks.

'Mr O'Rowde, he want leave soon. It just twenty-minute drive to Culmfield Estate, I home soon. My wife, she cook for me,' Amir laughs, 'but her cook not like meal you cook. Your cookin' good, Mrs M.' The man raises his thick brows, nods his head and rubs his stomach. 'Roasted potato and beef, so good. You remember car, I remember your cookin' – very, very good,' he says. Mum pats his broad shoulders and laughs too. I note how the man's English has improved since I last saw him. When Amir started working for Michael, you were lucky to get two words out of him at a time, and those were frequently, 'Yes, sir,' or 'Yes, madam.'

I assume Amir is trying to hide that he knows me, because he pays me no attention; he doesn't even say hello. The chauffeur was always tactful. I find myself staring at him now, fascinated by his odd body shape; he is wearing shorts and a football shirt, and his clothes emphasise how the African is out of proportion, he makes me think of an old painting of King Henry VIII, where the artist painted his head, hands and feet too small for the rest of his body. With Amir, it is the other way around; his skinny torso, arms and legs remind me of a top African marathon runner, but his hands and feet are huge, and his shaven head is far too big for his neck.

When Amir was driving for Michael in London, he would be immaculately dressed in a grey suit, pristine white shirt and a neat striped tie matching the red and green livery of O'Rowdes' – the chauffeur was always better turned out than his boss; Michael could crumple up a new thousand-pound jacket after a few minutes of wear. It's Sunday today, and I expect Amir thought he had a day off, so Michael wouldn't have made him wear his uniform.

I notice his muscled arms and legs and think how even though he is no taller than me, he could look after his boss if he needed to. If he *had* to, that is, because Michael is strong too, and could probably look after himself in most situations – there are not many people who would choose to pick a physical fight with either man.

Minutes go by before Michael gets out of the car and marches towards the house. Jessie meets him at the door, but he ignores her, and heads straight for me. His breathing is slow, as he looks me hard in the eyes. 'Take care of my daughter, Billy. The second Mary wants to come back to Culmfield, you ring me. My daughter must be home before school starts again, at the end of August.'

'Okay,' I say. Being close to him makes my heart thump.

'Good.'

I feel faint, so I hold on to the back of a chair. I want to face up to this bully; tell him to look after his wife, and stop him controlling everyone, but I say nothing, and I simply wait for him to leave.

Before he turns to go, he frowns at me, wordlessly conveying new terrible consequences if Mary isn't back with his family soon. I don't move until he is outside, and then I see that Jessie and Amir are already in the car.

Mary grips my hand as her parents are driven away. I am surprised that Jessie is leaving without her daughter, but maybe she thinks she has no choice, or perhaps Jessie believes it's best for Mary that she is away from Michael. Her mother's sad eyes remain fixed on her until the car disappears.

I send another message to Richard, telling him again how much I need him.

Mum lays out roast chicken and lots of other delicious smelling food on the top of the Rayburn. The over-spilling dishes seem to have appeared by magic, I hadn't taken in what Mum and Mary had been doing since Michael took Jessie away. I was in a fog; one moment worrying about what was happening to Jessie, and the next concerned why I still haven't heard anything back from Richard.

Three additional dinner guests have materialised from nowhere too; Freddy, William my helper, and William's sister Grace. Mum is badgering them to help themselves to food.

It seems when William heard about Mary staying, he asked if he could join us for dinner. Grace, being Freddy's girlfriend, didn't need an invitation – the girl follows him everywhere.

I watch William load his plate with potatoes, and think it's strange he wanted to have dinner with us. He makes no secret of the fact he prefers spending time with animals rather than people. I wonder if him being here might be something to do with his mother? Maybe, it's to allow his mum, Martha, to spend this Sunday evening alone with Sean, their farm manager? I don't know for sure, I am just guessing.

As I expect, William doesn't utter a word during our meal. In fact, few of us say anything because Grace doesn't stop talking. She tells Mary all about Fox Halt Farm, her home which is the farm next door, and all the local gossip in and around our village of Hamsgate.

We swamp succulent home-grown raspberries and strawberries with fresh cream from our dairy, while Grace tells me I must take Mary and her shopping in Exeter tomorrow, so I can buy Mary a whole new wardrobe of clothes to wear. I love Grace's straightforward manner. She makes me forget about Jessie and Richard. I take my eyes off the candle in the centre of the table with its hypnotic flame conjuring up so many memories for me; painful memories. I think, *if only life were so simple that buying new clothes would make things happy.*

Everyone goes to bed, but I sit at the table until the candle finally flickers and smokes itself out, its sweet, waxy scent lingering in the air. I have no idea how long Mary has been standing watching me. 'Can't you sleep?' I ask her.

She shakes her head. 'Would it be okay for you to sleep with me in my bed tonight, Auntie, I don't want to be alone.' Her eyes are red and staring. I guess she's been crying.

I get up so I can put my arm around her shoulder. 'Yes, darling,' I say, thinking how I don't want to be on my own tonight either.

'I will just let Crinkle out for a moment,' I add, wondering yet again, why Michael is allowing Mary to stay here. Is this a game he is playing with her, with Jessie, or with me? *What is he up to?*

'Can she sleep with us too?' Mary asks, pointing at the dog.

'No, Mary, Crinkle stays in her basket. Wallace curls up with her. The cat usually sleeps with his front paws around her neck.'

'Oh,' she says, not smiling. She heads back upstairs.

When I get to the bedroom, Mary is asleep. I set out a sleeping bag on top of the duvet next to her. I feel so sad for this unhappy girl. My thoughts turn to Jessie, then to Richard as I wriggle into my cocoon. Mary opens her eyes. 'We have to rescue them,' she says.

'What do you mean?'

'Mum and my brothers, they can't stay at Culmfield.'

'Did your Dad hurt you, Mary? Is he hurting your brothers?' I ask. I feel the hair on the back of my neck stand on end, I shiver.

'No, but he *is* hurting Mum. Dad is too clever. He will never let her leave him, and Arthur, Mikey and Max need to be with Mum. We must make a plan to help them escape.'

'Let's talk in the morning, we've both had a horrible day,' I say, too tired for this discussion.

'Okay, we will.' She closes her eyes. 'Love you, Auntie.'

'Love you too, Mary.'

Chapter 4

MONDAY 28 JULY

BILLY

At six o'clock, an elbow jabbing into my chest wakes me up.

'Grace, what are you doing here?' I ask. 'And stop jumping on the bed.'

'William is in charge of the cows this morning, so I came with him.'

'I thought I locked the front door last night. How did you get in?' I ask, thinking how Grace reminds me of Crinkle in overexcited puppy mode. I wish I knew how she always manages to be so enthusiastic about everything, no matter the time of day.

'Doh! Billy, I know where your mum keeps her spare key. The one under the flower pot by the front door.'

'Okay then. Why are you here waking me and Mary up?'

'I only meant to wake Mary. If she comes with me now, then she can watch the cows being milked. You can have a lie-in, Billy.' Her eyes sparkle.

'That would be nice,' I say, scanning my phone to see if Richard has sent a message or tried to call. The screen is blank.

'Do I have time?' Mary looks at me.

'Of course.' I say.

'Aren't we going in to Exeter this morning?' Mary says, winding her wild hair into a ponytail.

'No,' Grace replies, kneeling on the bed and making it rock violently. 'We are going shopping this afternoon, aren't we, Billy?'

I smile, thinking how I haven't the heart to refuse her.

Mum leaves Gloria and June, the Hamsgate Honeys, alone in the dairy, so she can come with us on the shopping spree. My van can only fit three people in the front cab, so I drive Mum's old Mini. Her treasured car is more than forty years old; Honolulu blue, speckled with rust. It's tiny, and I can't exceed thirty-eight miles per hour, because the rattling becomes too noisy to bear. I have begged Mum to buy a new car, but she is resolute that there's nothing wrong with the decrepit Mini. This is typical of her, never spending anything on herself and holding on to memories – like her journeys with my dad and grandfather in this car.

Grace adores everything we buy, complimenting Mary constantly. I agree with her; Mary's slender frame and freckles make her look like a young model in anything she tries on. Mum sums it up best. 'The girl would look great in a paper bag,' she says. Mary seems unaware of her beauty, and her reticence about her body makes her even more stunning. We all have a nice time together, and for fleeting moments, I forget Richard.

As we finish putting away the clothes we've purchased in Mary's new bedroom, Mary sits down heavily on the bed. 'I'll be fourteen on Wednesday,' she says. She is wearing a pink nightshirt with *'Wake me when I am a unicorn'* printed in glittery letters on the front. It swamps her body. I can't believe it's fourteen years since I first held her in my arms, minutes after she was born. So small and so precious.

'Would you like to go home for your birthday? I'll drive you.' I try not to sound too keen about returning her to Jessie.

'I'll just phone, thank you. I'll speak to them all in turn.'

'Are you sure?' I say, thinking how her birthday will be so different from the day Jessie would have planned.

When I lived with the O'Rowdes, the tradition for Mary's mid-summer celebration was a family picnic on a mud-coloured beach on the banks of the River Culm. The wide, lazy tributary winds its way in a huge 'S' through the middle of the estate, before flowing into the Exe. I close my eyes, remembering the family's ponies and horses with antique saddlebags laden with everything for an old-fashioned day out.

'Are you alright, Auntie?'

I open my eyes. 'Yes.'

'What were you thinking about just then?'

'Your birthdays when I lived at Culmfield.'

'You remember?'

'Yes, of course I do -- the horses tethered under a shady oak. I was recalling the rhythmic noise of the ponies crunching sweet dried grass out of stuffed-full hay nets, and all you children excitedly yelling when you splashed each other with the freezing water. I was picturing you and Arthur tiptoeing over the stony river bed and making dams. There was so much laughter.'

'Mum would have been planning the same family picnic for this Wednesday too. It's a tradition, you know.'

'So, don't you think you ought to go home, even if it's just for the day?' I ask, trying not to push too hard.

'I can't. I'm sorry but I can't.'

I nod and I close my eyes again, remembering Jessie telling me how Mary's birthdays were just like the ones she remembered as a child. Jessie's sixth birthday was her last one with her own mum, and she told me it was the happiest time she could remember. Every year Jessie arranged another picnic, trying to recapture the treasured moment from her past.

'Auntie.'

'Yes, Mary, sorry, I was just thinking about your mum and how disappointed she'll be.' Michael always made sure he didn't work on family birthdays, so the days would seem extra special with him around.

Lots of children from the local village of Barrowculme would be invited along, and Michael would collect them from their homes in an old London bus, one of many distinctive vehicles he owned in his collection. He'd drive his daughter's guests along the narrow lanes to an old footpath onto the estate, a short walk from the favourite picnic spot.

'I know it will upset her but I really can't go home. I'll just phone them.'

Later, as I climb into my sleeping bag on her bed, I see Mary is not asleep. 'I've been thinking,' I say. 'Would you like to ask some of your school friends to spend Wednesday with you here at the farm?'

'No thank you.'

'Alright, but if you suddenly think of something you'd like to do, you must tell me.'

'Okay,' she replies, then changes the subject. 'Tomorrow, Grace and I are going fishing.'

'Where?' I ask, frowning, wondering why she hasn't mentioned it before.

'Not sure. Grace called it the Trout Lake, I think?'

I cringe at this plan, because as children Grace's dad Tom and I used to trespass there too; onto the neighbouring Fox Hall Estate with our home-made rods. Trout Lake was our favourite spot, probably because we were not actually permitted there, so it became an even better adventure. Our parents used to get mad at us for going, and now here I am, wishing the two girls didn't want to spend the day at the lake either. I want to tell Mary she can't go, but I know it will be fun for her with Grace, and I know too, that if they get caught by the Fox Hall gamekeeper, Tom's daughter will soon talk her way out of trouble, just like her dad used to.

'Trout for tea tomorrow,' I say, disguising my worry.

'No, we will release anything we catch back into the lake. Grace said she can't bear to kill the fish. Afterwards, we are going to watch back to back DVDs all night in Grace's bedroom. Your mum is going to organise a midnight feast for me to take to her house.'

There is nothing more to say; tomorrow is obviously planned out, and Mary's birthday, the day after, won't be anything special.

I fall asleep – *Tom is creeping to the edge of Trout Lake. 'Watch out, Billy!' he shouts...*

FOX HALT FARM

TUESDAY 29 JULY

BILLY

*F*or a second morning I lie on Mary's bed, fathoming out reasons why I still have no reply from Richard – I am only kidding myself; I know why, he is mad at me, and has every right to be.

At ten o'clock, Mary mooches into the kitchen wearing everything Grace has suggested would be best for fishing. I think Grace has gone a little over the top because Mary looks like someone out of a high-class country magazine. I try not to laugh, while I suggest she is going to be too hot, and she should wear shorts instead. 'Take a coat too,' I tell her, 'just in case it rains; thunder and lightning are forecast for later this afternoon.'

'Alright, I will,' she says, as she heads back upstairs.

When Mary reappears, I ask her, 'Any more thoughts about your birthday tomorrow?'

'No.' Mary lowers both her eyes and her shoulders and sort of huffs. It suddenly feels awkward between us, so I am pleased when Grace bounces through the door with all their fishing kit. I note how the excited girl has on shorts and a tee shirt. I look at the bright yellow coat she is carrying.

'Grace,' I say, 'you must stop fishing if the rain starts, or if there is lightning. You know not to fish in a thunderstorm, don't you?'

'Don't worry,' she replies. 'We'll head for home as soon as the first little raindrop sploshes onto us.' She dances around in a circle holding her hands out. 'I so hope it pours down, this heat is horrid. *Sooo* many days now – it's got to rain later.'

Since Richard went to Cornwall, Freddy has been sleeping in the cottage across the farmyard but having all his meals with us. Richard invited Freddy to go with him, but his son said he wanted to stay at Fox Halt. I think Freddy thought his dad was being unreasonable about Jessie and Mary, and he wanted to make a stand. He thought too, he'd spend time with Grace, but now his young girlfriend is telling him, 'See you tomorrow morning, Freddy.'

'Have a great time, you two,' he says. I don't know who feels more dejected, Freddy or me, as we watch them leave.

My phone vibrates in my pocket, but I dismiss it, thinking that I am imagining a message. The ringer is off because I couldn't bear listening for it all the time. I have limited myself to messaging Richard every four hours, keeping him up to date with what's been happening. I yearn with every bit of me for a reply that says, 'I love you and I am on my way back.' I resorted to emotional blackmail this morning, texting him to say how Freddy had been usurped by Mary in Grace's affections, hoping if Richard wouldn't return for me, then he would come back for his son. I am desperate to see him, to apologise for what I did. I check my phone, just in case.

It really is a message. My heart races. *'Will be home tomorrow morning x,'* is all he says.

I quickly text him back. *'Can't wait to see you, all my love B xxxxxxxx'*.

I start to rehearse all my apologies to salvage his marriage proposal. I let myself dream about what it will be like when he gets back to Fox Halt Farm. I picture him asking me to go on holiday with him for the rest of the time we were supposed to be on our Greek island. In my mind, Richard and I head off to a quiet hideaway. I envisage Richard has it all planned out.

I have to do something for the rest of the day to keep myself from going mad, so I tell Mum I am going to sort out something for Mary's birthday.

Soon, I am driving my van out of the farmyard with our cattle trailer hitched up behind. I don't know how exactly I will accomplish what I have in mind, but I am heading towards Culmfield feeling determined.

Fox Halt Farm

Wednesday 30 July

Richard

As I drive down the potholed track to Fox Halt Farm, a sense of peace wraps around me. I see the familiar ramshackle buildings, which have evolved over centuries. Some of the earliest traditional cob-built ones are still in use, but it's only the farmhouse which has kept its original thatched roof. The outbuildings are mainly covered in galvanise sheeting, forming a patchwork of muted colours with varying amounts of orange rust.

As farm machinery has changed and grown, extensions and lean-tos have been added; with a tight budget of money and time. Daniella says that you'll never find a farmer who has time or money to build or repair things properly, but they always manage to do it again when it breaks or collapses. The new dairy has oak timber walls and a neat slate roof, so the new sturdy and precise building makes the surrounding ones look even more rundown. I remember decades ago, when I lived in Buckinghamshire and ran a multinational company based in central London, Daniella sent me an aerial photograph of the farm. She had noted on it each of the farm buildings, carefully labelling the *'cow shed'*, *'hen house'*, *'shippen'*, *'old caravan'*, and so on.

Daniella and I wrote to each other for years, recounting our very different everyday lives. But that's a whole other story. It's safe to say that I fell in love with the farm meticulously described in Daniella's wonderful letters long before I fell in love with Billy. So much has happened since. Now, here I am, having just moved to the place in that old photo, the place I came to adore. Fox Halt Farm feels like home, as I recognise each of the cows in the field on my right-hand side.

The storm yesterday afternoon has cleared the air, but this morning's cloudless sky seems to be promising another hot day. The grass is still parched to the colour of sand and my car wheels stir up a cloud of dust. It is as though the heavy rainstorm didn't happen here, but I don't know if there was thunder and lightning because I left my mobile phone on a table in a café on the Lizard Peninsula yesterday, so I haven't had any updates from Billy. The café was closed by the time I realised. I'll ring later, and I hope the phone can be posted to me.

Returning to the farm feels good but the thought of seeing Billy again fills me with apprehension. My time away has made me stand back and given me a new perspective. I realise now, that my number one priority has to be my son. I have been questioning if Freddy is truly content at the farm, or if he only came to Devon to make me happy.

I pull up in the yard as the seven o'clock morning news starts on the car radio, stopping next to William's Gator. William's sheepdog Benjy is in the back of his dusty vehicle, patiently waiting for his master to finish milking. The dog has no collar. In fact, no means of restraint at all. Benjy sits where he is voluntarily, knowing William will be back soon enough and they will drive off for another adventure.

William isn't in the milking parlour, instead I notice him with Mary. The pair have their heads bent over a stable door, peering in at Billy's old horse, Prince Sunshine. I wonder if the horse is ill, and I leap out of the car to see what is happening.

By the time I reach William and Mary, I realise that they are not staring at Billy's horse. The two of them are standing in front of the door next to Prince Sunshine's stable, which hasn't housed an animal for years.

When I left on Sunday morning, it was filled to bursting with various old or broken items, which Billy or her mum couldn't bear to throw away.

'Isn't he lovely,' Mary is asking William for his opinion of the stable's occupant. 'I wonder how he got here? Do you think Dad organised it as a birthday surprise? He loves doing extravagant things for birthdays.'

William shrugs his shoulders.

'I can bring him out,' Mary continues, 'you'll see him properly then.'

The teenagers are unaware of me beside them, both captivated by a new horse with its head in the granite manger in the corner of the old stable. I can hear it gobbling up some food.

'Go on then,' William replies, and opens the door. Mary darts inside and leads the horse out. Light reflects off its shiny chestnut coat. 'He's called Braveheart,' Mary says, pressing her cheek into the horse's neck.

I feel on edge, wondering if Michael did arrange for the beautiful creature to turn up at the farm, unnerved by the thought someone creeping around in the middle of the night; even if it is to deliver a wonderful surprise for his estranged daughter.

'Hello, boy.' William strokes the horse's nose. 'You're a beaut,' he says, and the horse puts his ears forward. 'I'll come and see you properly later. Sorry, Braveheart, but I have to finish milking the cows, they won't be kept waiting.'

The horse seems to nod at the boy.

'You can ride him later,' Mary tells William.

'Or I'll bring Star over here, and we can go for a hack together,' William suggests. I don't hear what they decide to do, because I walk away to go inside my cottage.

Billy had told me in one of her messages that it was Mary's birthday today, and I regret not picking something up for her.

I hope Billy will say the present she bought Mary is from both of us, but then again, I don't think any gift will be as good as Michael's.

Despite my misgivings about her being at Fox Halt, my first small impression is that I like Mary, she seems level-headed and well-mannered. I love Grace, but Mary seems gentler somehow, she reminds me of Harry, my daughter who has just married and is living in New Zealand now.

I miss my daughter's quiet thoughtfulness. I think, if Freddy and I do stay at Fox Halt, it will be nice to have Mary around for a little while.

In the hallway, I trip over a pink wellington left where it fell off Grace's foot, so I am not surprised when I find its owner in my kitchen.

Grace is looking out through the small window into the yard and when she doesn't turn around to greet me either, I wonder if I am dreaming being back here. Outside, I see William step away from Mary, while she lets her horse meet Prince over his stable door. Both horses have their ears forward. They seem to like each other.

The girl in my kitchen turns around at last. She looks up at me, pushing her lips out and down. I think she is trying to look sad, but all she really achieves is a resemblance to a clown. I try not to smile.

'Looks like Mary won't want anything to do with me, now,' she says, and I wonder if she is truly upset. I can never tell with Grace; she jokes, even when she's hurting. 'Your son will be pleased though,' she laughs. 'I'll tell him the good news.' Grace charges upstairs, two steps at a time. I follow her thinking how her name doesn't suit her. The girl is more Pocahontas with her brown-black hair in its usual two long plaits, the end of her braids held tight with unmatched elastic bands.

Grace scrambles onto Freddy's bed, waking him up. She doesn't seem to care that his father is watching as she kisses him on the mouth. 'Morning, my darling,' she tells him. I hope this is acting too, just like her earlier comical sad expression, but now doubt creeps over me.

I consider if this is the way my son is woken up every morning? I will have a fatherly word with Freddy later, and a word with the girl's mother too. She is only thirteen and this relationship with my son could be going further than Martha or I imagined.

There are raised voices outside, and instinctively I fear something is wrong. Grace must have heard them too, because we reach the bathroom window at the same time, both looking out onto the yard to see what's happening.

The new horse is back in its stable and Mary is with Billy and they both seem to be crying. Grace and I run down the narrow stairs side by side even though the staircase is only wide enough for one, our hips and elbows spiking each other.

Mary is sitting on the edge of a granite trough and Billy is sitting tight against her with her arms wrapped around her. Billy looks up from the girl and stares at me, her face ashen.

'Michael...' She pauses and looks down at my feet. She lifts her head again until her eyes meet mine. 'Richard, Michael has killed himself,' she says.

I stand still, unable to take in what she said.

'Jessie just rang me. I was on the phone when you got here.' Her words are rushed now. 'Charlotte found him.'

None of this makes sense. On autopilot, I move towards Mary and I put an arm around her too.

'Mary, I'm sorry,' I say, but my brain can't comprehend the news. I need more time. 'Tell me everything Jessie told you,' I say to Billy, but then I rethink, wondering if this is an appropriate conversation to have in front of Mary. I stare at the girl, who I saw so happy with her horse only minutes ago. Mary's face is tight against Billy's cheek, so all I can see is a mass of long red curls. Sobs come with each jerk of her neck.

'He-'

'No. Stop, Billy,' I say, running my hand along the crying girl's shoulder. 'I don't think Mary should hear this.'

Mary looks at me, her face red. 'Mr MarcFenn,' she says. 'I want to know too.'

'Are you sure?' I ask.

Mary nods, and then she turns to Billy. 'Please tell us what Mum said. Where was he? Did he hang himself from the rafters in one of the stables, is that why Charlotte found him?'

'Shall we go indoors?' Billy asks as she gently lifts damp hair away from Mary's face.

'No,' Mary shakes her head. 'Please, Auntie, tell me here.'

Billy takes in a deep breath. 'With the weather being so hot, Charlotte has been letting the horses out in the fields at night and keeping them in their stables during the day. She's been leaving home early each day.' She stops.

'Go on please, Auntie.' Mary reaches forward to squeeze Billy's hand.

Billy blinks and then she looks at me.'

'Go on,' I say.

'Michael's car.' She stops again.

Mary and I wait for Billy to continue, until eventually she says, 'Charlotte found Michael this morning; he was in his car. He was dead when she found him. The car was on the footpath that leads from the estate to the river, the place where Michael used to park the bus, when we had birthday picnics.'

'He was dead?' I check.

'There was a tube in the window. Michael's face was bright red. The vehicle was locked, so poor Charlotte couldn't get to him.'

'He was on the bus?' I ask, having lost track, my mind spinning. I've no idea where Charlotte found him either, other than it must be a path off the country lane that circles the estate. I know the bus though. I remember Michael showing me photographs before he bought it.

'No, he was in one of his Porsches.'

'Right,' I say, still struggling to understand.

'Charlotte uses the cut through to get to work each day: the poor woman didn't even know Michael was missing,' Billy explains.

'I see,' I lie, feeling quite dazed.

'Yes, she recognised the car and thought he was asleep at first, but then she noticed the pipe coming from the exhaust going into the passenger window. The car wasn't running, it must have been out of fuel by then, but the fumes had already killed him.'

'Poor Charlotte,' I shiver. I realise I ought to be upset about Michael too, even if it's just for Mary's benefit. 'Poor bloke too. Poor Michael, committing suicide like that.'

Mary pulls her hand away from Billy's and wipes her fingers under her runny nose. 'Was there a note, Auntie?'

'There was, darling, but it only said he was sorry.'

Billy turns to me. 'Mary says she still doesn't want to go home?' Her tone makes me think she wants me to talk to the girl, to see if I can persuade her to change her mind.

'Is that all it said?' Mary stares at Billy.

'Yes, darling. That's all it said. Your father was sorry.'

'Mary,' I say, 'you don't have to go home. Please stay at Fox Halt Farm as long as you want. Just say when you want to return, and we'll take you back to Culmfield straightaway. Any time, it doesn't matter.' Guilt has stung me, remembering how cold I was to the girl before. She must be scared, and I don't want her being afraid of me.

Mary makes a half smile. 'Thank you,' she says.

I look at Billy. 'Did Jessie tell you anything else?' I ask.

'The whole area is being cordoned off, and the police want to speak to anyone who saw Michael yesterday.'

'Is that when he went missing?'

'Yes, last night, sometime.' Billy pauses.

'What, Billy?' I probe. 'What else?'

'Jessie asked if you would go over there, she wants some advice about the business.'

'What? She's just lost her husband and she wants to talk to me about O'Rowdes'?' I frown. 'Are you serious?'

'Yes, she is very worried. Michael is everything to that company. Jessie thinks it could collapse without him. Look, Richard, she's a mess, and I don't think she really knows what she's doing right now. She's in shock, and it does sound nuts, but Jessie asked if you'd help her, and I said I'd ask if you would.'

'You know Michael's business better than I do, Billy,' I reply. 'Hell, you worked for him for years.'

'She didn't want me there. She definitely wanted you – not me.'

'Did you say I would help her?' I feel angry.

'I said that I'd ask you.'

'Good,' I say, feeling relieved that for once Billy hasn't taken me for granted, and hasn't offered my assistance without checking with me first.

'Richard, I am so sorry, I shouldn't have put Jessie before you. I want to marry you.'

'No, Billy, I am not discussing this with you now.' I sit down next to Mary.

'Mary, if I go and see your mum, will you come with me?' I ask. The girl doesn't answer.

'So, you will help Jessie?' Billy asks.

I nod at her, feeling relieved that she isn't pushing me about our future. Mary seems to be staring at me, but it's hard to tell. I look into her eyes. 'Will you come with me?' I ask again.

'No,' Mary replies. Her firm tone tells me she doesn't want to talk about this.

Going to Culmfield will give me some more time to think about my options too. 'I'm going to leave right away,' I say.

Chapter 5

CULMFIELD COURT, BARROWCULME, DEVON

RICHARD

I'm about to head off to check on Jessie, when I tell Billy about my lost phone. She isn't impressed, but unlike her, I feel quite content. It seems a good excuse for us not to communicate for a little while longer. I need time to think, and I still need to talk to Freddy.

Like Mary, my son refused to come with me to Culmfield. He reckons Mary will want to do horsey things now that she has Braveheart, and knowing Grace has no interest in horses, he thinks he'll be 'flavour of the month' with her again.

Culmfield Court is impressive; the magnificent brick mansion with its twisted chimneys fills the valley bottom with its presence, while the noise of the deep gravel under my wheels make it feel exclusive.

Gargoyles watch me from the high roof, while granite lions guard the front steps. I don't want to knock, assuming that Jessie has opened the heavy door many times this morning to different people involved with the aftermath of Michael's suicide. I have stayed at Culmfield before, so I know my way around. I let myself in. I am expected, after all.

Beautiful Persian rugs on the shiny wooden floors fail to stop my footsteps echoing around the panelled walls. Massive canvases painted by a fifteenth-century Dutch master don't absorb the hollowness either.

I find Jessie and her three young sons in the main drawing room with two strangers. Arthur, the eldest child, is the only one of the family who is dressed. Despite it being the summer holiday, the boy seems to be in his school's white shirt, neat striped tie and dark grey trousers. He looks out of place, especially because Jessie and his brothers, Max, and Mikey, are still in their dressing gowns and slippers.

The strangers, a man and a woman, have on expensive dark suits but they both lack any remarkable features. I can't help wondering who they are: police, Michael's business associates or something else official? Arthur comes up to me and shakes my hand. 'Hello, Mr MarcFenn, thank you for coming.'

No-one else turns away from the BBC news report. A familiar television presenter is reporting 'the sudden death of the well-known businessman and entrepreneur, Michael O'Rowde.' She tells the world that 'he was found dead on his family estate in Devon this morning.'

Dead. Somehow, the television broadcast makes it real. I cannot comprehend the range of emotions that seeing this news item evokes. It's like a blow to my chest. I can't breathe.

'I am so sorry,' I whisper, but inside, I feel no regret.

'Thank you, Mr MarcFenn,' Arthur replies, and I wonder how many other people are happy that Michael is out of their life.

With everyone's attention fixed on the TV, I scan the three children. I guess they are twelve, ten and eight years old. I recall the time when their father and I worked together, Michael would often talk about his kids. He gave such a good impression of a doting father and husband, but that was before I found out about his affair with Billy and discovered what he might have done to Tom.

A business correspondent is talking now. I start to listen too.

'On Thursday last week O'Rowdes' revealed its worst sales performance since the recession, and concern has been mounting that many of the major supermarkets are facing financial collapse. All the big-name retailers are being hit hard by three new discounters, who have recently opened new stores in the UK.

'O'Rowdes' shares have fallen fifty-four per cent in the past year, with growth prospects in the UK being hit by the latest Competition Commission's ruling making it hard to open new stores.

'Last Friday, Michael O'Rowde blamed nose-diving house prices and growing unemployment in both the UK and America for lowering sales margins. It seems O'Rowdes' were struggling in the worst economic conditions for years. There are also unconfirmed reports that the supermarket owner has experienced major and costly setbacks with his recent expansion plans into two new Asian countries.

'Dealing in O'Rowdes' shares is suspended at present. The sudden death of its founder, and majority shareholder, must make the future of the company uncertain.'

'Turn it off, please.' Jesse's voice is croaky.

'Okay.' Arthur does what his mother asks. He watches the screen turn black and then turns back to me. 'You got through all those people with cameras at the gate then, Mr MarcFenn?'

'Yes, Amir was with a policeman down there. He helped.'

'Amir is great. He is going to identify Dad's body for us.' Arthur doesn't give any indication that he is upset that the chauffeur is about to confirm that his father is dead.

'Where's my sister?' he asks.

'Staying at Fox Halt Farm for now.' I see disappointment in his face. I glance at Jessie for her reaction too, but I don't think she is listening.

An uncomfortable silence stretches out for minutes, until I decide to ask if any of them have had breakfast. I imagine they have all been ensconced in this room since they heard about Michael. I say I am happy to find some food or drinks for them, if they would like anything.

Arthur replies immediately. 'It's fine, Mr MarcFenn, Nala and Sharmarke are already in the kitchen sorting something for us. I'm sure there will be enough for you too.'

'Nala and Sharmarke?' I ask, frowning at Arthur.

'You remember, Nala, Mr MarcFenn? She is our...' he pauses, 'sort of housekeeper. Amir's wife. You must have met her before?'

'Sorry, yes of course I know her,' I say, surprised at my forgetfulness. My mind is still whirring over Michael's suicide. He never seemed the type to let anything worry him too much, but I guess this proves you can never tell. 'And Sharmarke is Nala and Amir's son, that's right, isn't it?' I check.

'Yes.'

On cue, the pair walk in with trays laden with drinks and sandwiches.

Nala is striking; dressed in a duck blue shirt with a long navy skirt. Her hair is wrapped in a silk hijab, the same duck blue tone as her shirt. I notice a few black springs of hair have escaped around the edges of her headscarf. She doesn't smile but her manner seems a little more assured than I remember.

Sharmarke is different too. He is about my son's age, and no longer the straggly child from my last visit to Culmfield. The boy has filled out and must be a foot taller than Amir now. Like Arthur, he's wearing a white shirt with the same stitching design. Unbuttoned at the neck without a tie but still, I wonder, if Arthur and this boy go to the same school.

I recall Billy telling me about how she used to give Mary and Sharmarke riding lessons; Billy always had a broad smile on her face whenever she mentioned it to me; they were obviously happy times for her, sharing her knowledge of horses and riding. Something she would have done with her own children; if she'd been able to have a child.

I realise that Sharmarke and his mother are staring at me. I think they might be trying to recall who I am, or they are silently questioning why I am here.

Arthur reads their faces and straightaway, he introduces me. 'You remember Richard MarcFenn, Dad's friend. Mr MarcFenn owned the property company Dad uses,' he corrects himself, 'used.' Nala still looks blank, but

•

Arthur continues. 'Richard is here to talk to Mum about the business, now Dad's not here.' He sounds confident and still gives no indication he's upset.

'Yes, hello, Mr MarcFenn,' Nala smiles and then quickly dips her head, casting her eyes towards the floor. Her reaction suggests that she doesn't want to have any further conversation.

It is Arthur, not Jessie, who invites everyone to help themselves to food and drink, and again it's he who introduces the suited couple. 'Mr MarcFenn – our family solicitor, Mrs Stephens. This gentleman is O'Rowdes' Company Secretary, Mr Khatri.'

We shake hands, and out of habitual business convention, we provide our first names and repeat our surnames, smiling politely.

'Mum is in charge of O'Rowdes' now,' Arthur tells me. He scratches the palm of his hand which makes me think he is a little unsure of himself.

'She has to make some important decisions about the business. I hope you can help her, Mr MarcFenn. Please will you give her some advice, I don't think my mum can think very clearly at the moment.'

I reconsider the boy's behaviour; scratching his palm was not a sign of weakness, he was thinking how to express what he needed to say. Arthur has resurrected his father in my mind, I can picture Michael doing the exact same thing in our business negotiations. Arthur's confidence makes me think how I would have reacted if my father had died when I was just twelve years old; not like this, that's for sure. I would have been in pieces. I'd still be in bits, if it happened today, and I'm forty-seven. I just can't imagine my father not being around.

I venture onto a new guilt trip about my father and how I ought to see him more often. I hardly see Father these days. He lives four hours away at most, so there is no excuse. He is still in the house I grew up in, and just a short distance from my former home. Until Harry's recent marriage, my ex-wife checked up on my father every weekend, but Janette is in New Zealand, on an extended campervan holiday with

Harry's twin sister, Sid. My thoughts divert for a moment, to my late mother, and how she nicknamed our twins girls Harry and Sid. My wife and I chose beautiful names, Ariadne and Cressida, but I don't know why we bothered, when nearly everyone uses their nicknames.

Janette and my father are still close, and I used to receive regular updates about him from her. But she has been away for weeks, so I don't know how he is at the moment. I console myself that Father still has lots of people around him, keeping a watchful eye, and he'll be fine. I will ring him this evening. Jessie or Arthur will let me use their phone. I begin to think what I will say to my father, and when I can arrange to visit him.

'So, Mr MarcFenn.' Arthur breaks into my thoughts. 'Will you talk through some of the business stuff with Mum please?' I detect a slight reticence in his voice. 'I think Mum needs help getting her hands on some cash too.'

I turn to Jessie, but she is still paying no attention to me or Arthur. 'Mrs Stephens will help with the money,' I say.

'Yes, she could but Mum wants your help, Mr MarcFenn.' Arthur is firm.

I don't understand why Jessie wants my advice. I can only imagine that it's because I helped her a long time ago when she first inherited Culmfield, that was before she met Michael. Her dad had employed my father to advise on property matters, so when her dad died, she sought advice from MarcFenns too. I had just started to work for the family firm, and my father asked me to work with Jessie. I am sure I can assist a bit, and it will be a good excuse to stay away from Fox Halt Farm a while longer.

Without waiting for my reply, Arthur indicates for me to sit next to his mother. Jessie is perched at one end of a red velvet chaise longue. She is so thin that I feel I am taking up the whole seat.

'I'm sorry about Michael,' I tell her, speaking softly.

Jessie nods to acknowledge me.

'It will be no trouble, if you do want my help,' I say.

She nods again. 'Thank you, Richard.'

Jessie looks at me for the first time since I arrived. 'Thank you,' she says again, as though she has forgotten her first words.

'It's no trouble,' I repeat.

'Ask Mrs Stephens and Mr Khatri to go,' she whispers.

'Really, you want them to go?'

Jessie raises her eyebrows to confirm she is certain. '

'Alright,' I say, standing up, and then I ask the pair to leave.

Fox Halt Farm
Tuesday 5 August
Billy

William is with me in the milking parlour. 'You're doing that too quickly,' I tell him, as he wipes a cow's udder before attaching the milking machine's teat-cups. 'Please make sure it's really clean.'

'Stop nagging. I know what I'm doing,' he replies.

'Gently, William. What's the rush? Is there somewhere else you need to be?'

'No, it's just that I'm getting a bit fed up with you.'

'What do you mean?'

'Fed up with you looking over my shoulder. Lecturing me every few minutes about things I already know.' He moves to the radio, turning the volume up.

I step towards him. 'That's too loud, the cows will get stressed,' I say, leaning forward to turn the music down.

'It's you who's stressing them, Billy. Just go, leave me and the cows alone.'

William is right, my mind is not on the milking. My brain keeps churning over how everything has turned against me. The worst is that Nala and Amir believe I may have killed Michael.

Richard said they came up with a scenario that I could have murdered him, making his death look like a suicide. Amir told Richard how Nala gave me the access code to open a side gate to the estate on the same night that Michael died. I did get the code from her, but it was so I could spirit Braveheart away without permission. I didn't want to risk a refusal from Michael or Jessie. All I wanted was for Mary to have a wonderful birthday surprise. I asked Nala to keep quiet about seeing me, but my request to keep my 'burglary' a secret must have led Amir and Nala to the notion that I might be a killer, as well as a thief. Luckily, the police haven't knocked on my door, so the pair must have kept shtum about their suspicions, and it seems I have upset everyone else too.

It's nearly a week since Richard left to help Jessie at Culmfield and he has moved out of the farm cottage to stay at his former home. He told me Freddy missed his friends and was worried about moving to a new school to complete his GCSEs. His son said he liked being at the farm at weekends but living permanently in Devon wasn't the best for him. Now they are both staying in Richard's ex-wife's house, while she's away in New Zealand. I know that with Richard acting as Jessie's nominated person at O'Rowdes', it's much easier for him to be living near their head office in central London, but it's difficult thinking of him living in his old house. He said it was just for now, but I still hate it.

I was shocked when Richard explained to me about his trip to Culmfield, and surprised about how comfortable he was with all the business questions he said he was looking at. He was obviously enjoying helping Jessie, sharing his knowledge with her. Before this, I thought he was happy to let go of the reins of his own massive company to move to the farm, but as he talked about O'Rowdes', I could hear he was relishing being back in the world of big business.

Richard says he will be back here on Saturday morning and he can stay until Sunday evening, but at the moment that is all the time he will commit to spending with me.

I am miserable, and I keep taking it out on William. My problem is that he is so like his dead father; the way he moves, his black, unruly hair and his kind brown eyes. I treat him like I did Tom, who didn't care how badly I behaved. I'd shout at his father, and he would just shout back, but William takes everything to heart. I know I should be more careful about what I say to him. He is a great boy; Tom would have been so proud of his son.

Mum can't understand why I let Richard leave. She doesn't see why I couldn't allow Jessie and Mary to stay at the farm with her, while we went on our romantic holiday. I can't explain to Mum why Richard was so angry about Jessie staying. I just can't trust my mother to keep the secret about how Tom died. In my mother's world everything is black and white, there is no guile with her. Life is straightforward. She loves everyone, and everyone loves her. Mum is always open, caring and honest, she tells family and friends everything. She has no secrets. My mother has to keep on believing Tom died in a terrible farm accident, or she will tell the truth to the whole world. The police believe Michael's death is a straightforward suicide, and that's how I want it to stay. I don't want anything from his past stirring up an investigation. I want Jessie to be able to organise a quiet funeral, without a media storm about Michael being unfaithful, or with allegations he might have killed someone.

Jessie has frozen me out, still hating me for not telling her about Tom. Loathing me too, I suspect because Mary is still living with me, and not back home with her.

Grace blames me for Freddy's departure, because if I hadn't caused Richard to leave then his son would still be at Fox Halt Farm. The poor abandoned girl is also upset that I fetched Braveheart, because now Mary is more interested in her horse than her.

'Do you want me in the dairy, or the farm shop, this morning, Auntie?' Mary is suddenly beside me, shouting above the din of the milking machines and the radio, which William has turned back up. I move, so I can answer without yelling, but Mary doesn't wait for a reply. 'William wouldn't let me help him. I don't think he trusts anyone,' she says. I don't explain about William, not telling her how withdrawn he became after he found his dad dead. I rest my back against the parlour wall, trying to steady myself.

'Let's get some breakfast, then we'll sort the dairy, then the shop. Is that alright?' I ask her.

Mary seems the only one who is pleased to spend time with me, she's been helping me as much as she can.

'Yes, okay, Auntie.' I hear her reply, but it's fuzzy.

It's not okay, I think. Nothing is okay anymore.

Chapter 6

SATURDAY 9 AUGUST

RICHARD

Recollections of my life with Janette lurk in every corner of Beechwood. Good memories mainly, but it's still a relief to be driving to the farm for the weekend.

My passenger is texting. *Ping,* and another message from Grace arrives. The lack of conversation between Freddy and me allows my mind to wander.

Beechwood is pretty much the same. In a way, I wish my ex-wife had made changes, then maybe I wouldn't think about her, and how our life together could have been different. I remember our children growing up and I wish I had been at home more with them.

The neighbour, Jayne McLaughlin, is delighted that Freddy and I are back. She always treated Beechwood as an extension to her own house. With Janette away, I think she missed her sanctuary next door, away from the chaos of her five children, their boyfriends, girlfriends and friends. It's no surprise that Jayne's home is overrun because the woman fusses over everybody – even Freddy disappeared into her house as soon as we arrived back, and I have hardly seen him. He reappeared as I was ready to leave this morning. No doubt he is being spoilt rotten.

Jayne was a good friend to me too, when Janette and I divorced. Her husband works abroad for long spells at a time, so she was always dropping into my new home at the other end of the village to make sure I was coping. I like her, even though she does nose into everything. Each time I park up, Jayne is at her front door offering me tea. I am sure she is desperate to know why I'm living in my old house. She'll be dying to offer advice, but I have been up to my neck at O'Rowdes', so I have politely refused all her refreshments. I imagine she isn't impressed.

I rented out my cottage when I decided to move to Fox Halt, so I can't get my tenants out for six months. I am not sure what to do. I have no idea what the future holds. Perhaps I should seek Jayne's counselling after all?

I know I want some space away from Billy for a while longer. I have to think everything through, and there is a whole list of good reasons to stay at Beechwood for now; Janette won't be back for three or four weeks. The house is close to London, Freddy can go to his old school, and if I want to, I can see Billy regularly. I miss her, but I am forcing my head to rule my heart. I need to know being with her is the one hundred per cent right thing to do. I keep questioning her love for me.

When I reflect on my marriage to Janette, I see that she just needed me for the security she thought I would provide for her and our family. Janette and I are far better apart, and we are friends now. There is no pretence and no misgivings. I fear the same mistake again with Billy. I want her to love me, not want me just for all the support and help I give her.

I am longing to see her and hold her in my arms. I love the farm and being there with Billy, but I need reassurance that she *really* is the woman of my dreams.

We pass the turn-off to Bristol, and my mind turns to Billy's wonderful mum. Daniella's been like a mother to me too; I miss sitting at the farmhouse kitchen table chatting to her about all the little things in our lives. She has emailed me so many times asking me to come back. In the end, I had to tell her I was too busy to reply. I explained about sorting out all the administration at O'Rowdes', and I promised we would talk today.

Just past the junction for Bridgwater, I start analysing the O'Rowdes' nightmare. Michael's death has left a complex jumble of different issues to sort out. Everything was in Michael's sole ownership and his will is a one-liner leaving everything to Jessie. There are offshore accounts, trusts and companies with names that make no sense. I am not even certain they are all legitimate. I keep thinking how unlikely it was that Michael should kill himself, but then my past experience proved I knew little about him.

Michael was my business associate, but I also believed he was a close friend. Yet over the years he duped and double-crossed me, and I suspect he did the same to many people. Maybe in the end, his conscience, or his pride led him to suicide. Perhaps he anticipated the downfall of his empire, or losing his wife and children? Perhaps he foresaw his wonderful life, and everything he'd worked for and built up from nothing, crashing down around him? Could the mighty Michael O'Rowde not bear the humiliation of it all?

Jessie can't get hold of any money at the moment; the amount she will inherit is massive but there are many hoops to jump through first. Jessie is so wealthy, yet she has no means of paying for anything right now. With a place as big as Culmfield, bills soon mount up, and loaning my bank card to her has been an easy solution.

Jessie trusts me to do the best to help her and she is trying to see what needs to be done. She is astute, but her confidence has been shot to pieces. I have to keep reassuring her that she will be fine.

Arthur helps at every turn. He listens in on our phone calls, asking lots of questions. The boy is doing so much to help, that it makes me wonder what it was like in the house before his father died; Michael was only at Culmfield at weekends, so I wonder if Arthur has been propping up his mother for a long time.

When I first saw Jessie at Fox Halt Farm, I was angry, assuming Michael had broken his beautiful wife. My initial conversations with her felt like I was talking to an empty shell. I thought of her as a helpless victim; captive in her castle-like home. I saw only anxiety and fear, but as I have continued to discuss things with her, I detect an undertone.

I am beginning to suspect that there are glowing embers of a fire still inside the woman that Michael tried to smother.

There is something else too; I feel a connection with her. Like me, Jessie is wary of Billy; her voice stiffens if I mention her old friend. I am guarded about Billy too, she reminds me of my knee that I hurt while I was in Cornwall. Before then, I moved without conscious thought. On the surface my damaged joint looks unblemished but before I sit or stand now, I hesitate, wondering if it will work properly, wary that it may give in, or I will suddenly suffer from a stabbing pain. I no longer take my knee for granted, and this is how I view Billy now. I am unsure of her. I question her motives. When she texts, I read each word carefully, scrutinising every sentence for its true meaning.

I wish I could go back to automatic trust, but the injury is there. I hope it heals, but at the moment, I am too scared to love her.

Fox Halt Farm

Billy

When my phone pings, Mum looks at me. 'What's he saying?' she asks.

'It's Freddy texting. They are at Granada services getting fuel.' Then I laugh.

'What, Billy?' Mum is frowning at me.

'He's asking if there will be any of your world-famous Battenberg cake waiting when they get here.'

'Tell that young man it's already on the table. He can have as big a slice as he wants, three or four slices even. Tell him I can't wait to see them too.'

I send the reply as instructed, and then return to gazing at Grace, who is standing in the yard. She has her head bent over her phone, constantly typing. I guess she and Freddy have communicated throughout his journey. I think how Richard and I might have managed to type two messages at most, before we would have given up the laborious task of key pressing and called each other.

I have only messaged Richard at bedtimes, saying a little about what's happening here and always finishing with *'I love you'*. He replied each morning, *'Missing you'*. Six identical two-word texts in total, since he left to stay at Beechwood.

It was Freddy's idea that they went to stay at his mum's while she is away. I've not seen Beechwood or even been to the village of Jordans, but I reckon it's nothing like Hamsgate. I picture executive style homes and lawned cul-de-sacs. Nothing like the mismatched cottages crammed on either side of Church Lane. In Jordans, I imagine precise tiled roofs, swimming pools and tennis courts, so different from our village with its lumpy thatched cottages and leaning stone walls where tractors have nudged them to make the potholed lane a bit wider.

I don't like the thought of Richard and Freddy back in their old home, but the lack of communication has been good in a way, because I didn't want to talk in texts, or even on the phone. I have so much to tell him, but I want to say it directly to Richard's hazel eyes. I want him to see how sorry I am.

I see his empty cottage every time I step outside the house. I see Mum and Grace looking miserable and it makes me want to crawl back to my bed and cry. I miss him with all my heart. There is only one thing that's making each day bearable, and that is Mary. I love having her back in my life.

At last Richard's car pulls into the yard, and Grace and I rush at it from different directions. I expected my mother to follow me outside, but she hasn't.

'Hello,' he says, as he climbs out. He is slow to stand up; his knees seem stiff from the long journey.

'Hi, sweetheart, I have missed you.' I am relieved as he takes my hand in his. 'Billy, I hoped we could perhaps walk up to High Willhays. I'll be ready to go in ten minutes, could you find something for a packed lunch?'

I am shocked by the sudden instructions. I expected him to come inside, sit at the table, drink tea and eat two slices of his favourite cake. I wanted things to be normal. I try to hide my disappointment. 'That sounds amazing, Richard,' I say, 'we haven't been up on the moor for months. It's been so dry, I'll just wear my trainers. Have you got sunscreen?'

'Yes, here.' He waves an orange bottle at me. 'I picked up some just now at the services. See you in ten minutes.' He hasn't moved away from the car. I stare at him, wanting to ask him to come indoors but my mouth is too dry for any words.

'Will you drive?' he asks. 'I've had enough of driving for one day.'

'Yes,' I reply. I turn to go back into the house, disheartened that our first conversation was about footwear, sun protection and who will drive us to the start of the walk. Now, I am thinking that Richard plans to find some remote spot up on the hill to tell me that he has decided that we are finished. He came back to say goodbye, that's all. He'll leave Fox Halt Farm later and this time it will be forever.

In the kitchen, Mum has left me a note. *'Gone to help in the shop. Mary is coming with me. Herbie says it's really busy. Dinner at seven, Richard's favourite steak and kidney pie. Have a great day both of you'.* I scrawl a sentence on the bottom of the paper. *'Going for a walk on the moors – taking dog – we love you xxx'.*

I fill an old rucksack with everything I can think of that I might need for the day, and then I rush outside with the bag on my back and Crinkle in my arms. I smile at Richard as best I can, with the fob of my van keys gripped between my teeth.

'Piggy can't come.' Richard has refused to call our dog her proper name since she was a pup. He says she only thinks about food. I tell him off for using such a cruel name, arguing she is not greedy, and she is far too pretty to be called Piggy.

I spit the keys out of my mouth. 'Why not? She loves it up on the moors.' As I reply, Crinkle wriggles out of my hold and gallops towards Richard at top speed. The Border terrier is so happy to see him that she wees over the toes of his walking boots. He picks her up.

'Alright, Piggy, you can come. I've missed you, little one.' Richard stares into her black eyes, and she winks back at him. I wish he was holding me saying how much he missed me.

'Have you got her lead?' he asks.

'Yep,' I reply.

The number of tors on Dartmoor is difficult to say exactly because it depends on how you define a tor, but there must be around two hundred. Not all the summits have rocky granite outcrops, some are just rounded heather moorland. Some are simply marked with a pile of rocks built up into a cairn, or a sheltering wall. Richard and I have climbed most of them in the last couple of years. Our hikes were a way to unwind from the work on the farm and gave us time to chat through ideas. We always race to the tops, walking until we are nearly there, and then, making a sudden sprint for the last few yards, hoping to catch the other unawares.

'I am going to win,' I goad Richard. 'Come on. Are you getting old?'

'No, I just want to go at this pace, it's been a tiring week and we haven't done this for ages. I'm not as fit as you.' Richard sounds serious. I'd hoped a dash for the summit of High Willhays would lighten the atmosphere between us, but it doesn't, and we stomp up the last few feet apart and in silence.

A three-hundred-and-sixty-degree view greets us. This is the highest point on Dartmoor: we can see thirty miles at least, and maybe into Cornwall, even with the heat haze obscuring the far away coastline. There are dots in the distance that we know are the cows at Fox Halt Farm, and the metal farm roofs are glinting in the sunshine. It is rarely this still or sunny up here, yet I don't feel any elation.

'Shall we have something to eat?' Richard is opening his backpack.

'Great idea,' I say, then my voice trails off because I have spied inside his bag. I can see that Richard purchased more than sunscreen in the motorway services. He has bought delicious looking snacks too, enough for both of us.

'What's wrong?' he asks.

'Nothing, don't worry,' I say, not wanting to explain because I know I am probably being silly. I was looking forward to us sharing all the lovely food I'd gathered up in the minutes I had to get ready for our adventure. I wanted to watch Richard smiling while he enjoyed the special goodies I've carried to the top of this hill. I had been delighted with what I had found in the kitchen, which had included some pork pies which Mum brought back from the farm shop yesterday. She said they had a few left over, and someone was bound to drop in and eat them. She even suggested that Richard might enjoy them for lunch. Yesterday, I hadn't imagined a picnic up here, I thought we would be sitting at the kitchen table with Mum fussing around us, making tea and producing all sorts of things from cake tins, or extra-large Tupperware containers.

Mum is always prepared for visitors; friends, family and neighbours all know they are welcome anytime at the farm, there is no need for an invitation. Since Dad died the number of people who turn up on our doorstep has doubled, maybe even trebled, but in seconds, Mum will always find sustenance for them all.

Richard watches me place all my provisions next to his. Neither of us speak. This is horrible; everything is wrong. We are not the team we used to be. As we walked, I answered his questions about what I've been doing, and the various faces Richard pulled made him look interested, but he made no particular comments.

Richard said that the police have confirmed Michael died from carbon monoxide poisoning. However, Jessie can't organise his funeral yet because the coroner hasn't released his body.

We skirted the subject of our relationship, aided by Crinkle, who seemed to sense our unease. It was as though the dog wanted to make us laugh. She kept jumping around or wrapping herself around our legs. All the time, her tongue was hanging out, and she looked like she was grinning her head off.

Richard has put the happy dog on the lead, securing one end of her tether under a heavy stone. Crinkle settles down in the only bit of shade while I pour water into an empty food container and set it down next to her. The intuitive dog laps noisily, and I wonder if she is trying to interrupt the edgy silence between Richard and me.

'Billy, I love you,' Richard says at last. I close my eyes and take a slow breath in. I have waited for those words for so long. My reply rushes out. 'Sorry, Richard, I am so sorry that I didn't send Jessie away.'

'I know you are, Billy, but how could you have done it?' Richard has his eyes fixed on mine.

'Look, please understand. I am so sorry. It was just such a shock seeing Jessie again. I wanted to help her. I didn't think.' My cheeks are on fire.

'No, Billy, you *did* think. I asked you not to let her stay, but you went ahead anyway.' He pauses. 'Billy, you knew what you were doing. You knew helping Jessie could put your Mum at risk, or Grace, or William – even Freddy could have been in danger. You knew what Michael threatened to do if you saw Jessie again.' He stares at Crinkle and she wags her tail.

I move to the dog, hoping I can make him look at me again. 'How could I tell them to go?' I ask.

'How could you *not* tell them?'

'I'm sorry. I just couldn't.'

'You're not sorry, Billy. If it were happening now, you'd do it all over again. Wouldn't you?'

I rub the coarse hair under Crinkle's chin. 'Not if I had known what would happen to us,' I say. 'I wish I could turn the clock back. I had no idea I was choosing Jessie over you.'

'Stop lying, Billy.' His tone is sharp. 'You decided not to go on holiday with me. You said you had to stay with Jessie. I had a taxi organised for her. I would have paid for Mary and her to go somewhere else for a few days. Billy, we could have gone to Paros.' Richard shakes his head. 'You knew what you were doing.'

'Okay. You're right.' I hold out my arms and stand up. Crinkle paws at my knee because she wants me to scratch her neck some more, but I ignore her. 'Yes, Richard, I should have sent Mary and Jessie away. I am sorry. Please forgive me?'

He doesn't reply, so I try another tack. 'You say you love me, so please forget my stupid decision.' I step towards him, but he moves away.

'Forgive, yes. I can forgive you. Forget, Billy? No, I can't forget what you did.'

This is hopeless. 'You can't accept that I made a mistake?'

'No, I thought I was your priority. Hell, I asked you to marry me, didn't I? Billy, this is tearing me apart. I feel like I don't know you anymore.'

'Can't we just get back to where we were?' I say.

'No.' He shakes his head again.

'Not *ever*?'

'Billy, I wish we could go back, but what happened has happened. It can't be undone.'

'But I love you. I want to be with you forever, be your wife. Our love is stronger than an argument over Jessie.'

He doesn't reply.

'So that's it, we give up?' I whisper. 'All those years, the heartbreak, all our history together, and our love for one another? You want to walk away from all of that?'

'I don't want to walk away.'

'Don't then.'

'But I don't want to feel like this.' Richard sounds like he is beaten. 'Marriage is about loving the other person without conditions. Your partner has to come first, but I believe that in our relationship, Billy, it's you who always comes first. *You* wanted Jessie's forgiveness. *You* wanted her and Mary to see you were sorry for abandoning them, for lying to Jessie and cheating on her. *You* wanted them to stay, so *you* could feel better about yourself.'

'I just wanted to help them,' I argue. 'Surely, you know that?'

'But you didn't care about my opinion, did you, Billy?'

'I did, I knew you were angry, but I thought you loved me so much you would help. That we would help Jessie together. I didn't think you'd abandon me and head off to Cornwall. I didn't think you wouldn't reply to a single one of my texts, when I apologised and said I was wrong.' I pause, feeling close to tears. I am angry. 'Nor did I think for one minute you'd let me get through Ross's birthday and the anniversary of Saffi's death on my own either!'

Richard can see I am upset, but he doesn't ease off.

'You didn't, did you? You expected me to come running. Just like I always do.' He puts his head in his hands for a moment, then he stares at me. His eyes are watering now. 'I lit a candle too, Billy, and I remembered Ross and Saffi. I sat on a lonely beach with Marcus, and I cried too.'

His reply about the candle on the lonely beach wipes away my anger in an instant. I had made up my mind that his absence last Sunday was heartless. I thought he had forgotten the birthday that might have been if I hadn't miscarried our baby. The very same date that Saffi died.

On Sunday, I placed my candle in the centre of the kitchen table marking the sixteenth birthday of the son we never got to meet. That same night, I looked across the table at Freddy, and imagined the child I wanted to name Ross, sitting in his place. Richard too, how I wished he was there with me, sharing my heartbreak of what might have been.

I didn't tell Richard I was pregnant with Ross. I loved him, but our affair was over, and I planned to manage without him, while he tried to mend his marriage. When our baby bled away, I fell into a bottomless pit of despair. It was my life at Culmfield that helped me climb out. It was Michael and Jessie who rescued me from the desolation that overwhelmed me for months afterwards.

My candlelit vigil was for Ross and Saffi, and for my dad and grandad, Tom and Ed too - all the amazing people in my life who I'll never forget. I felt so alone that night, but never considered that Richard might also be watching another candle somewhere, slowly burning.

Chapter 7

HIGH WILLHAYS, DARTMOOR

BILLY

On top of the highest hill on Dartmoor, my mood is at its lowest. Knowing that Richard was also grieving has turned my anger to angst. I know deep down that everything Richard has said is true. I was finding excuses for helping Jessie, and the way Richard has seen through me empties me of hope. I breathe slowly, determined to stop my tears. 'We are finished then?' I ask.

'No, darling. I'm saying I don't know how I feel about you anymore, I won't lie to you. I love you, but I am not sure you love me in the same way.'

'I love you with all my heart.'

Crinkle stretches her head on her paws, her eyes fixed on Richard – it seems she might be pleading with him too.

'I have been thinking a lot about this, Billy,' he says. 'I don't want to give up on us, but I don't want to be taken for granted either.'

'Don't give up on me.' I shake my head.

'I'm not. I've decided that I will come back to the farm every Saturday, and we can do something together. Go on a date, I suppose, and let's see if the magic comes back.'

'Magic?' I frown at him.

'I mean the sort of blind love, and the thrill of being with you.' He grabs my hand and holds it.

'Thank you, Richard,' I say, squeezing his hand.

He changes the subject, nodding towards our untouched food. 'Look, are you going to eat any of this?'

'I'm sorry, can't eat anything,' I reply. 'My stomach's inside out.'

'Same here,' he says. 'What should we give Piggy for her patience? Look at her, she doesn't understand why we are in this perfect spot on such a beautiful day ignoring all this delicious food.'

My mind slips back to something he said before. 'Every Saturday. Do you promise?'

'Yes.'

I feared the worse, but now I have a little bit of hope, at least.

A few feet below the summit of Yes Tor, Richard is suddenly lying on the peaty ground beside me. Straightaway, Crinkle thinks it is a game, and she jumps on him. I laugh, but he swipes the terrier away. He rubs his knee. 'I tripped into a rabbit hole in the sand dunes in Cornwall,' he explains. 'My sore knee is why I let you beat me to the top of High Willhays. I was too frightened to run, in case it gave in.'

'What can I do to help?' I ask.

'Can we just stay here for a moment?'

'Of course, we can. It doesn't look like you have a choice. You shouldn't have hiked if your knee was bad. Have you had it looked at?' I am wondering if we should call Dartmoor Rescue to stretcher him off the hill.

'It'll be fine. It's a twinge, that's all. Just give me a moment,' he says, and I shrug because I am not confident in his prognosis.

We sit for a while, and eat the pork pies, until Richard stands up on his injured leg. 'I reckon it will be okay now,' he says, 'as long as we take it gently on the way back.'

That's what we do; we walk slowly, and somehow, things start to feel a bit better between us.

Our evening meal is friendly enough, but Mum seems unusually quiet. I think she is desperate to ask how Richard and I got on, but she doesn't ask. I wouldn't know what to tell her anyway. Freddy hardly speaks either, because he is texting Grace throughout.

Grace wouldn't join us for dinner. I suspect she still can't bear to be anywhere near me, the person who ruined her summer holiday, possibly her *whole* life. She blames me for Freddy leaving, and that Mary has Braveheart too.

It's Mary who keeps conversation dribbling along, as she asks easy questions requiring simple answers from us all in turn. She even musters a few laughs. I wonder if the atmosphere around the table tonight is similar to the meals she used to experience at Culmfield. Mary may well be a practised peacemaker?

Once we finish our apple and blackberry crumble, Richard gets up. 'Daniella, that was amazing, thank you. I'll load the dishwasher before I go,' he says.

'You don't need to go yet. Do you?' Mum glances at me. I guess she wants me to make him stay.

I don't want to beg. I know the dinner hasn't been easy, and I am sure we'd all like to leave the table, but I don't want him to disappear either. I try not to sound desperate. 'Richard, can't you stay a bit longer, it's not like it's far for you to get to bed.' I smile, wondering if there could be a tiny chance he might come upstairs with me later instead of sleeping in the cottage.

Richard doesn't return my smile. 'I'm staying at Culmfield tonight,' he says. I am shocked, I assumed he would stay in the cottage across the yard tonight.

'We aren't going to Culmfield now. Are we?' Freddy has looked up from his phone, and he seems as surprised as me.

'You can choose, Freddy,' Richard replies. 'Stay here if you want and I'll pick you up tomorrow afternoon, or you can come to Culmfield with me now.'

'Why do you have to go tonight?' I haven't heard these two argue before. They usually just rub along together, happy to do whatever the other wants to do. Richard moves behind Freddy's chair and he places a hand on his son's shoulder. 'Freddy, I am not going to lie, I don't want to stay next door without Billy, and I don't want to be upstairs with her either.'

Freddy's annoyance turns to embarrassment; he leans forward in his chair. 'Dad, stop. Please.' But his father doesn't stop. 'You aren't stupid, son, you know Billy and I are having problems–'

'But–'

'Jessie has a nice bedroom for you to stay in,' Richard says. 'If you want to come with me tonight, and…' Richard waits for Freddy to look at him.

'And what?' Freddy snaps.

'Freddy, if you choose to stay here, then please remember what I said about Grace. You are not to sleep with her.'

Freddy stands up, so he is face to face with his father. 'Dad, Grace and I are not doing anything, okay?'

'Alright, I trust you,' Richard says quickly. 'Are you staying at Fox Halt then?'

'Affirmative.' Freddy sits back down, before he turns to me. 'And I will stay in the farmhouse, if that's okay with Billy and Mrs May.'

Mum and I say yes at the same time.

'Daniella.' Richard is looking at my mum now.

'Yes,' she replies.

'There is something you need to know.'

My mother catches my eye. 'What do I need to know, Richard?' She speaks slowly.

'I'll be coming back here each Saturday, but I won't be staying overnight again. Billy and I need some time apart for a while.' He is staring at me now. 'Billy, this affects you too.'

'Go on,' I say, frightened what bombshell he will drop on me next.

'I have re-advertised my cottage here as a holiday let with bookings available from next Saturday,' he says.

'Next week?' Mum frowns at him.

'Yes, Daniella,' Richard nods. 'I'm sure you will get some enquiries soon, so I've organised a cleaner for Monday.

The guests can use my furniture, and Freddy and I will collect all our personal bits tomorrow, before we head back to Beechwood.'

Mum opens and closes her mouth, and then she sits back in her chair.

'You're not going to have Sunday lunch with us tomorrow, then?' I murmur.

'No, thank you, Billy. I'm taking Jessie and the boys out for a roast dinner. It's all booked. A change of scene will do them good.'

Mum stands up now. 'You seem to have it all worked out, Richard. Do I get a kiss goodbye?'

'Of course, Daniella,' he smiles, 'but there is something I need to check first.' He turns to Mary, who has picked up the *Okehampton Times*, and looks engrossed in an article on the front page. 'Mary,' Richard says, but there is no sign she has heard. He speaks louder.

'*Mary.*' This time, she looks up.

'Sorry, Richard, were you talking to me?' Mary asks, smiling sweetly at him.

'Will you come with me now, to Culmfield? It would mean the world to your mother to have you back home again with her and your brothers.'

Mary shakes her head. 'No thank you,' she replies, 'but please tell them all that I love them.'

'Are you sure?' he asks.

I answer for her. 'Yes, Mary's certain. Richard, please don't press her. Tell Jessie she is fine here. She'll be back when she is ready.' I get up from the table to stand next to Mum. 'Are you sure, Richard?' I ask him.

'About what?'

'About giving up the cottage, that's what.'

'Yes, Billy, I am.'

'And Mary's sure she doesn't want to go home, so please just go, will you? Freddy is staying here too, so just go. Go on your own.' I feel uneasy, having no control over what's happening.

'Okay,' he says. He kisses me lightly on the cheek, then he kisses Mum too. 'See you tomorrow afternoon.'

Freddy follows his father outside and I hear their faint voices before Richard's car starts up.

'Thank you, Auntie.' Mary touches my hand. 'Thank you for caring for this little cuckoo chick.'

I savour the touch from another person. 'It's lovely to have you here, darling,' I reply. 'Stay as long as you need.'

'Thank you.' Mary smiles at me and then looks away. I know that this is all she wants to say for now. She is still not ready to explain her reasons for staying with a surrogate family and adopting their nest.

CULMFIELD

RICHARD

It's dark when I phone Jessie using the hands-free in my car. 'No, Mary is not with me,' I say, whilst watching the enormous wrought-iron gates shake open in front of me.

There's a long pause before Jessie speaks again. 'I'll meet you by the front steps,' she says before cutting off our call. As I get out of my car, Jessie snatches at my elbow. She grips my arm tightly, and without a word steers me across the wide forecourt to the building immediately opposite.

The chapel isn't locked, and as we step inside, Jessie clicks on the lights. 'It's magical isn't it?' she whispers. She's right, it is spectacular inside. The walls and the high-domed ceiling are covered in murals of fantastical creatures and plants. I drink it all in, as though I've not seen it before. In truth, it is the first time I have noticed the decoration, because last time I was here, I couldn't take my eyes off Saffi's coffin.

'You've only seen the interior in daylight before, haven't you?' Jessie says, still holding on to me, 'but Grégoire painted everything in here to be at its most spectacular in candlelight.' She gazes up at the ceiling, and a mythical bird grasping fruit and flowers in its mighty talons. Jessie sighs.

'This place is my sanctuary,' she says. 'I call it *My Place of What Ifs*.'

'Yes, Jessie.' I look up at some ripe strawberries hanging out of a pelican-like bill, and it feels as if I could reach up and snatch one of the succulent looking fruit. I imagine its sweet taste on my tongue. 'Grégoire Laurent is a talented artist, that's for sure.'

'Were you thinking about that dreadful day?' Jessie asks.

I nod at her. 'Yes,' I say. 'That day, I stood here, wishing Saffi would storm down the aisle in his high-tech wheelchair and thank everyone for coming. My friend was always joking around, so I kept hoping I'd hear him laugh, and then he would lead us outside to a surprise party on your lawn, where a string quartet would play his favourite arias. You know, Jessie, Saffi is never far from my thoughts.'

She touches my face. 'I wish I had met him. *She* talked about Saffi all the time, saying what an amazing friend he was to her.' Jessie is talking about Billy, she hasn't used her name since I first started helping with the business. She continues. 'Poor Grégoire too, he has never been the same. His death affected him very badly too.'

'You should have met him, Jessie. Saffi was so full of life. It's no wonder I can't believe he's not around anymore.'

'What if I had met him, and he'd fallen in love with me?' She is smiling, and I smile back. I notice how her blue sweater drowns her thin frame, and I imagine her jeans are belted tight over her hip bones. It's as though Jessie borrowed the clothes from someone else. I wonder if they are Nala's, but the legs and sleeves are too long.

'You wanted to speak to me privately, Richard, and I considered this would be a good place to talk,' Jessie says.

'Are your boys alright on their own?' I check.

'Don't worry,' she says. 'They are in the drawing room glued to the *Bee Movie*.'

She sees my surprise, and laughs. 'Richard, it's a film for kids, about bees. The DVD arrived yesterday, and it seemed like a nice idea. Nala, Amir and Sharmarke are watching it too; it looked good, from the bit I saw.'

'Oh, I see,' I say noticing how Jessie looks worn out.

'You said you needed to discuss something with me, and not to include Arthur, so here I am, on my own. Talk to me.'

'Tomorrow morning will be fine, Jessie, if you're too tired now, or you want to go back inside with your boys…' I say.

She frowns, making me suggest another option. 'Or we could just stay here for a while in the quiet. Light some candles, or something? Whatever you'd like to do?' I am not talking to Jessie in the reserved way I did with Billy earlier. It's nice not to have to choose my words carefully, trying to get my point across without hurting her feelings.

'No, please tell me now, what is it?' Jessie lets go of my arm and sits down on a long wooden bench running along the back wall.

'If you're sure?' For a second, I recall my stilted conversation with Billy just before I left Fox Halt Farm. I could tell that despite my attempts not to upset her, I still caused hurt. Jessie isn't moving, waiting for me to continue.

I sit down next to her. 'I'll get right to the point, I'm too exhausted for small talk,' I say.

'So am I, Richard. Much too tired for niceties, just carry on, please. Whatever it is you want to say, tell me it straight.'

'There's been an offer to buy O'Rowdes', and a strong suggestion that there will be a second bid from another rival supermarket on Monday.'

She leans back, resting her spine against the wall. I am not sure she has grasped what I've said, so I check. 'Jessie, would you sell?'

'What do you think?' She tips her head to one side.

'I am not sure, Jessie. I don't fully understand Michael's business yet, and I don't know who to trust within the company to advise me. I don't know if my would-be advisers have an inherent self-interest, and I am uncertain who will give me the true picture.'

Jessie lifts her head upright again, sliding forward on the polished seat. 'Funny,' she says, but she is not smiling.

'What's funny?' I ask.

'Not funny.' She pauses. 'That was the wrong word. I suppose I meant ironic. You sound like Michael.'

'Why?' I shrug my shoulders.

Jessie copies my movement, but in an exaggerated way. She looks uncomfortable, as though the memory I have evoked is painful for her.

'That's what Michael said when he got *her* to work for him – Michael said he wanted someone he could trust.' She sighs deeply. 'I thought I could trust her too. You never know, do you?'

'Sorry, Jessie, I didn't mean to–'

'It doesn't matter,' she cuts in. 'Forget it, Richard. Please just tell me what you think I should do.'

'Don't sell,' I reply quickly.

'Why not?'

'Well, I think—' I pause, running my fingers over my chin, and feeling my end-of-day bristles. 'From what I have been able to find out so far, O'Rowdes' can weather this current downturn, and you should have a lot more money in the long-term by holding firm.'

Jessie recognises an uncertainty in my voice. 'You aren't sure, Richard?' she says. 'What are you uncertain of?' She holds my gaze, waiting for my response.

'If you don't sell,' I say, 'then O'Rowdes' needs to recruit some first class people to take it forward. I don't know who those people are, how you get them, or indeed how long it will take to put them in place. I'm not certain what will happen to the business in the meantime. O'Rowdes' is facing serious competition and it needs to get some exceptional people in place to lead it into the future, and those people need to be found as soon as possible if the company's going to survive.'

'It's a minefield, isn't it?' Jessie says.

'Yes.' I change track, wanting her to look at this from another angle. 'How much money do you need for a secure future for you and your family?' I don't wait for the answer. 'Personally, if it was me, I'd hold out for the best offer, accept it and run. But it's not me, it's you who has to decide.'

Jessie's answer is immediate. 'Sell. I don't want it. I am not interested, and the family will be better off without the business. Just like we are without Michael.'

'You don't mean that,' I say, a little half-heartedly because I know she might be right. I can see what Michael has done to her.

'I mean it, Richard, we're being honest with each other, aren't we? I'm glad he is not here.'

I don't want to debate this with Jessie. I go back to the sale. 'Think carefully. It is a big decision. Don't have regrets later,' I say.

'I *am* thinking carefully. Do it please, Richard. Get rid of it.' She stands up. 'Let's go and watch the film.' But I stay where I am. I don't want to leave this conversation so suddenly. Emotion has taken over, and the future of O'Rowdes' is too serious for that. I tell her, 'Let's see what happens on Monday.'

I am surprised how quickly Jessie's confidence is returning. She is so much stronger. I wonder if it's because she believes in me and feels assured that I will look after her interests. I hope she does because I am trying my hardest to help her. I remember Jessie before she met Michael, and to see her like she was, when she turned up at Fox Halt Farm was shocking.

When I first introduced her to Michael, she was beautiful, fearless, and enthralling. That was just after she inherited Culmfield Court. Back then the estate was run down with too many bills to pay. Jessie came to MarcFenns for advice. Michael was my client too, so I arranged for them to meet so he could discuss purchasing some of Jessie's land for a housing development. Michael bought the land, and he asked Jessie to marry him that same day. I feel guilty that the introduction I organised had such unpleasant repercussions. I knew Michael was clever and that he got everything he wanted. It looks as though Jessie's life turned into one of relentless control, with her feistiness and charm squashed out of her.

'Jessie, I need you to clarify something for me,' I say.
'What is it?'

'Sit down again, please.'

'Alright,' she says, sitting back down on the bench. 'What do you need to know?'

I am uncertain how to phrase the question. I don't want to embarrass her. Jessie sees my unease. 'Come on, Richard, tell me. I won't cry, I promise.'

I feel my face and neck reddening. 'Why did you let Michael put absolutely everything in his sole name?' I ask. 'Why did you let him take control of it all? Has Michael forged your signature over and over again? We have one hell of a journey ahead of us, to undo what he did. Were you aware of what he was doing, Jessie?'

'He didn't forge my signature.' She smiles. 'He coerced me.'

'How do you mean coerced?' I ask.

'Michael didn't force me, nor did he threaten me,' she explains. 'It was gradual. Fifteen years of relentless persuasion, until I just went along with anything he wanted. He was clever.'

'You are too, Jessie. Surely you realised what was happening?'

'Constant criticism and arguments wear you down, Richard. I began to doubt myself, and our disagreements weren't rows, they were silences. Quiet is unbearable after a while. Michael wasn't one for discussion, and it just became easier to give in to him. He was only at Culmfield at weekends, and I didn't want the children to see we weren't talking.'

'I see,' I say, remembering my business meetings with Michael when things weren't going his way. He didn't listen to people telling him there were problems, or time delays. He expected difficulties to be dealt with, and somehow things always turned out as he planned.

'My husband always got his own way.' Jessie looks at me. 'You know that as well as anyone, don't you?' I nod, then she continues. 'Michael manipulated everyone, even me.' She pauses. 'I think *she* was probably the first person to say no to him. When their affair ended, it stung him to his core.

Michael made sure I couldn't desert him too. Sorry, Richard, you don't need to hear about my marriage.'

'Jessie, I want to know. I would like to understand why the finances are set up like they are. Was he ever violent?'

She shakes her head. 'Nope, I just rolled over. He just did what he liked, and I let him. It was all mind games; he never physically hurt me, never hit me. No, he simply found fault in everything I did – looking back now, I think he even created situations to make me believe I was going mad – It was only our children that kept me from killing myself. I felt so worthless. Nala looked after most things for me, while I just surrendered, doing anything he wanted. Agreeing to everything. Mary running away was like a fog lifting for me,' Jessie continues. 'It felt like her anger was directed at me. My daughter wanting to leave really shook me up. She made me want to fight back.'

'Listen, Jessie, do you really want to talk about this now? I see how upset you are,' I say, touching her hand, but she keeps going.

'I grabbed hold of Mary, refusing to let her leave. I think I must have hurt my daughter because I clawed at her hair, to stop her from walking out the door.' Jessie suddenly changes the subject. 'If I sell, I won't sell the name, no-one is using O'Rowdes' name again. It goes with him,' she says.

'We can't do anything about that yet, Jessie,' I tell her.

She switches back to Mary. 'Why do you think she won't come home?' she asks.

'I don't know, Jessie,' I say.

'I thought it was her dad who drove her away, but it can't be – If it was Michael, then would Mary be home now.'

'I really don't know,' I say again.

Chapter 8

CULMFIELD COURT
RICHARD

Jessie rests a hand on the old font, focusing her attention on the glowing night-lights arranged evenly around the top.

'Did something unusual happen that morning?' I ask her.

She is not listening.

'Jessie, did anything unusual happen that morning?'

'What, Richard?' she asks, looking up.

'The morning when you found Mary packing her case, did something happen beforehand?'

'No, nothing, as far as I remember,' Jessie replies, her concentration returning to the flames.

'So, what exactly do you remember? Maybe we can find a clue to what upset Mary.'

'It was pretty much like every Saturday.' I feel like Jessie is mesmerised by the candles, and I wonder if I should click my fingers to get her to listen. I try raising my voice instead. '*Jessie*. Tell me about that morning, please.'

Jessie turns to look at me. 'Sorry, Richard, I was thinking about Mary, wondering what she was doing right now.'

I check my watch. 'I expect she is in bed. She helps with the milking most mornings, so she's usually up pretty early.'

'She likes it at Fox Halt?' Jessie asks.

'Yes, I think so, I don't know for sure, but in her texts to me, Billy makes it sound like Mary is always busy helping her.'

'I can't bear to think of Mary being unhappy,' she says.

'She's alright, Jessie, I'm sure she is, and she'll come home soon,' I say, trying to stop Jessie worrying, even though I have no real clue about when, or if, Mary is going to return. So far, each time I have offered to drive her back to Culmfield, she has immediately refused.

'Please, Jessie, tell me about that morning,' I say, distracting her from her thoughts of her daughter at Fox Halt Farm.

'Don't lie to me, Richard,' she says. 'I can see it in your eyes. You aren't certain Mary will ever come home, are you?'

'Jessie, Mary will be home soon, I am certain,' I say again, trying to sound more convincing this time. Shocked she realised what I was really thinking.

Jessie laughs. 'Don't worry, Richard, I'm sure she will too. I have to be patient. Mary will come back when she is ready. You asked me what happened that morning. I remember Sharmarke and Mary practising their show jumping first thing, and I saw Mary after their lesson. She was her normal happy self. The two of them were supposed to be at Bicton today, they were practising for the show.'

'Bicton?' I frown.

'Bicton Arena, it's a local venue for jumping competitions. Some of the big qualifiers for both show jumping and horse trials are held there.'

'Right,' I say, 'and she was okay?'

'Yes, I remember her boasting to me how she was going to win. Sharmarke and Mary always try to beat one another. Mary's horse is more experienced, whereas Sharmarke's is headstrong. That morning, Sharmarke was finding it difficult to get his horse to settle, and Mary told me he was knocking jumping poles left, right and centre. Yes. After their lesson, she was fine.'

'And after that?' I ask.

Jessie shakes her head. 'I suppose that was probably about an hour before I found Mary packing. She was red-faced from crying and she was very angry.' Jessie stops. I wait several seconds for her to continue, but she doesn't say anything else.

I ask a new question. 'Did Sharmarke go to Bicton today? To the competition, I mean?'

'Yes, and he won. He said Mary wasn't there. Surely, *she* could have taken her? *She* must know how important the competitions are.'

'I don't think your daughter has talked to Billy about competing at Bicton, or anywhere else for that matter,' I say. 'I think Billy would have mentioned it to me if Mary had wanted to go. I know for sure that Mary spent today working in the farm shop.'

'Isn't she riding?'

'Yes, every day. The boy next door has some jumps she's been using, and Billy's found Mary a top-notch riding instructor too.'

Jessie sits next to me now. It feels too close, so I ease myself away a fraction. Her eyes fix back on the candles. 'Good, I'm glad she is riding,' she says. 'It's all Mary wants to do. Michael kept on nagging her that she would inherit Culmfield one day, and he kept on telling her she had to concentrate on her school work instead.'

She touches my hand, but I don't move it away. I think Jessie just wants to make sure I am listening, before continuing. 'Mary doesn't want a big country house, she dreams of travelling the world on the show jumping circuit. Riding and winning, that's all she wants to do, but Michael scoffed, kept saying it was all a big fantasy, and she'd never be good enough, or he would explain how much hard work would be involved to get to the top of the sport, and stay there.'

'Mary will inherit Culmfield?' I ask.

'Yes, she is our eldest child. Did you think Arthur would inherit this place?' Jessie presses my fingers as she takes her hand off mine.

'No. It's just that I didn't think Michael was looking at things that way, everything I have seen so far makes it look like Michael thought he would keep control forever.'

'What do you mean?'

'His will, and the way he organised things here. It's the same at O'Rowdes'. It's as though he never really considered that he wouldn't be in charge.'

'No, that's wrong. Michael often talked about the children, and how the boys would run the business together in the future.'

'So, how can you think about selling it?' I ask.

'Why did you sell MarcFenn? You had children to take it on, it was a multinational company just like O'Rowdes. Your company had been in your family for six generations. Is that right?'

I nod.

'But you still chose to sell, didn't you?' Jessie says.

'Yes.'

'O'Rowdes' has no lineage like MarcFenn, and the company has no sentimental value to me either.'

'Look, Jessie,' I say. 'Yes, MarcFenn was big, but never on the scale of O'Rowdes'. Selling out is a monumental decision.'

Jessie is unperturbed. 'Same principle though, you didn't want your kids forced into taking on the family firm. You didn't want them duty bound to follow in your footsteps? You wanted to allow the twins and Freddy to choose their own future, didn't you?'

'How do you know that?' I am shocked again, I have never spoken to Jessie about my decision to walk away from my property company. I turn to face her, and she mirrors my move. 'Michael told me. He said you discussed it with him for hours.'

'Yes, sorry, I had forgotten about that.' I feel a sense of relief, I was finding her ability to almost see through me unnerving.

Jessie speaks quickly now. 'Michael and you were friends for years, Richard, have you forgotten that too?'

'We *were* friends,' I say.

'And you chucked Michael away for *her*?'

'Billy didn't destroy our friendship.' I feel agitated.

'Really?'

'Yes truly, Billy was *not* the reason.'

'So, why did you and Michael split?'

I stand up; this is not what I want to talk about. 'It's late,' I say. 'Let's stop now.'

'No, tell me, Richard.' She looks up at me, reminding me of Crinkle when she wants food. Jessie's eyes are black, round and pleading. 'I would say if I could, but I can't. Please leave it,' I tell her.

'Why can't you say? I've had enough of secrets. I trust you, Richard, and you must trust me too. I am stronger now. Whatever it is, you must say, don't try to protect me. Whatever happened, I won't be shocked. Look what he did to me. I know what Michael is capable of. Tell me, please.'

I shake my head, keeping my eyes on the floor.

'If you can't talk to me, then I don't want you representing me anymore.' Jessie stands up and tries to pass me in the aisle.

'Fine by me,' I say, stepping back to let her through. 'I wish you and your family all the best.'

Jessie is in front of me. 'I didn't mean it,' she says. 'I know anyway. I just hoped you'd tell me.'

'What do you know?' I say, sitting down again.

'*She* told me.'

'Billy told you?'

'Yes, when I was at Fox Halt. She said Michael was responsible for Tom Westcott's accident.'

My heart stops. It feels as though Jessie has kicked me in the stomach. I can't believe Billy would reveal to anyone our terrible secret, there is so much at risk. I feel I don't know the woman I wanted to marry anymore.

'Please don't go, Richard, I am truly sorry. You're not the only person who won't explain things to me. For pity's sake, my own daughter won't talk to me. I understand why you didn't want to tell me what my husband did.'

Jessie folds forward towards me. It is as though her stick legs have snapped. I catch her, sitting her down beside me. 'It's okay, Jessie, I won't abandon you,' I reassure her. I look around at all the weird creatures on the walls and notice how the candlelight casts shadows that make them seem to move. 'You're right, Jessie, the candles do make Grégoire's work even more admirable,' I say, trying to make her feel more at ease, but she doesn't seem to need further reassurance. Jessie has a new question.

Richard, why did you want to stay at Culmfield tonight? Why aren't you with *her*?'

'Could we talk about that in the morning?' I ask.

'Sorry. Yes,' she replies, 'it's a long time since I had a proper conversation with anyone. We can leave the what ifs, for now.' Jessie lifts herself up. 'I'll show you to your room.'

As we climb the steps up to the house, Jessie stops and turns to me. 'Do you put the yellow gerbera on Saffi's grave each anniversary of his death? Were you here last Sunday? Is it you, who sows the sunflower seeds so that there are always golden blooms standing tall against his headstone on his birthday?'

'No,' I reply. 'Might it be Grégoire? He lives on the edge of the estate, it would be easy for him. I can picture him now, inconsolable at Saffi's funeral.'

'It's not him,' Jessie says.

'I don't know, who it might be, but I wish it *was* me,' I tell her. 'Saffi would have loved the flowers.'

Fox Halt Farm

Sunday 10 August

Billy

The heatwave continues, so we are starting cheese-making early in the morning, as the roasting daytime temperatures would make the cheese sticky and hard to mould. It's just after five, I couldn't sleep, so the dairy seemed a good place to take my mind off Richard.

I am planning to test out the different sized heart-shaped moulds that arrived last week. The new shaped cheeses will be ready by Valentine's Day. I also want to experiment with them, so I can offer our customers a new alternative to wedding cakes.

The shape of the mould affects the cheese. Height, width, and surface area ratios change how it ripens, and how easy the truckles are to handle. Our cheese ripens from the outside in, so if we make them too thick, the truckles won't be ripe in six months' time. If they are too big, they will be awkward to keep turning over, and difficult for shop assistants and customers to handle. Too small and shallow, and the cheese loses moisture too fast.

As I begin lining the new moulds with cheesecloth, the low buzzing of the pasteurising machine, and the germ-free milk dribbling into the cheese-making tank sound soothing.

The room is well lit, and the wet floor reflects light up into the airy space. Slowly, the work, rhythmic background noises, familiar smell and the brightness make me feel less miserable.

'Stop!' I shout at Mum as she bends down to tip the required dose of good bacteria into the pasteurised milk. 'It's not warm enough yet.' I checked the tank a few minutes ago, so I know that the milk hasn't reached the temperature for the micro-organisms to ferment. The carefully controlled process gives Foxy Lady its distinctive taste and texture.

'Sorry, darling, I was just trying to help.' Mum straightens herself back up.

'You should have checked,' I tell her. 'You could have ruined our whole day's production.'

I am shocked that my mother didn't read the thermometer floating in the milk. She is normally so careful about everything. It would be nice if we could use raw milk, so we would not need to reintroduce some of the bacteria that would have been in the milk before we pasteurised it, but the risk of tuberculosis is too high. Our cows are tested regularly for the disease, but outbreaks are still common in Devon. We can't take the chance.

I see Mum's eyes. 'Have you slept?' I ask her.

'No, Billy. Have you?'

'No,' I say, shaking my head. 'In the end, I gave up and decided to come out here instead. I can't stop thinking about him. I've lost him, haven't I?'

My mother stuffs her hands into the shallow pockets of her white coat. 'Maybe,' she says, 'but that's really up to you.'

'Mum, it's Richard who decided to go,' I tell her. 'I couldn't stop him leaving. Surely you see that?'

'You pushed him away, darling,' she argues. 'Just look at what you've done, and what you're *still* doing. It's you, not Richard who can solve this rift. You must show that wonderful man that you love him.'

'I keep on telling him, but he just won't listen,' I say.

'Telling's no good.'

'What?' I ask.

'Billy, sit down and listen. You need to see things through other people's eyes for once. You only ever think about yourself.'

'Mum, I don't,' I say perching myself on the only stool in the preparation area. My mother stands next to me. I look up at her.

'You do, Billy,' she tells me. 'You're spoilt, and you're selfish, and you're thoughtless. You are so lucky to have Richard. You need to wake up and see what you're doing.'

'Don't say that. I do lots of things for people. I'm looking after Mary, I fetched her horse here, I got her a riding coach, I–'

'Shut up, Billy, just listen for once. I'm your mother, I have known you all your life. I see your every move. I know you, and if you let Richard dump you it will be the biggest mistake of your life. And if he does dump you, I shan't blame him.'

My mother never speaks to me like this, she is easy-going and usually agrees with me. I don't say anything, expecting her to relent. In a moment or two, Mum will soften what she has just said with some of my good characteristics.

'But I am *not* selfish, Mum,' I tell her. 'There are things that have happened that you don't know about, there is a terrible secret pushing Richard and me apart.'

'*More* secrets, Billy? I thought you didn't keep things from me anymore? I thought you realised that secrets always get you into trouble? You said you wouldn't lie to me again?'

'Mum, I can't tell you. It won't help if I do,' I reply.

'So, you're not going to tell me that Richard and you believe Michael killed Tom.'

'You know? How? When?' I stumble for words. 'How long have you known?'

'Since late last night, when Richard emailed me.'

'He messaged you?'

'Yes, we have been emailing each other since his daughter's wedding in New Zealand. Unlike you, Billy, Richard talks to me. Sometimes, I think he considers me more of a mother than you do. He misses his mum. He was desperately sad that she wasn't there to see Harry getting married. Did he tell you that?'

I shake my head. I hadn't even thought about how Richard had been feeling that day. I just kept telling him I was missing him, upset because he was there with his ex-wife. Mum lifts her eyebrows. She continues to explain. 'When my phone beeped, I thought it might be a booking for Richard's cottage, and I was curious, hoping it would be one of the regulars.'

'But it was Richard,' I say.

Mum nods at me. 'Yes, he said, he was sorry he had not told me how much he enjoyed the steak and kidney pie. He also apologised for not having the chance to talk.'

'And?' I say, hoping she'll get to the point. I am impatient, desperate to know why he told my mother the truth about Tom's accident, when he knows she won't be able to keep it quiet.

'And when I replied, he emailed again almost instantly. He told me that you shared your secret with Jessie. His message was line after line about how disappointed he was in you.'

'That's it then,' I say. 'I have *really* messed everything up now. I have lost him.'

'No, Billy, stop.'

'Mum, Richard is never going to forgive me.' I slide off the stool onto the floor. I don't feel I can take any more. It's wet and cold but all I want to do is sit here forever, and slowly fade away. I have one last thing I have to say.

•

'Mum you mustn't tell anyone about Tom.'

'I won't, Billy. Believe me that's the last thing Martha and the children need. They don't need the horror of knowing that Tom could have been murdered. They are only just coping now; a big investigation digging everything up won't help them at all. Billy...' She gives me the *Mum Stare*. I know I am about to be told off.

'Yes,' I say.

'Get up, please,' Mum puts out her hand to help me, but I don't take it, she is not strong enough. I get up slowly onto my knees and then sit back on the stool. 'Yes,' I say again.

'You should never have told Jessie, that was very wrong of you.' She looks serious, shaking her head and staring at me. 'Billy, you must realise the truth – you *are* selfish.'

'But, Mum, Mary and all those other things I have done.'

My mother is not listening to me. 'Mary is here because you have a vain hope Jessie will thank you for looking after her daughter. You do nothing unless you think you'll get something in return. And there is something else I need to say to you.'

'Go on then.'

'You don't need Richard. You're strong, clever, and hard working. You don't need a man in your life propping you up all the time. Stop thinking that if there isn't someone there for you, you can't manage.' She touches my cheek. 'Look, Billy, your whole life has revolved around being with someone. Darling, you have to stop thinking that you *need* to be in a relationship. You don't need anyone. Billy May, you're a single person capable of anything you want to do – on your own.'

'But I love Richard, I can't live without him,' I say, jumping off the stool and then sitting back down again.

Mum shakes her head. 'Billy,' she says, 'you can live without him, I assure you, you can.'

'But–'

'Please listen, I have gone on living without your dad, and I'm not saying I don't miss him all the time. I wish he was here now helping me to talk to you. Your father was half of me, and that is never going to change. However, I have you, and the farm, and Hamsgate, and so many friends and family. I can live, and I am happy. I still love Jack, but I am my own person, not just your dad's widow.' Mum looks so deep into my eyes that I can feel my face heating up.

I stare back at her, wanting reassurance that she still loves me, even if I am so weak and egotistical.

'I know you love Richard, and I understand why you do; he is a generous caring man,' Mum says. I see the deep lines around her eyes and around her thin pale lips. There are so many lines etched into her face; many brought about by the worry I have caused her over the years. She smiles at me, but it doesn't make me feel better. I feel ashamed.

'Billy, I can see how Jessie coming to Fox Halt Farm has messed things up between you and Richard, but please don't give up. You can get him back, I'm sure. But it mustn't be because you need him, it has to be because he can't live without you. You have to make being with you the most special thing in the world to him.'

'Will you help me, Mum?' I feel like a four-year-old again, desperate for all her care and encouragement.

'Please believe me, darling. Between us, we will sort this out, I promise you it will be okay.'

'Thank you,' I stand up to hug her. 'I love you.'

'I love you too, Billy,' she replies, wrapping me in her arms.

Eleven hours later, the strap of a heavy, insulated bag cuts into my shoulder. My other arm holds up a crammed-full carrier bag. I asked Mum if I could make two trips across the yard to the cottage, but she insisted I had to carry them in one go. Mum and I have talked and talked, about how I can make Richard believe in me again. I am not sure if a problem shared is a problem halved, but I feel more positive.

As I get to the door, Freddy brushes past me. He stops, calling back to his father. 'Ten minutes, I'm going to say bye to Grace.'

'Is everything in the car?' Richard calls after him from inside.

'Yes, Dad, just give me ten minutes, will you?'

A quadbike comes into the yard and I see Grace is driving it. I lift my hand to acknowledge her, then I step into the cottage putting my bags down just inside the door.

'How are you?' I ask Richard when I see him coming downstairs.

'Shattered,' he replies, sitting down on the steps. His shoulders are rounded over, and he looks washed out.

'Have you finished packing?' I ask. 'Is there anything…' I stop mid-sentence, thinking this is impossible, but then I tell myself I have to carry on. 'Can you come over to the farmhouse for a cup of tea, just for a minute or two? Have a quick break, before you do all that driving?'

'Sorry, Billy, I can't, we need to get back. I told Freddy we're leaving at five.'

'What do you need help with then?' I ask.

'It's okay, I have to do a final check, but I think it's all done in here.'

He isn't going to let me help him, so I try another question. 'How was Jessie, how is she feeling?' I set my eyes on Richard's, waiting for a reply. Mum has gone over the rules, and I promised her I would stick to them. There are only two rules I have to follow, but I think they are going to be difficult. Her rules are; firstly, I mustn't use the words 'I', 'me' or 'my'. And secondly, ask one question at a time, and then wait for an answer. If I get no reply after thirty seconds, I must repeat the question, I mustn't change the question or rephrase it, and then wait for a response.

For forty years, I never realised Mum had a formula to get people to open up to her. I didn't know the reason why she had so many friends, and why people turn up at our door all the time. I didn't appreciate why her bed and breakfast guests came back year after year. I didn't know she applies two simple rules.

I was too busy answering her questions, telling her all about me, convinced she had to know the answers because they were important to her. Mum said it is second nature to her now, and the only thing that surprises her is the in-depth detail about their lives that strangers sometimes divulge to her. My mother becomes a friend or a confidant in minutes.

Mum's words run through my mind, as I wait for Richard to answer. 'You must give generously and selflessly,' she said.

'Climbing back,' Richard replies. He doesn't elaborate, and I think what a clever expression for her to use, it reminds me of Jessie telling me about her childhood and her climbing trips with her father. The first time I spent time alone with Jessie was on a climbing adventure in Snowdonia, Michael refused to join in, too terrified of heights to go with her. But the sport was Jessie's passion. She loved the exhilaration, the fear of falling and the high open spaces.

'Did she actually say, she was *climbing back*?' I ask.

'Yes, it was the last thing she said before I left. I am climbing back, Richard, that's what she told me.'

'That's good to hear. Jessie is lucky to have you helping her.'

'It's hard, Billy, Michael tied everything down. I haven't found a single asset in their joint names, and there is so much to sort out before Jessie can get her hands on any of the money. I thought I'd just help her fill in a few forms, that's all really but it's endless. And the more I do, the more I discover needs doing. The more I find out, the more questions I have. It's crazy, but I want to help her.'

'How are you managing to do it all?'

He shakes his head. 'I'm fine,' he says. 'Don't worry.'

Freddy charges back in and grabs my two bags. 'Are these the last bits? I am not sure there is any space left in the car,' he says.

'Sorry, I don't know what they are,' Richard replies, as he gets to his feet.

'They are full of provisions that Mum wanted you to take back to Beechwood,' I explain.

Freddy smiles. 'Brill, I'll put them out of reach, so we have something left by the time we get home.' He heads outside, cradling the bags in his arms. His delight stings at my heart; the word *home* was the worst. I want this cottage to be his home, not Beechwood. I wish too, that the provisions had been my idea. But most of all, I regret that it was I who made all the pies and the Battenberg cake that Freddy is so carefully stowing away in the car.

Mum's cooking is always delicious and mine will be a disappointment. I can't say it was me who cooked everything because, I have to give anonymously. Mum said I mustn't seek gratitude or compliments.

'Please thank Daniella,' Richard says.

'I will.'

'I'm sorry, I can't go and see her, but if I do, it will be another half an hour before we get away, maybe an hour; you know what she's like for keeping me talking. Tell her I'll message her when I get back. She will want to know we arrived safely.'

'And she'll need all the details of the whole journey, I expect?' Damn, I broke the rule! I must have cringed, because Richard says, 'Don't worry, I'll text you too.'

'Please don't if you're too tired and want to crash. Mum will tell me everything anyway. Text in the morning to say hello. That will be perfect,' I say.

'Thank you, Billy,' he says. 'Sorry, but we have to go.'

'Hug?' I say, stretching out my arms to him.

He steps forward, kisses the top of my head and then moves back. At the same time, he hands me the keys to his cottage. I try not to look upset at the tiny amount of contact. 'Drive carefully,' I say. 'Look after yourself and your wonderful son.'

As his car drives away, I catch Grace who is about to scoot off. 'Darling, you must miss Freddy so much,' I say.

She nods at me.

'Will you come in the house? Mum needs you to cheer her up. She misses you making her laugh. We both miss you.'

Grace is already texting Freddy, but she looks up. 'Is there any Battenberg cake left, or has Freddy taken it all?'

'There is plenty left for you, and Mum might tell you something about the cake that Freddy took. She can explain why he and Richard may not be so thrilled when they unwrap it.'

'What?'

'Ask Mum,' I say. 'Come indoors, will you?' I expect her to refuse, but I stand still and wait for a reply. I stare at Tom's incredible daughter, wishing he was here to see how she's grown. If her dad was around, then maybe Freddy wouldn't be so important to Grace. How Tom loved her. He was so proud of both his kids – I wish Tom was here, and Richard too, if only he'd come back and stay. A cold tear runs down my cheek.

Grace jumps off the quadbike. 'Let's go inside,' she says. 'It looks like I need to make you laugh too.'

Chapter 9

BERKELEY SQUARE, LONDON
MONDAY 11 AUGUST
BILLY

It surprises me how easily I lie, but I don't use my falsehoods and half-truths to control and manipulate others like Michael did. For as long as I can remember, I have practised deceit. When I was little, lying was easy for me because my parents and grandfather took one look at my innocent face and believed me, instantly. I can hear Grandad boasting, 'Her's like George Washington, our young Billy; her can't tell a lie.'

I considered my grandad's unwavering faith in me as a wonderful compliment, even though I knew it wasn't true – but then, my grandfather was always my biggest fan, I miss that gentle and kind man so much.

Nothing but trouble has come from my guile, yet I still lie. I'd prefer not to, but life is a rush sometimes, and the truth can take too long to explain. A tiny fib is often so much easier.

It was an early start for me, much earlier than I get up to do the milking. I don't like being in London, but I'm here now, so I'm going to make it count. 'Mr MarcFenn has arranged for me to have his parking space today,' I lie.

Reg Syke, the security guard recognises me. 'They've not told me that. Now't new there, Miss May,' he laughs.

I nod at him and smile.

'Look, go ahead,' he tells me, 'the space is over there.' He points to a gap between two expensive cars, and I see a large glass plate etched in foot high letters that reads '*Director*'. It's where Michael's car would have been parked. Richard will be catching the train in today from Beechwood, so it's empty.

'Nice to see you again, Miss May,' Reg says, as I climb out of my dusty van.

'And you too, Reg,' I reply. I am not lying now, it *is* good to see his familiar face. Some of Richard's employees didn't want to move from the former MarcFenn offices to Richard's new headquarters in Docklands. So, when Michael's company took over the vacated building, the sale contract stipulated that any of Richard's staff who didn't want to move had to be retained by O'Rowdes' for at least two years. That was seventeen years ago, so it is nice to see Reg looking so well. It feels good that he remembered me, especially when I'm unsure of the welcome I am going to receive in a minute or two.

'Will I see you later, Reg?' I ask. 'I expect I'll be leaving around six this evening.'

'No, just work mornings these days,' he replies. 'Will be here tomorrow though.'

'Well then, maybe I'll see you again tomorrow.'

He smiles and nods so violently his shoulders shake.

'Do you know, Reg, you haven't changed a bit,' I tell him. 'You look really well. It was lovely that you remembered me.'

'Yes, you too, Miss May,' he says quickly, as a car pulls up at the barrier and the driver signals that they need his help. 'See you tomorrow,' he says. 'Goodbye for now.'

'Is he expecting you?' The receptionist taps her immaculate fingernails on the desk.

I planned to arrive before Richard, I reckoned that if I was sitting in the reception area, he wouldn't make a scene, and would have taken me straight up to his office. But the traffic was far heavier than I expected, so he has beaten me here. 'Yes.' Another untruth. I check my watch. *Damn, it's not working* – I only put it on because I thought it added to my business-like appearance.

I notice a crease down the front of my old suit jacket and speckles of farmyard dirt on one of my patent shoes. I feel like the imposter that I am. I was going to read the time out loud to give some credence to my fib. Luckily, the receptionist misinterprets my glance at my watch, and my shining of my shoe on the back of my leg as frustration with her question, and she phones Richard without further interrogation.

'Please go up, Miss May,' she says at last. 'Mr MarcFenn said you know where Mr O'Rowdes' office is, he is working in there today.'

As the all-glass lift raises me up through the familiar floors, memories flash through my mind of all the time I worked for Richard here. Days spent slowly falling in love with my caring boss; a man I couldn't have because he was devoted to his wife and children. I remember our business meetings, the turmoil and finally, our all-too-short affair.

Years later, I was one of O'Rowdes' managers too with my own office a street away. Michael arranged the nearby location, aware that my history with Richard made it too painful for me to work in this building again.

'Hey! What a wonderful surprise.' Richard is smiling.

'Mum's idea, she's got all the troops organised at home. Everyone is mucking in again. She thought you could do with a hand.' This is something I rehearsed to say. The *'I, me, and my'* rule seemed to work yesterday, and constructing each sentence carefully before I say it out loud stops me saying how I really feel, how scared I am of losing him, how I want him to love me again and how very sorry I am for everything I've done.

I use another phrase, which I practised in the van. 'Michael O'Rowde's former business strategist at your disposal, inside information, contacts, business structure, intelligence, statistics, facts and figures all available here, just as you need them,' I say, pointing to my head. I start to take off my jacket. Richard smiles again, and I feel my toes tingle in my uncomfortable high heels.

'Have you had breakfast?' he asks.

'No.'

'Me neither, I'll ask Sarah to organise some bacon rolls and cups of tea for us both.'

'Sarah?' I frown, wondering if I might know her from when I worked for O'Rowdes' before.

'She was Michael's personal assistant,' Richard explains.

'What's her surname?'

'Sarah Lancaster, I don't think you would know her, Billy. She said she started working here two years ago, that was after you left. She's very helpful though.'

'That's good, she must have been able to answer lots of questions for you,' I say, thinking how it's *not* good because I fear the woman will have already assisted him more than I can. I was hoping Richard would appreciate me being here to help him.

'Yes, it is.' Richard is writing something. I wait for him to finish, assuming he has remembered something he must do later, making a note before he forgets, but he pushes his writing pad towards me.

There are three tiny words on the page. *'Don't trust Sarah.'*

I write beneath, in the same sized lettering. *'Is she listening?'*

The notebook is passed between us three more times. Our small messages read,

'Don't trust Sarah.'
       'Is she listening?'
'Maybe?'
       'Bugging the room?'
'Maybe? And there might be a camera too.'

Richard rips the page out of the pad, folds it and puts it in his pocket. I think he is joking about Sarah, but I am not one-hundred per cent sure. I stare at his face trying to get a clue, but his expression gives nothing away.

'It's nice to have you here, Billy,' he says. 'You worked with Michael for a long time, he trusted you.'

'Good to try and help,' I reply.

'So, do you want tea and a bacon roll, or not?' He sounds pleased that I am here, despite Sarah helping him. I wonder again if she really is spying on us.

'How about grabbing a quick breakfast in the wine bar?' I say remembering the bistro opposite the entrance to this building.

Richard picks up a file on his desk.

'Brilliant idea,' he says, standing up. 'Gary will make us bacon sandwiches, I'm sure.'

He presses his speaker phone, and I guess it is Sarah who answers. 'Yes, Richard,' she says.

'A friend has just popped in, we're going to get some breakfast, we'll be back in a short while.'

'Can I get you on your mobile, if I need you?'

'You can.'

'Very good.' She hangs up. Her voice seems faintly familiar.

'I have some dodgy looking Battenberg we can share later.' Richard grins at me. I notice the three deep lines on the outside of his eyes, and a tiny wrinkle each side of his mouth. I love the way this happens when he smiles. I like his description of the cake too, it did look dodgy.

'Did you make the cake?' he asks.

'Yes, sorry,' I say. 'Hope you're not too disappointed, here's hoping that it tastes better than it looks.' I cross my fingers and hold them up in front of me.

'I am sure it will. It was a wonderful thought. I'm really grateful. Thank you.'

I don't say you're welcome, I just smile at him. I want to say baking kept my mind off him, but that would be about me. I must be gracious.

'Shall we get some breakfast?' I ask.

'Yes,' he says, waving the file he is still clutching. 'Let's go.'

The wine bar is pretty much as I remember it. Richard speaks to the man behind the counter, while I find a table for us to sit at in the corner of the empty room. The dim light makes Richard look even more tired than he did in the office.

'Are you alright?' I ask as he sits opposite me.

'Yes,' he says.

'You're not, are you?'

'No, not really.' He shakes his head. 'O'Rowdes' is set up in such a different way to how MarcFenn used to be.'

'What do you mean?'

'Well for a start, MarcFenn had department heads, who I relied on, but it seems Michael delegated little and trusted no-one. It's been hard to find my way through everything.'

'Yes,' I say.

'Billy, I want to give Jessie guidance but getting hold of information has been tricky. I meant it about Sarah.' He pauses and opens the file he's brought with him.

'What, that she is spying on you?' I laugh.

'I think she only lets me see what she wants me to see.' Richard looks up from the file. 'And she seems to guess exactly what I am going to ask her for next. I know it's probably just my imagination, and she is just good at her job.'

'And she is trying to protect her job too,' I suggest. 'Knowledge is king, after all.'

'That's true,' he replies.

'Sarah's not spying.'

'You think?'

'No, I'm sure she isn't.' I shake my head. 'Michael wouldn't have employed her if she wasn't thorough. He would have expected her to have everything to hand, ready for him the second he asked her for information. He never suffered fools.'

'You're right, I'm being paranoid,' he says. 'But still, I'm glad you are here, Billy.'

'Good,' I say.

'I'd like your opinion on this please.' Richard lifts a sheet of paper out of the file and gives it to me.

'What is this?'

'An offer for the whole company. It arrived here just before you,' he says. 'I can't do anything formally, until the extraordinary general meeting, but I want to get it sorted in my mind.'

I read slowly. The takeover bid from the rival supermarket is huge. There are a few conditions, but they seem reasonable.

'It's a fair whack, don't you think?' Richard asks.

'Would Jessie sell?' I ask, trying to recall the last valuation I saw for O'Rowdes'.

'She says she wants rid of the company.'

'You've asked her already?' I check. 'Have you called her? Has Jessie made up her mind so fa–'

'Slow down, Billy, please.'

'Sorry.'

'I haven't spoken to Jessie about *this* offer,' he says.

'There are others?' I ask.

'Yes, this is the second. The first came in on Friday from Webers, and Jessie and I have only discussed that one.'

'Was she really up to making such a big decision?' I ask. 'It's a lot to consider. Jessie seemed so insecure at Fox Halt, and with Michael's suici–'

'Billy, she is a different woman from the person who turned up at the farm. It's as though someone has switched her back on. She is determined to wipe away anything to do with that man.'

'Totally get that.' I nod, wondering if Richard has noticed my odd sentence structure. The forbidden words are messing up my grammar. I wonder if I sound like some pretentious city slicker now? I hope not, but if Richard has noticed, he doesn't comment.

'Jessie is set on selling, and she wants the O'Rowdes' name gone too. No future owner will be allowed to use it again.'

'Right.' I nod again, thinking how I'd feel that way too.

Richard continues. 'As I see it, Jessie is focused on just two things at the moment. She wants to erase everything associated with Michael, and she is yearning for Mary to come home. That's all she's been talking about since I showed her Weber's offer.' He pauses. 'Billy, you have to find out why Mary won't go back to Culmfield. Whatever has happened to her, Jessie will be hell bent on sorting it out.'

What I want to say starts with 'I', so I try to work out another way to phrase it.

'Billy, aren't you going to say anything?' He frowns.

'Mary will tell us soon enough,' I reply. 'Look, we better find out how much O'Rowdes' is currently worth, so we can decide which offer is the best one for Jessie to accept. Do you have the first bid to hand? Are there any special terms?'

'It's in the office,' he says.

'Okay, we'll take our breakfast back there, so we can get started right away,' I say, thinking how much I like the word 'we' – it sounds so much better than 'I'.

As we walk into the office, a young man approaches us.

'Yes, Matthias,' Richard says to him.

'Sarah asked me to let you know that she has gone home.'

'Oh,' Richard replies.

'She has a migraine.' Matthias sounds flustered.

'Thank you.' Richard shuts the door to the office. 'Right, I'll show you Weber's offer,' he tells me, opening a drawer in his desk. He closes it and opens another and then a third before he finds what he is searching for. 'Here it is,' he says as he hands me a crumpled A4 sheet.

My sandwich remains untouched as I start making notes about the two deals.

'Thanks for this, Billy.'

Looking up from my frantic scribbles, I speak slowly and carefully. 'It's surprising how much is coming back,' I say. 'Funny the things we remember; all the stuff we think we'll never need again.'

'I'm not surprised,' Richard replies. 'It's not that long ago since you worked for Michael, and you were involved in a lot of his business decisions.'

'Yes,' I nod, thinking how I loved my job at O'Rowdes'. However, my relationship with Michael is not something I want to recall. I try to appear calm even though my insides are churning.

'It won't have changed much,' I say. 'Michael had a definite plan for the future. It was simple. He was pulling out of all his other business ventures to concentrate solely on the supermarket. That was the part of the company he knew best.' I sit back in my chair; my mind skips back through time.

It must be about ten years ago, when I started working for Michael. At the time, I was living at Culmfield helping Jessie with the refurbishments of the estate and helping her with the children too. It was such a beautiful place, and my life seemed quite perfect back then. That was until Michael started to worry about O'Rowdes'.

At that time, the company was heading in many different directions. So many that Michael couldn't keep track of it all. He wanted someone he trusted to help him, and Michael decided that person was me. I had a first-class business degree, and tons of previous experience working with MarcFenn. Michael stole me away from Jessie, Mary and Arthur and my wonderful life at Culmfield. He engineered it, so I had no choice but to work for him in London.

Richard is staring at me. 'Are you okay?'

'Yes,' I say, forcing a smile.

'Billy, would you explain Michael's long-term plan? It would help me if I understood his strategy better. Could you do that?' he asks.

I nod, deciding it's impossible to provide a coherent account if I continue with Mum's difficult rules, so I give myself permission to suspend them for a while. 'I started at O'Rowdes just before the millennium,' I say. 'That was when Michael first told me about his fears for his company. He said it was growing too big and too fast.' I stand up and move to the window. A taxi in the street below catches my eye, and another time when I worked in this building jumps into my mind.

'Billy.' Richard is next to me.

'Where was I?' I ask.

'Michael told you the company was growing too fast.'

'Yes, he said he had created a monster, and that it was out of control. I didn't realise it at the time, but it wasn't the monster that scared Michael, it was the fact that he couldn't manage its every move. The talented puppeteer had tangled strings, as it were.' I pause, wondering if I need to try to describe this better, but Richard doesn't seem to have any questions.

'Please go on,' he says.

'Well, as you can imagine, Michael couldn't cope with not knowing every microscopic part of his business. O'Rowdes' had a wide range of interests from the airline to pharmaceuticals, and research, to a zoo for endangered reptiles.' I pause again. 'Did you know about the lizards?'

'Not until last Friday, when I looked in one of these files.' Richard waves his hand towards a book shelf with neatly labelled folders, standing up in perfect rows. Michael's files fill one wall completely.

'Yes,' I say. 'Everything's meticulously recorded. Michael researched every scheme to the nth degree and implemented each plan with precision. But he wanted to oversee every single process, in all of his multifaceted enterprises.'

'You're right about that,' Richard says. 'I've never worked with anyone else like him. Michael knew so much about his developments and property investments. He paid MarcFenn vast amounts of money to manage his portfolio, and to advise him. But he still investigated every detail himself, and he always knew exactly what he wanted. I felt superfluous a lot of the time.'

'Well, he was like that with everything,' I say. 'I know the plan when I left was to focus on the supermarkets, but I guess things weren't going so well lately. Michael thrived on new challenges, and I wonder if he opened too many new supermarkets in too many new places. He always had to be first, and the biggest. He wanted O'Rowdes' name all over the world. I wonder if he took his eye off the competition, and his existing business.' I pause as Richard returns to his desk. 'Does that tie in with what you have gathered so far?'

'I think so,' he replies. 'I was thinking Michael had been complacent, he was underestimating the competition and he thought he could railroad his way into places like South Korea. He believed he was invincible, but he wasn't, was he?'

'No, he wasn't,' I agree. 'He should have been pretty worried recently. He built O'Rowdes' from scratch, it meant so much to him, he would have struggled with it failing.'

'Talking with you about all this makes it clearer to see what was going on,' Richard says. 'Thank you, Billy.' He gets back up and comes over to me. As he looks out of the window, I think how strange it must be for Richard to be back here, this was his office once; the current neat and tidiness is very different from the muddle it was when he was heading up MarcFenns, but the view onto Berkley Square won't have changed much. I wait for him to turn back to look at me, but he doesn't, so I talk to his cheek. 'It took me years, not days to suss O'Rowdes' out. It wasn't until Michael told me about his childhood and how he started the business that I really grasped what O'Rowdes' meant to him. After that, I appreciated his passion for it. Michael had some tough times growing up, did he tell you?'

'No.' Richard turns around to face me, 'he didn't.'

'I won't tell you it all now,' I say, 'but it was pretty grim.' I change the subject. 'Look, we ought to get on,' I say. 'Have you got any figures together at all?'

'Tell me?' Richard stares into my eyes.

'What?'

'About Michael. You said his childhood was grim.'

'I can't, not in a nutshell, it's too long a story. Let's just say he was a victim of unlucky circumstances. Horrible,' I change my mind, 'no horrific circumstances, which made him focus on the business.'

'Was he abused?' Richard asks. 'Do you think that's why he abused everyone else? They say that's what happens to people, don't they?'

'No, he wasn't abused, not in the way you might be thinking. You want the whole story, don't you?'

'Yes.' He sits down at the desk, spinning around in his chair to look at me. I decide to sit too, choosing a low easy chair in the corner of the room. I don't know where to start. It was years before Michael trusted me enough to talk about his past. I need a few moments to get the story in order, I want to be brief and factual, cutting out the emotion that ran through it when Michael told me what had happened to him. 'Can we get some coffee and maybe try the cake first?' I ask.

Richard picks up the phone, and when Matthias answers, he asks for some drinks to be brought in to us. 'Billy, tell me,' he says.

I point to two large paintings hanging opposite the files. The pictures stand out for two reasons; firstly, because every other bit of wall space is plastered with small architectural drawings of different flagship supermarket stores, all with the name O'Rowdes' emblazoned across them, and secondly, because they are so beautiful, they were painted by an artist who was commissioned to paint the Queen's portrait a couple of times. 'Look,' I say.

'What am I supposed to be looking at?' Richard frowns.

I stand up again to touch one of the paintings. 'These are his parents, the painting is based on an old photo Michael had, it was taken on the day they got married.'

'So, he did get on with them? I take it they are both dead; he has never mentioned them to me.'

'Yes, they're dead. They both died when he was very young, Michael never knew the original Michael O'Rowde, his father. He died when he was two. His mother was very young, she had no family to help her, and she became a prostitute, to support herself and her toddler. She was murdered by one of her clients, when Michael was just eight or nine, leaving him completely alone.'

'God, his mother was killed, was the man caught?'

'No, he wasn't. Richard, this is difficult to explain. Until recently, Michael had flashbacks and nightmares about her death. He believed his poor mother had killed herself. He remembered how unhappy she was, and he thought she jumped from the balcony of the block of flats they lived in.

Michael thought his mum had chosen to abandon him.' Telling this story is hard, my throat is dry.

'That is awful,' Richard says.

'Yes,' I say, remembering the day when Michael opened up to tell me this. Michael hadn't told Jessie about his early life. When I saw how vulnerable he was, I felt I loved him. I believed he loved me too. *Maybe he did?*

Matthias comes into the office with two cups of coffee and Richard waits for his stand-in assistant to leave before speaking again. 'Where did his money come from then?' he asks.

'His maternal adopted grandmother,' I reply, 'but it's complicated. I'll try and explain – Michael's mother was called Marilena, sorry I don't remember her surname. She was from Germany. Mary is named after her.' I pause, realising I am going off track. I sip some coffee. 'As a tiny baby, Marilena was evacuated from a German orphanage to London. Her parents perished in a concentration camp, and she was adopted by a British couple. Michael's original capital to start O'Rowdes' came from the lady who adopted Marilena.'

'Billy, this isn't making sense, you said when Michael's father died his mother had no family. Where were her adoptive parents?'

'Sorry, Richard, I am trying to keep this short. I have missed out quite a lot of the detail. Marilena and Michael's father were just fourteen or fifteen when Michael was born. Her new parents insisted Marilena got rid of the baby, but she refused and ran away. Her adopted mum and dad disowned her. Michael's father's parents helped to start with, but they had a big fall out over their son's drinking.'

'Right.'

'Michael's parents tried hard to make it on their own, they even got married but where they lived was pretty rough. Michael's dad got into fights when he was drunk. No-one is sure what happened to him. Michael hired a private investigator to find out, who concluded that his father was stabbed and killed in a brawl outside a pub, and his body was dumped in the Thames somewhere. Going back to his mum, the bit I remember most about what Michael told me was how he lay down beside her dead body, and pretended they were both sleeping. It was heart-breaking him telling me that. Can you imagine it?'

Richard shakes his head. 'So, his grandparents took him in after Marilena died, is that what happened?' He doesn't sound sympathetic.

'No, it wasn't like that, Michael was alone, he lived rough for at least a couple of years, terrified he'd be put in an orphanage, or he'd be rehomed with a horrible new family. He didn't go to school and stole what he needed to survive. He lived like that until he was eventually reconciled with his adopted grandmother; his grandfather was dead by then. She really looked after him, but she died too. Michael inherited her money when he was sixteen, and that's when he bought a rundown shop on Streatham High Street.'

'I knew that was where he started, but that's all,' Richard says, getting up to study the portrait of Michael's parents.

'Sorry, but there is something else I need to explain, it's important,' I say.

'Tell me.'

'It's this next bit, which made me understand Michael. He told me what he loved most about that first shop was putting up a huge O'Rowdes' sign above it. The sign was his memorial to his parents. He said his life was dedicated to growing his business so he could display their name everywhere. There you have it, the abridged version, Michael O'Rowde – his early years.'

Richard carefully unwraps a large piece of cake. 'Thanks for telling me that, Billy,' he says. 'It does help me.'

'I hope so,' I say, keeping my eyes on the cake while Richard splits it, putting each half on a fresh sheet of paper from his printer.

I watch his face as he samples his share. Richard nods at me. 'Delicious,' he says.

'Glad you like it.' I smile. I decide to revert back to my talking restrictions, I did promise Mum I would stick to the rules.

'Billy, before we do anything else, can I ask how long you're staying?'

I work out my sentence as I go along. 'Mum and William said they could manage for two days. Is that good with you?'

'Very good,' he says, wondering if he is talking about the Battenberg cake or me staying. I decide not to check.

'Mum's booked a room tonight at the Fitzclaine Mayfair.'

'For you? The room is for you, I take it?'

'Yes, it's for me,' I laugh. 'Mum says it is a lovely hotel. She insisted on paying but it's on the condition that she gets to hear every last detail about the place.'

'That's sweet of her, you knew Daniella and I met there for lunch years ago? It was the day you started work for me.'

'Yes,' I reply. 'She is always going on about it. Mum loved it there. She was so happy you had given me a job. It was rare for my mother to leave the farm and she had such a special time with you.'

'It was special for me too. She is one amazing person.'

'Too amazing sometimes, I have a lot to live up to,' I say and I laugh.

'She shouldn't be paying for the hotel. You're here to help Jessie, so when her money comes through, I'll make sure Daniella gets her money back.'

'It's not to help Jessie, it's to support you,' I say.

'Yes, it's nice to have you here. In fact, I wonder if I could join you for dinner at the Fitzclaine this evening?'

My pulse quickens and I grin inanely. 'Yes, you're welcome to,' I say.

'Excellent. It will be nice to have something to look forward to after we have chugged through all these files.' Richard points to the bookshelf again.

'That shouldn't take too long,' I say, thinking the information we need will be easy to find. Michael's filing system was impeccable.

'We just have to decide what information we need,' Richard says as he starts up Michael's computer.

'Can you imagine if we were looking for something in here when this was your office? We were as likely to find a half-eaten meat and potato pie as much as a vital deed for a particular property. Do you remember what it was like?' I ask.

'Indeed, I do. *The Shambles*, that's what you used to call my office.'

'That described it pretty well, don't you think?'

Richard laughs. 'Right then, ready,' he says. 'What shall we look up first?' He pushes up his sleeves.

Chapter 10

FITZCLAINE MAYFAIR HOTEL, MAYFAIR

RICHARD

It's just before seven o'clock, and I wish I was catching the train back to Beechwood, not stepping into the gilded foyer of the Fitzclaine Mayfair.

An hour ago, as she was leaving the office, Billy offered me an out, saying she could see I was exhausted, and it might be best if we didn't have dinner together. We were both up early, and all the reading and double checking had been tiring, but Billy had worked so hard all day, I didn't want to disappoint her. I was imagining her sitting alone in the grand dining room so I told her I was fine and looking forward to a good meal – I am not particularly hungry, and I think I would prefer to be heading for my bed. But then again, I would only lie awake for hour after hour thinking about everything. Sleep hasn't come easily recently.

I wait for Billy by the smart reception desk. I phoned her just before I walked in here, she should be with me in a minute or two.

'Are you alright?' I turn around and see it's Billy, she must have seen me pressing my fingers across my forehead.

I nod. 'You were quick,' I say.

'Been waiting for your call, expect you're famished. Mum's been on the phone for half an hour; she had to tell me the exact table to book for dinner. She insists we have to ask for the same table you two had all those years ago.'

'And she told you all about her experience that day too, I expect. I know Daniella never tires of describing the tea cups, and the quality of the tablecloths, does she?'

'She did, and she told me all about the waiter who knew Okehampton because he'd once worked at The Gidleigh Park Hotel. I've been told to find out if he is still here, apparently he was very thoughtful and has deep blue eyes.'

'He was from Belgium, I remember that,' I say.

Billy laughs. 'You know, it's really my mother who should be here. She would love every second of it, just like she did last time.'

I wonder if Billy is nervous too, she doesn't seem herself at all, her sentences keep stopping and starting. Maybe she is just tired.

'We'd better go and check it all out for her then,' I say.

She touches my arm. 'Can I just say something?' she asks.

'Go on.'

'Do you mind if we just talk about Mum and you bringing her to this swanky place? Nothing else, we don't need deep discussions about our future.'

'Sounds like a fine plan.' I place my hand over hers, the one she still has rested on my arm. Her skin is cold. 'And also,' I say, 'would it be okay if I leave pretty much as soon as we have finished our main course? I don't want to be late, it's going to be another hard day tomorrow.'

'Do you wish you weren't trying to help Jessie?' Billy asks.

'No, Michael's death has so many consequences for her. I am glad I can do something to make it a bit easier for her and the children.'

'You're a good man,' she says, staring deep into my eyes.

'Thanks for coming to London, Billy,' I say. I have forgotten everything that's happened between us these last few days, and I am suddenly aware of the sweet smell from the coconut conditioner she smothers on her hair. I look down at her mouth. I lean forward to kiss her.

'Miss May, Mr MarcFenn?' I turn around, unhappy this moment with Billy has been broken. I expect to see a concierge wanting to help us. I have used the Fitzclaine for many business lunches, so I am not surprised that a member of staff has recognised me and used my name.

But the person who has addressed us does not look like a hotel employee, neither waiter nor manager, instead The Fat Controller from *Thomas the Tank Engine* stories comes in to my mind. The man has a shiny bald head and a long, tailored coat with wide black and grey stripes.

'Hello,' I say, still wondering who he might be.

'I am Detective Sergeant Hughie Bawen,' he says. 'We would like to talk to you both. We need you to come to the local police station.'

'Sorry?' I say, unsure I have understood him.

'We need to ask you both some questions about Mr O'Rowde's death,' As he is explaining, an official looking woman and two uniformed police come into the lobby. I try to stay composed as my mind shouts, *Christ, he's the police!* 'Do you mean right *now*?' I check. My cheeks are burning.

'Yes, we'd like Miss May and you to come with us now, please, Mr MarcFenn.'

'Of course, we will. I am sure we're both keen to help with anything you need to know,' I say, my heart thudding.

Billy cuts in. 'What do you need to know, Detective Brown?' She has her elbow pressed on the reception desk, and it doesn't look like she is about to go anywhere.

The man corrects her. 'My name is Bawen, Detective Sergeant Hughie Bawen.'

'Sorry.' Billy smiles at him. 'It's been a very long day, I wasn't concentrating.'

'Don't worry,' the policeman replies.

'We were about to get something to eat. Could you sit at our table and talk to us there?' I offer.

'No, Mr MarcFenn.'

'No,' I check.

'We would like to speak to you individually, it is easier at the station. It would be helpful if you come straight away.'

'Will it take long?' I ask, as a film of sweat coats the back of my neck.

'That depends.' He shrugs his stripy shoulders.

'Then, the sooner we answer your questions, the better.' I step forward and Billy moves too.

My hands are trembling as we are driven away in separate cars.

Charing Cross Police Station

Billy

One evening last Christmas, I was driving in Exeter when I became aware of a flashing blue light behind me. I pulled in to let the emergency vehicle pass, but they stopped behind my car instead. A policeman asked if I had been drinking. I said I hadn't, which was true, but I was still frightened that his breathalyser might light up anyway and I'd be arrested. I knew I was innocent, but it didn't stop me fearing the worst. I was stopped because my car headlights weren't on, so I apologised for my oversight and I was allowed on my way. Until now, this was my only encounter with the police, and just like last time, I feel anxious.

I stand in one corner of a small room with just a desk and four chairs for company. I am worried, tired and hungry. My empty stomach sharpens my mind, but I was up at four this morning, and I have been with Richard all day trying to help. Trying all day to make him see how sorry I am, without being able to tell him how I feel. Overall, exhaustion dulls my thinking more than my hunger stimulates it. I am struggling to think clearly.

'Please take a seat, Miss May.'

I stand still. 'I want to go,' I tell the detective sergeant. 'I want to go right away.' I frown hard.

'Billy May, I am arresting you–'

This appalling response makes me drop onto the offered chair. The detective's words are bubbles rising from the bottom of the sea. I am drowning.

I try to understand. I think he believes I killed Michael. He is telling me my rights. Everything feels fake, as if I am a suspect in a crime series on the television; Detective Sergeant Bawen is an actor, not a real policeman. I listen in a fog of make-believe, as he informs me that I am entitled to a solicitor.

My thoughts are chaotic. I worry if I go to prison Fox Halt Farm will have to be sold. I think about Mum and what this will do to her. One dread into the next. Each imagined nightmare scenario more terrible than the one before.

I tread water, searching for a lifebelt. 'How do I get a solicitor?' I ask Bawen, glaring at him, trying to guess his thoughts.

He stares back at me, giving nothing away.

'Can I get free advice?' I ask, not waiting for his reply.

'Yes, Miss May, we can get the duty solicitor for you.' His response lacks expression.

'Thank you,' I say, and then I make more demands. 'I want to speak to him before I say anything to you, and I'd like something to eat, please, while I wait for him to get here.' I mimic the detective's flat voice, but my mind and heart are racing. Bawen agrees to sort out some food, before he leaves me alone.

My mother's voice floats into my head. *Trouble, Billy, that's all that comes from secrets and lies.*

I think how everything is starting to unravel. 'Big trouble, this time, Mum,' I say out loud.

Richard must be in a neighbouring room. I imagine his shoulders tensing up, as Bawen begins questioning him too. I wonder what he will say. I start to think everything through again. At first, I thought the detective was arresting me for murdering Michael, but now I feel unsure. I think I could be here because Richard and I withheld information about Tom's death from the police. *That's a crime,* I think – *that's why I was arrested?* Maybe someone has reported our version of how Tom could have died, and now Bawen has to investigate if Michael murdered my friend. I tremble, worrying if we will both be incarcerated because we didn't inform the police about our suspicions. I imagine Freddy and Mum visiting us in prison.

I wonder if it was Jessie or my mother – or someone else Mum told – who contacted the police. Now, a new thought smacks me so hard that I feel like I have been hit with a plank across the base of my neck. I flinch. Maybe I have been arrested for Michael's murder. *Has Bawen decided that Michael's threats gave me good reason to get rid of him?* Nala knew I was at Culmfield the day he died, and I asked her not to say I was there. I wonder if she has told the police about my visit to fetch Braveheart, and that's why I'm here.

Kavara Neil, the duty solicitor, looks haggard when she comes into the room. I quickly contemplate who else she has counselled this evening and what horrible crimes they may have committed. How different her work must be compared to mine; this smartly dressed woman has never worried about the consistency of yoghurt, or the acidity of fruits to be added to a mix.

I recognise a smell of antiseptic as she approaches me. She seems to blink more often than most people, and when she places over-large reading glasses onto her thin nose, she reminds me of a frog.

'Hello, Miss May,' she says, looking up from the page of a notepad. 'Should I call you Billy?' Her voice is calming.

'Yes, Billy, please,' I reply.

'Call me Kavara.' She reminds me of my teacher in infant class, the ever-reassuring and kind Miss Devlyn. I feel I like the frog woman. The tingly sensation in my nose from her chemical scent seems soothing too. I rush in with my first question. 'Tell me, is your advice wholly independent?'

'Yes.' She smiles at me, and I trust her immediately.

I explain about Michael and Tom, and then I ask if she thinks I have committed a crime by not reporting what I suspected.

'It depends, Billy, on the circumstances. You may have had a good reason to keep quiet,' she says.

'Michael threatened to harm my mother or the children if I went to the police,' I tell her.

'Your children?' She sounds shocked.

'No, Tom's children,' I say.

She nods slowly. 'So, did you destroy any evidence?'

'No,' I reply.

Kavara looks me in the eyes. 'Billy, you *should* tell me everything.'

'I have,' I say, wondering if she detected hesitation in my last response. 'I have told you everything.' I'm worrying if I ought to own up about Michael's muck-splattered car that Richard has hidden somewhere. I don't know where, because I haven't asked him. Richard persuaded Amir and Nala to allow him to drive the car away from Culmfield. I know he hid it in a place where he believed Michael would never look. I consider telling Kavara, but then dismiss the idea. I won't say, not yet anyway.

Kavara looks at me from under her glasses. It's as though she's deciding if I am telling her the truth. She blinks four times before she says. 'So far, with what you've told me, I think you're probably okay.'

I feel a sense of relief but now Kavara asks me a new question. 'Is Tom's Westcott's death the reason why you are here, Billy?' She is frowning.

'I'm not really sure,' I reply. 'I was so shocked when I was arrested that I didn't hear a word the detective said. At first, I thought it was because he believed I killed Michael. But he committed suicide.'

'So, were you arrested because of Michael O'Rowde's death?'

I don't know what to say, surely Kavara knows why? Bawen must have told her, it must be written on a form somewhere, I wonder if she just wants me to confirm it? 'Maybe,' I tell her.

She sighs. 'I suggest you tell me everything that's happened lately. I'll sit with you whilst the police interview you. I can advise you before you respond to each of their questions, if you feel you need me to.'

'Can I ask you something else, Miss Neil?'

'It's Mrs Neil, but just call me Kavara.'
'Alright, Kavara,' I say.
'What is it you want to ask?' She speaks softly.
'This evening, I was brought here with a friend, and I think he is being interviewed too. Could you advise him as well?'
'Not unless he requests legal advice.'
'But he may not know you can help him. He could be telling the police things that will make matters worse.'
'For you?' she asks.
'For himself. Both of us. I don't know.' I shake my head and shrug at her.
'Sorry, there is nothing I can do to help your friend,' she tells me.
'Nothing?' I check.
'Nothing.'

RICHARD

*I*t's stuffy in this tiny room even with the air conditioning on full blast. The detective sergeant removes his jacket and carefully rolls up his shirt sleeves, exposing flawless pale skin. I decide his brilliant-white shirt is brand new because it has the tell-tale creases from being folded up in its packet. I note too how Bawen's head seems to rest on his shoulders; he appears to have no neck, maybe no spine either, because his body sags. His albino skin and rounded body give the impression that The Fat Controller has mutated into a snowman.

'Mr MarcFenn,' the snowman says. 'I understand that you believe Tom Westcott's death was not an accident?'

'Yes,' I reply.

'And you believe that Michael O'Rowde might have been responsible for Tom Westcott's death?'

'Yes,' I say again. Bawen makes me feel it is best for me to confirm everything. I want to be back at Beechwood, and his slouched posture reminds me of a drunk colleague who I should put in a taxi so he can get home. He doesn't feel threatening.

'So, Mr MarcFenn, you deliberately kept this information from us. And this was because Mr O'Rowde made threats to harm Mrs Daniella May or Tom Westcott's children if you didn't keep quiet?'

'Well...' I say.

'May I remind you that we have spoken to others, and we have their accounts. It will be best for you, and everyone else concerned, if you tell us what you know – the truth,' he says.

I stay quiet, so he repeats his question. 'Mr MarcFenn, did you deliberately keep information from the police because Mr O'Rowde made threats?'

'Yes.'

'Thank you,' he smiles, and I notice the deep laughter lines around his eyes.

'You know it's an offence to withhold information from the police?'

'But, detective–'

'You help me, and I'll help you,' he says. 'So, do you know you should have reported your suspicions?'

I stare at the snowman, not really listening to what he is saying because I am engrossed in his features, realising he has no hair at all. Not just on his head, but his eyebrows and eyelashes are missing. *Has the policeman had cancer treatment? Or is it alopecia?* I ask myself.

Bawen raises his voice a fraction. 'Mr MarcFenn, do you kno–'

'Yes,' I say, trying to concentrate.

'And Miss Billy May was having an affair with Michael O'Rowde at the time of Tom Westcott's death.'

'Yes.'

'Their affair had been going on for some time?'

'Yes.'

'You were aware that Miss May was at Culmfield Court the day of Michael O'Rowde's death?' I note a subtle difference in Bawen's tone, it's slightly frosty, unlike his earlier statements and suppositions. Of course, I knew Billy was at Culmfield; she was fetching Mary's horse, but I feel unnerved. Wondering why the snowman has asked me this.

'You were aware Miss May was at Culmfield on the twenty-ninth of July this year?' Bawen stares at me. His pressing manner, and the leap in time from Tom's death to nine days ago, makes my tired brain race. *Why is he asking me this?* A new frightening thought enters my head; *does he suspect that Billy may have killed her former lover?*

Bawen has given me no clue that Michael's death might not be suicide. He might not even mean it now, but alarm bells ring in my brain about why he is interviewing me. I speculate whether Michael's death is now being considered as suspicious, and if the investigation has been taken away from the local police. Is that why CID are now talking to Billy and me?

Earlier, I supposed Bawen had obtained his information from Jessie or Daniella. But now I decide that someone must have said something else, or something new has been discovered. I wonder who the informer could be, or what the police have found? I try to guess what may have been reported, what new discovery has been made and when this might have happened.

'Mr MarcFenn, did you know that Billy May was at Culmfield the day of Michael O'Rowde's death?' Bawen's tone is friendly again. He is smiling at me. 'Just a yes, or a no, please.'

'I'm not answering any more questions, not until I've had some sleep. I'm very tired. You know, detective, I've been up since five this morning, worked all day, and haven't eaten since before lunchtime.' I want to ensure that whoever hears the recording of this conversation, knows the condition I am in. Maybe it could be deemed I was unfit to be interviewed this way?

'I must warn you, Mr MarcFenn, that refusing to answer questions can be seen as incriminating.' He pushes his chair back and smiles again.

'Can I go?' I ask. 'I want some legal guidance before I say anything else.'

'Yes, but we will need to interview you again. Tomorrow, perhaps?' The snowman pulls on his jacket.

I step towards the door, before turning back to face him. 'Is Miss May waiting for me here?' I ask.

'She'll be here for a while longer.' His grin makes me want to knock his smiling head off his round shoulders.

'Have you arrested her?'

Bawen shakes his head and shrugs at me as I leave. My brain is fried, and even if I did get hold of a lawyer, I would not have the concentration to talk things through rationally. I will write down everything I told Bawen and seek advice first thing in the morning.

On the train, I see another passenger's evening paper and its headline. *'Woman in Custody over O'Rowde Death'*.

I lean back in my seat and stare up at the roof of the carriage. *What will I tell Daniella?*

BILLY

*K*avara is still with me, when the detective comes back into the room. He acknowledges the solicitor with a nod, and then checks his watch.

'Miss May,' he says, 'it would not be fair to you to interview you now, it's too late. Get a good night's sleep. You'll have a clear head in the morning.' He smiles at me.

I smile back, trying to hide my anger. I imagine this is just a game for him – Detective Sergeant Bawen believes that I won't get any rest.

'We'll talk in the morning,' he says.

'Yes,' I reply. Something inside me makes me determined to sleep. I won't be beaten by this man.

Chapter 11

CHARING CROSS POLICE STATION
TUESDAY 12 AUGUST
BILLY

The detective shifts forward in his chair and stares at me for a few seconds. 'Billy May, on Tuesday twenty-ninth of July – two weeks ago today, you left Fox Halt Farm and drove your van with a cattle trailer to Culmfield Court. Tell me why you went there?' he asks, keeping his eyes fixed on mine.

'No comment,' I reply again, staring back. This must be the tenth question he has asked.

'And when you arrived at Culmfield Court, you spoke to Mrs Nala Bileh, and she provided you with a security code, so you could access the gate on Wall End Lane, the side entrance into Culmfield Court. Tell me what you said to Mrs Bileh?'

'No comment.' I want to answer, but Kavara says if I do, Bawen will keep probing. She said the Crown Prosecution Service take a dim view of a case with flaws, or incomplete or questionable evidence. The police need proof. Nothing goes to court unless the prosecutors are pretty sure they will secure a conviction. Responding to questions in this way is my best option for now.

'You were heard arguing with Mr O'Rowde. Tell me what you were arguing about.'

'No comment,' I reply…

After forty-five minutes, Detective Sergeant Hughie Bawen gets up slowly to his feet. He puts his head on one side and shakes it, still gazing at me. 'Don't think this is the end of this, Miss May. We will be making further enquiries, we will need to talk again, and for now, don't contact anyone connected with this investigation.'

Kavara stands up, 'Come on, Billy, we can go,' she says.

Five hours and twenty-five minutes later, Crinkle is under my feet. 'You're a ninja dog,' I tell her, as I walk into the kitchen at Fox Halt Farm. I lift her up into my arms and bury my face in her warm neck. This is the happiest I have felt since yesterday, when I thought Richard was going to kiss me. All the way home, I have been desperate to reach this sanctuary, and for my mother to tell me everything is going to be fine. But Mum has a visitor. Charlotte Westcott-Laurent, Tom's sister, is standing by the Rayburn.

'Hello,' I say to her.

Charlotte scowls back, and sips some tea from the mug she's holding.

'Have one of these,' Mum says, offering her a cookie from a heaped-up cooling rack but she shakes her head. 'No thank you, Mrs May,' she replies.

I breathe in melted chocolate, noticing how the warm smell pacifies me a little, but I still wish I was alone with my mother.

'This is a nice surprise,' I lie. Yesterday, before I was arrested, this would have been a true statement, I should have loved to have seen her. Like Jessie, Charlotte and I were close once, but my affair with Michael wrecked our friendship too.

'You know I was arrested?' I ask her. 'Should you be here? Should you be talking to me?'

'Not really sure,' she shrugs. 'I was just the person who found the body, that's all. I don't see what harm it will do if I speak to you.'

'Okay.' I shrug too, but I am only mirroring her action. I am not relaxed about this.

A smile starts on Charlotte's face. 'Hey, you nearly got away with it, Billy,' she laughs. 'Maybe you still will, if they've let you go.'

'You believe I murdered Michael? Is that what you think?' I ask. 'No, you can't believe that!'

Charlotte places her mug carefully on the table. 'I don't know you anymore, Billy.' Her voice is breaking up. 'I don't know what you might have done. I still can't believe you didn't tell me that hateful man probably killed my brother.'

I stare at her, not knowing what to say.

She looks at my feet then into my eyes. 'Billy, do you think I would have continued to work at Culmfield if I thought for a moment that my boss had murdered Tom?' she asks.

'But he threatened to hurt your nephew, or your niece, or Mum, if I told you,' I say, trying to explain.

'I don't care, I have worked for *him* all this time, for a man who may have killed my wonderful brother!' How could you?' she speaks so harshly that saliva sprays from her mouth. She wipes her chin with the palm of her hand, a slow movement, with her eyes fixed on mine. It feels menacing.

'Charlotte,' Mum cuts in, 'you said you came to see Mary. She'll be in here, in a minute.' Her voice is soft, trying to break the tension. She has known Charlotte since the day she was born. Back then, my mother didn't think she would have children, so her friend's baby next door has always had a special place in her heart. This confrontation must be hurting my mother to the core.

'Where is Mary?' Charlotte calms her voice down, but she still doesn't look away from me.

'In the dairy, I expect,' I reply. 'Mary is researching all the local and artisan cheeses in the country. She wants me to change our logo too, she keeps showing me her ideas for new packaging.'

Charlotte raises her eyebrows, but says nothing. I keep talking, trying to take her mind off Michael and Tom. 'She's contacting different retailers asking which cheeses they stock, saying it's for a school project.'

'Mary's drawn up a long list of questions, like why they have chosen to stock particular products, what sells best, and how much dairy produce their typical customer buys. Asking them to name their own favourites too.'

I can't believe Charlotte hasn't asked me to shut up, but maybe she doesn't want to return to the original subject either. *What more is there to say?* She looks at Mum. 'Could you take me to the dairy to see her?' she asks. I feel relief at the thought of her going outside, leaving me in peace.

'No,' my mother shakes her head. 'Mary will be in here soon enough. She'll know my biscuits are out of the oven, and will be in to fetch some. Give her five minutes,' she says. 'Sit down, Charlotte?'

'Thank you, Mrs May, but I'm fine here,' she replies.

'*Please* sit down.' My mother is determined but so is Charlotte and she remains standing.

New thoughts start to tumble in my mind. I am remembering the detective sergeant and the way he wouldn't tell me what he knew about Michael's death. He made lots of hints, and asked questions that seemed wholly irrelevant. It felt like something was wrong with what he was speculating, and I wondered if he might be bluffing, hoping I'd confess.

The man is going to keep digging, so I think I could benefit from Charlotte's help, she could give me some background information. I sit down, thinking how to frame my first question. I don't want to stir her up again. I look up at Charlotte. 'What did Jessie tell the police?' I ask.

'Everything,' she snaps.

'*Everything?*' I check, worried how Charlotte will react; she seems like a crocodile I am poking with a stick.

'How you used to be best friends. That you helped her with the children when they were small.' The crocodile stares at me, hungry. 'Gave the dates she believed your affair began and ended. Said you thought Michael killed my brother, and Michael threatened you about reporting him.'

I rub my hands together as if I am trying to cover them in soap, maybe wash off all the guilt I'm feeling.

'It was me who told them that you were at Culmfield the day Michael died,' Charlotte says.

'Why did you or Jessie say I argued with Michael? I didn't see him that day.'

'That wasn't us. I just said I saw you and I helped you take Braveheart away. I told the detective I found his saddle and rugs, and all the rest of his things for you.'

'So why does the detective think I saw Michael?' I ask.

Charlotte shakes her head. 'Who knows?' She isn't concerned.

'When Detective Bawen interviewed me,' I say, 'He said that someone heard me arguing with him. Who else has he talked to?'

'Everyone. Everyone who works at Culmfield.' She turns to Mum. 'Mrs May, are you sure Mary's coming in?'

'One minute,' Mum replies. 'She likes them best when they've cooled, she says they taste more chocolatey then. She's experimented with timings, temperatures and taste a lot, lately.'

I am frightened now that Charlotte will go outside to find Mary when I have more questions. 'You know Nala gave me the entry code?' I ask her quickly.

'Yes.'

'Well, I didn't want her to get in to trouble for helping me, so I asked her not to tell anyone. She wouldn't have misunderstood, would she? Do you think Nala could have said I was arguing with Michael when she meant something else? Her English seems pretty good now, but do you think she might have made a mistake?' I ask.

'Billy, I don't know.'

'Believe me, I simply got the code from her, and then I drove to the side gate. This doesn't make sense – something seems wrong,' I say. 'Did Jessie tell the police anything else?'

'I don't think so.'

'Nothing?'

'She told the police about her coming here with Mary, and she said how worried you and Richard were that she was at Fox Halt Farm. How you were both scared Michael might carry out his threats, if he discovered her here.'

•

133

'Were they pressuring her? That detective? Did Bawen trick her into telling him everything?'

'No. She wanted to tell him,' Charlotte replies.

'Why?' I frown.

'Because they asked her who she thought might have killed her husband.'

'She thought of me?' I am air-washing my hands again, pressing my fingers so hard into the base of my thumbs that it hurts. 'Why? He killed himself. You saw the exhaust. You saw him. It was suicide.'

'We don't know that for sure, not anymore.'

'Surely it's obvious what happened.'

'There is something you don't know, Billy – Grégoire saw someone with Michael in the car,' she says.

'Grégoire what?' I ask, not understanding.

'That night, he saw someone with Michael in the car.'

'When?' I check.

'The night before I found him dead, Grégoire saw the person with Michael. After you collected Braveheart.'

'And your husband thinks it was me?' I ask. 'If he does, then he's wrong. It was *not me*!' I am virtually shouting.

'No?' Charlotte replies, sounding sarcastic. 'Well, when they saw Grégoire, *whoever* it was ducked out of the way. Grégoire didn't want to pry. He guessed Michael had another woman on the go. He turned around and came home along the road instead, not wanting to get involved. Grégoire didn't even tell me about what he'd seen until last Friday. He asked me if he ought to tell the police.'

'And you said he should?'

'Yes, definitely, Billy. I had just found out from Jessie that you didn't tell the police about Tom's death. I was still reeling from that revelation. I dialled the station straightaway, and when they answered, I handed the phone to my husband.'

'I see, so, it's Grégoire who threw doubt over everything.'

'Yes, and a second post-mortem will be undertaken now.'

'But I didn't see Michael. I didn't. I *promise* you. I never laid a finger on him. The last time I saw him was when he came here.'

Charlotte smirks. 'Well, Jessie told the police that you hated Michael, so I can see why she pointed them to you.'

'But all I wanted to do was help her, to show Jessie how much I regretted the affair.' My miserable plea riles Charlotte up, and I watch as her face reddens.

'You betrayed us both, Billy. We were all friends. You and Jessie were like twins, that's what you used to say. Have you forgotten? And then one sorry day you drop us both, deciding Michael was more important. You abandoned us and,' Charlotte slams a hand hard onto the table, 'then, Billy, after your sordid little affair ended, you betrayed us again. You didn't tell the police, Jessie or me about Tom's death.' She smacks the table again, causing some of the biscuits to fall off the cooling rack. Her ferocity makes me shudder.

I defend myself. 'Michael threatened to harm Grace and William. I couldn't inform the police, or get in touch with you.' I pause. 'What would you have done, Charlotte?' I ask. 'Listen, I truly believed Michael would harm them, arranging whatever he did to look like another accident. You didn't hear him making those threats. Believe me, Charlotte, he meant them.'

'No excuses, Billy,'

'But–'

'No buts. You should have at least made sure Jessie was alright, but you didn't. Nope, Billy, you just got on with your perfect life. You were fine, and that's all that mattered. You were growing your business with Richard's support at every turn. You didn't give poor Jessie a second thought. Neither of us will ever forgive you.'

'Charlotte. Don't give up on me. I didn't mean to hurt you.'

'But you *have*.'

My reply is too loud, but she's still not listening. '*Please* understand. We all make mistakes. I made bad choices, I was selfish, but please, *please* forgive me. I'm so sorry. I didn't kill Michael, believe me...'

Mary walks into the kitchen with her hands pressed over her ears. The girl jumps up and down, yelling at Charlotte then me. 'Stop! Stop.' She stands between us. 'Dad caused all this trouble.'

Mary speaks softly now. 'My father caused heartbreak everywhere he went, just so he could be happy. Don't let him win again.' The girl sits down at the table next to me. 'I remember how we all used to be so happy,' she says.

'I know,' I say, touching her hand.

Mary smiles at me. 'When I was small,' she says, 'it was like Billy and Mum were my two mothers, they both loved Arthur and me so much. Culmfield was full of joy and Mum used to laugh all the time. Charlotte, please don't be angry with Auntie. She dropped me too, but she loved Dad, and she needed him when Saffi died. I know she couldn't have killed him.'

I am stunned at how Mary has rationalised all this, shocked by her confidence that I wouldn't have hurt Michael, and how she thinks that I loved him too much to murder him. She obviously has the version of events that Michael told Jessie, the one where I was devastated when we broke up.

Charlotte's shoulders drop. She looks at Mary, speaking gently. 'Darling, will you come home? Your mum misses you.'

'I can't,' Mary replies instantly.

'Why not?' Charlotte asks.

'No, I can't tell you.'

'Is it your mother? She is worried she hurt you.'

'No way!' Mary replies, making it sound like this suggestion is ridiculous. 'Mum is wonderful, it isn't her. Just leave it. Tell her I'm happy here.'

Charlotte suddenly puts a mobile phone on the table in front of Mary. 'Your mum asked me to give you this,' she says. 'It's on a contract, so you'll always have credit, and you can phone anytime.'

'Thank you.' Mary says picking up the phone, and rolling it gently in her hand.

'Your mum's mobile number is already in your contacts,' Charlotte explains to her. 'My number is in there too, and Arthur's, Nala's and Amir's. If you want to talk to any of us, you will be able to get in touch right away. And-' she pauses. 'If you *do* want to come home, someone will be here in thirty minutes.'

'Mum and Arthur have mobiles?' Mary swipes her fingers over the screen, giving the impression that she knows what she is doing.

'Yes, your mother got them all yesterday.'

'Awesome,' Mary smiles, quickly slipping the phone into her pocket.

'Look, Mary, I can wait if you want to grab your things, I can take you back to Culmfield now, if you like.'

'I said no – I am staying here,' Mary says. 'Just tell them all I miss them. Tell Mum I love the phone – say thank you for me.' She heads into the hall and I hear her run up the stairs.

When Charlotte leaves, Mary comes back down. 'Hasn't William gone home?' Mum asks her as she starts making two mugs of tea.

'No, he is in the dairy,' Mary replies. 'When he heard Charlotte getting mad at Auntie, he told me to grab a few cookies and bring them back out to him.'

'I didn't want to upset Charlotte,' I tell her, but Mary doesn't say any more about the argument.

'Do you want tea too, Auntie?' she asks me, then she turns to Mum. 'Do you, Nan Dan?'

'Nan Dan?' Mum frowns at her. 'You mean me?' she asks.

'Yes, I made the name up this afternoon, do you like it?' Mary grins at her.

'It's lovely, very clever,' Mum says. 'I know you didn't like calling me Daniella.'

'No, I don't like to.' Mary screws up her nose. 'I know William, Grace and Freddy call you Mrs May, but all my grandparents are dead, it's nice to think of you as a nan. It's like how I call Auntie Billy, Auntie, when she's not my real aunt, she's just special to me, just like you are Nan Dan.'

'Thank you, Mary. You're special to me too.'

'So, do either of you want a drink?' Mary smiles.

We both say no.

Mary is about to go back outside, and while she holds a china mug in each of her hands, Mum fills the pockets of her white coat with biscuits. 'Thanks, Nan Dan,' Mary says.

'You're welcome, my darling.' Mum winks at her. I feel concerned about Mary. She was already upset, and now she has heard Charlotte and me rowing. She must know too, that last night I was locked up in a police cell. I'm too tired to think how to explain everything to her at the moment, so I decide to make time to have a long chat with her in the morning. I want to show her that I care about her though. 'What are you and William doing?' I ask her as I open the door to let her out into the yard.

Mary answers in an easy tone, befitting a normal aunt who never had an affair with her father, who never abandoned her, or her mother, and certainly not an aunt who is a murder suspect.

'Nothing much really, Auntie. We're just hanging out,' she says. I consider her answer carefully, thinking how William doesn't 'hang out' with anyone; he is always busy working, mainly helping Sean, his mother's farm manager. Martha took on Sean to help her temporarily after Tom died, but Sean stayed on, mostly because he is as infatuated with Martha as she is with him.

The farm manager is ten years younger than Martha, and neither tells the other how they feel, even though everyone else sees the sparks between them. William and Grace like Sean too; he manages next door well. The neighbouring farm is huge, so in turn, Sean appreciates William's help.

William likes being busy, so if there is anything that needs doing, he is first to offer. Stillness lies uncomfortably with the boy next door. Action Man, that's him, rushing to finish one job while looking for the next. Avoiding socialising by keeping his iPod's earphones constantly buzzing in his ears, discouraging people from talking to him. That is why I am surprised when Mary says they are 'hanging out'. I wonder what the pair are really up to. Mary may read suspicion in my face, but she provides no more detail. 'We'll be another hour, I expect,' she says, darting outside, spilling tea as she walks quickly away.

Crinkle follows her, but Mum calls her back. The dog stops immediately, spins on her front legs and yaps at us. We both laugh at her. Mum turns to me. 'Are you okay, Billy?' she asks.

I shake my head. 'No,' I tell her. My mother holds her arms out.

'Come here,' she says.

Chapter 12

BEECHWOOD, JORDANS, BUCKINGHAMSHIRE

RICHARD

Jessie says she looks forward to our evening phone calls, and if she wants to talk then I am happy to listen. However, tonight I am finding it hard to pay attention. My mind keeps slipping away to Billy instead.

Both Bawen and my solicitor told me not to speak to Billy until I had volunteered myself for more police questions. I want to find out what the detective knows before I am interviewed again, so I said I was too busy to make an appointment to see him again until Thursday. I am struggling to think about anything else, constantly trying to guess what new questions he might ask.

'Jessie, tell me everything you know about the investigation. Start at the beginning. Don't leave anything out,' I say.

'How's that going to help me sleep?' she replies.

'I think talking it through could help you put things in perspective. I'm sure it will make you feel more at ease, rather than having everything churning over and over in your mind. I find talking to someone else generally makes things seem less difficult,' I explain. I am not going to admit to Jessie that I want to find out all she knows before I face Bawen again.

'Where shall I start?' she asks.

'How about why the police think Michael may not have killed himself, why they think someone may have murdered him and staged his death to look like suicide?' I say, surmising that if Billy is a suspect then this must be what the detective is thinking.'

'Well, that's probably down to Grégoire,' she says.

'Why?'

'On Friday, he told the police there was someone in the car with my darling husband…'

'*Darling* husband?' I check.

'I was being sarcastic, Richard.'

'Oh,' I say. 'When was this? When did he see someone with Michael?'

'The night before Charlotte found him dead, and the person with him, whoever they were ducked down as soon as they saw Grégoire. He didn't see their face.'

'Jessie, stop, why was Grégoire on the estate, he doesn't work for you anymore, does he?'

'No, not since Saffi died, but he often comes over to see Charlotte when she's with the horses, or he will go for a walk on the estate in between his painting. He says he gets the opposite of writer's block.'

'Sorry?'

'Grégoire says if he doesn't stop for breaks then his art can get slapdash. He can ruin his paintings if he starts rushing them.'

'Right,' I say, 'so where was Michael's car parked?'

'On the footpath, it's a short cut between here and their home.'

'I see,' I say, as Freddy comes in the front door, grabs a coat and goes out again without a word to me. 'You said Michael was with a woman? Did Grégoire recognise her?' I ask, wondering if I should check where my son is going.

'No, I said he saw someone in the car with Michael. He thought it was probably a woman. He is not a hundred per cent sure, but she or he tried to hide as soon as they saw him. He guessed Michael might be having another affair. It was the day that we had that big thunderstorm, do you remember?'

141

'Yes,' I reply.

'The car was a bit steamed up too. It was just a fleeting glance, he has no idea what they looked like.'

'So why did he wait so long to tell the police about this woman?' I correct myself. 'This other person?' Then I check. 'You did say he reported this on Friday, last Friday, that's what you meant?'

'Yes, last Friday.'

'So why so long?'

'As you can well imagine, Richard, both Charlotte and Grégoire are under no illusions about Michael, they both knew about his affair with Billy. Charlotte still works here, and Grégoire didn't want to get involved either,' Jessie explains. 'When he saw the car and its occupants, he backtracked and walked home along the road instead, deciding to forget what he'd seen. It wasn't till Friday that he even mentioned it to Charlotte, and she made him contact the police right away.'

'So, then,' I say, 'basically, Grégoire has opened up a can of worms, but that's all the police have?'

'Yes, but the detective is determined to find out who was with Michael. I get the impression from him that he won't leave any stone unturned.' She stops.

'What, Jessie?'

'Richard, the detective really is not certain Michael killed himself.' Her voice sounds flaky like she is about to cry.

'Are you alright?' I ask.

'Yes, I'm fine. Don't worry.' Her tone is level again.

I try to sound casual. 'Do you think it might have been Billy in the car? Is that what you told the detective?'

'Why not? She was here that day.' I hear her swallow, she must be drinking something. Jessie continues. '*She* was pretty mad about Michael, and maybe she wanted to find a way to help me? Maybe she asked Michael to stop bullying me. They could have argued. Perhaps she didn't mean to kill him?'

'She couldn't have done it,' I say, but a voice in my head asks, *could she?*

'It's amazing what someone will do when they are backed in a corner,' Jessie says. 'Even murder. She hated Michael.'

'Not Billy, she wouldn't,' I argue. 'Besides, how on earth could she make it look like suicide? No. That's crazy. And Billy would not be strong enough to have overpowered Michael. He was pretty tough, you know.'

'She's clever, and she'd have liked him out of all our lives,' Jessie replies.

'If she did, which she didn't,' I say. 'How did she make it look like carbon monoxide poisoning? That would have taken planning. No, Billy didn't kill him.'

'Richard, face it, she could have made it look like an accident. Have you spoken to her?'

'The police say I can't. They could look at our phone records. I don't want to make things worse.'

'Charlotte saw her this morning, she told me *she* looked alright then,' Jessie says.

'Charlotte went to the farm?' I check.

'Yes.'

'Didn't the police warn her not to communicate with Billy?'

'I don't know,' she replies. 'But I needed to give my daughter the mobile phone I bought with your credit card yesterday. Charlotte volunteered to take it to Fox Halt Farm for me. I didn't question whether she should go, I just needed to get the phone to Mary.'

'Was Mary alright?' I ask.

'Yes. I think so.'

'Did Charlotte ask her to come back with her?'

'She wouldn't come home – but at least I know she can ring me now, whenever she wants to.'

'That's good,' I say, changing the subject. 'I want to see her.'

'Mary?' Jessie asks.

'No, Billy,' I reply.

'Message her mother, if you don't think you should contact her,' Jessie suggests.

'I can't, Bawen might be monitoring her too.'

Another question suddenly flashes across my mind. 'Jessie, why didn't Charlotte discover Michael until the morning? Surely she would have noticed the car on her way home when she finished her last check at the stables?'

She answers quickly. 'Charlotte walks here first thing. She does a lot of work with the horses in the mornings and when she's finished – around lunchtime, she walks home.'

I frown, unsure she has answered my question.

Jessie continues to explain. 'When she comes back later, she's not here long, so she often drives instead. Look, Richard, I'm tired. Could we quickly discuss the two offers? You said you need me to sign something, and I was hoping you could bring the papers here, tomorrow maybe?'

I consider how Jessie and I can talk more easily face to face, and how it would be nice to get out of the city.

'I could be there by mid-morning,' I say, wondering why it is so difficult for me to say no to her.

CULMFIELD

WEDNESDAY 13 AUGUST

RICHARD

A brand new Range Rover towing a horsebox charges up the middle of the Culmfield drive. At the last moment, the driver veers to the side to let me pass. She lifts a hand to acknowledge me, but I don't recognise the woman under her Indiana Jones style hat.

'Who was that?' I ask Jessie, as she wipes some bird muck off one of the stone lions guarding the front steps.

'Eleanora Walters.'

'Who?'

'I don't know her. She is Charlotte's friend. I just wrote her name on the receipt.' Jessie doesn't look up.

'Receipt for what?' I ask.

'For Michael's horse. The animal needs exercise and he's far too good to be stuck here, not being ridden.' Still no eye contact.

'But, Jessie, you can't sell anything. Not until the legal issues have been sorted.'

'I can't keep using all your money.' She stays focused on the lion.

'You can, it's fine,' I say to the back of her head. 'It's not like you're throwing money around, you're just paying for things you need.'

At last, she turns to me. 'I don't *need* new clothes and a hairdresser, do I?' she asks.

'What?' I frown, not understanding what she means.

Jessie smiles. 'Richard, it may have escaped your notice that every time you see me, I am wearing this.' She pulls at the hem of her sweater.

'You're right, I hadn't noticed,' I reply.

'These are the only clothes I have that weren't chosen by Michael. I'm putting on weight too. If I did wear any of the designer clothes, he bought me, they'd be pretty uncomfortable.' She pats her stomach and pushes out her cheeks.'

'You're not putting on weight?' I say, thinking she might have but I hadn't noticed that either, I thought she looked healthier, but that was because she wasn't so stressed.

'Michael kept implying I was getting fat, he would say it all the time,' she says. 'He'd tell me that I shouldn't eat this or that, because I'd lose my figure, especially after having the children. He chose everything I wore, scouring away my self-belief in tiny layers. I found these clothes in the drawers under our bed, I had forgotten about them. They are all I can bear against my skin now. Everything else feels like a tight blanket he is wrapping around me, so tightly that I can't breathe, is that stupid?'

'No, it's not, Jessie,' I reassure her. 'But you can buy new clothes and have your hair done with my money, I don't mind.'

'But *I* mind,' she says. 'I don't want to rely on anyone anymore. The cash for that horse will buy me a whole makeover, and I hope you will take me back up to London tomorrow, so I can spend the day frittering away every last note that Mrs Walters just handed me. I'll catch the last train home.'

'Yes, Jessie, of course you can come with me.' I hold out my hands, palms up, trying to emphasise what I want to say. 'But don't sell anything else. Please wait, it should only be a couple more days and you'll have some interim funds to use. I need to ask you to put up with the situation just a little longer.'

'Alright, alright.' She stamps her foot on the marble step.

'Thank you.'

'I won't sell anything else until you say I can.' Jessie rubs her hands together. 'But I think, Richard, when you *do* give me the green light, there is going to be a very big sale.' She laughs. 'Maybe I'll have a charity auction, the money from his cars could help a lot of people. A women's refuge – that would be a good cause, don't you think?'

'Sorry, Jessie, I was worried for you,' I say. 'I didn't mean to boss you around. That's the last thing I wanted to do.'

She smiles, and my heart jolts a little. After all she's been through, it is good to see her happier. I can almost make out the dimples she used to have and the old sparkle in her eyes. I remember how she used to be one step ahead of me, ready to joke, or dive straight into something new. She was like my friend Saffi, he led me into all kinds of trouble. I can hear him now. *'Come on, Richard, don't worry, it'll be fun.'* Jessie was like that too, she could get you to agree to nearly anything.

'Richard, I don't want you to worry, I'm doing okay.'

'Yes, I know,' I reply.

'Do you want to know why I was so desperate to see you?'

'To sort out some of the paperwork?'

'No, not just that.'

'What then – for my good looks and charm, I suppose?'
'No, sorry, but that's nice too.' Another smile and another quickened heartbeat.

'Tell me,' I say.

'I need to take the boys into Exeter to buy some climbing gear, and then I want to take them to Haytor Rock and get them climbing.'

'I know nothing about climbing.' I shake my head. 'I won't be any help to you there,' I say.

'Charlotte will come too. Three adults with the three boys. It will be brilliant. Come on, you look dead on your feet. Dartmoor and the fresh air will do you a power of good. Please?'

This is what I meant, she is like Saffi. I feel this won't end well, but I can't say no. I imagine the trip is something Jessie has wanted to do with her children for ages. Something else Michael controlled and refused to allow.

The enthusiasm on the bus is rubbing off on me. I am surprised how much I am enjoying driving it. I can understand why Michael bought the old London vehicle. It's quite late when I pull the bus up in the car park below Haytor Rock. The shopping trip was an in and out exercise because Jessie had phoned the outdoor shop on Fore Street with a list of everything she needed. It was manoeuvring out of the Culmfield coach-house which delayed us.

I'm certain Amir would have got the bus out in seconds, but I was unfamiliar with both its size and the controls. Michael's chauffeur has found some extra work helping in a garage in Taunton, so he wasn't around to help. I think he needs to get his mind off Michael's death too.

Before he died, Amir fitted his life around his boss. Although he is still on hand to fix anything that needs repairing around Culmfield, I expect getting away from the place for a few hours is helping him adjust to his change in circumstances. But still, if Amir had been around to fetch the bus out of the coach-house, we would have left about an hour earlier.

'It's good we are late,' Jessie says, stepping off the bus.

'Why?' I ask.

'No crowds. Look, the hordes who are normally attracted to this beautiful place have left for the day – we have just got Dartmoor ponies and some black and white Belted Galloway cattle for an audience.'

Jessie has climbed Haytor lots of times before, so she is familiar with each route to the top. She tells us she started coming here with her father when she was about four, and I can see how she is enjoying sharing her knowledge and passion with her sons. I watch her with the ropes and the other bits of climbing equipment, noticing how she is totally at home with it all.

She shows me how to 'belay' her youngest son, Max. Jessie makes it look easy, but I find it tricky keeping the rope taut while the boy charges up the rock.

Charlotte suggests where Max should put his feet and hands, while Jessie keeps a careful eye on me. I like the gentle way she corrects my mistakes so I don't feel stupid or clumsy, and with her help, I soon get the hang of it.

The boys climb and climb, trying ever more challenging ways up. All three clearly love it. We all need this. Jessie is enjoying her sons trying her favourite sport. Grégoire left this morning to run an art retreat somewhere in Southern France, so Charlotte says if she wasn't here, she'd be moping at home missing him.

The boys are happy, using up energy that has been caged up for days. Every day since Michael died, there has been at least one reporter or a long-lensed camera hanging around Culmfield, so the family have been reluctant to leave the house. In a way, Jessie is still a prisoner in her own home.

Jessie is right, it is relaxing being on Dartmoor, having something different to concentrate on rather than thinking about Billy and whether she might be a murderer.

As we clamber in the bus to go home, we all agree we have to do this again.

'Let's get McDonald's,' Arthur says suddenly.

'No,' Jessie tells him, 'I have already phoned Nala, she is sorting out hot chocolate and sambuusas for us all. They will be ready as soon as we get home.'

I wonder what sambuusas are, but I am not going to ask because I need to concentrate on driving. My passengers are all at the back, so conversation is tricky anyway. I imagine they are something from Nala's African heritage. Whatever they are, the children seem pleased.

'She didn't do it.' Charlotte has come up to the front to talk to me.

'What?' I say, unhappy with the distraction. This is the last mile before we get back, the road is narrow.

'Billy didn't murder Michael. I believe her and, Richard, you should too. Surely, you know she wouldn't be capable of something so awful?'

'I don't know anything anymore,' I reply. 'I'm not good at judging people, Charlotte.'

'What do you mean?' she asks.

'I thought I knew Michael once, and Billy too,' I say, keeping my eyes on the road. 'I didn't realise my ex-wife wasn't happy in our marriage. I trust what my friends and my loved ones tell me, and I get caught out.'

'But surely you trust Billy? She says she's innocent. She says she didn't see Michael at all that evening.'

'Charlotte?' I say. 'How do you know when someone is lying to you?'

'I know Billy,' she replies. 'I have known her all my life, and I honestly believe her when she says she didn't see Michael that night.' Whenever someone uses the word honest, alarm bells ring in my mind, and I immediately suspect them of being untruthful. Over the years this hunch has generally proved correct, so I check. 'You *honestly* believe Billy, do you?'

'Look, Richard, all I can say for sure about that day is that Billy found me in the stables and I helped her move all Braveheart's tack. I watched her load him in her cattle trailer.' Her voice trails off.

'I want to believe Billy,' I tell her.

'Right,' Charlotte says, and she scratches her head, lifting her hair where the climbing helmet pressed it down.

'I can't talk to Billy to get her version of events,' I say. 'I can't ask her what happened because the police have asked me not to.'

'Okay,' she replies.

'Look, I withheld possible evidence from the police about your brother's death. I'm probably in enough trouble about that. I don't want to make things any worse by ignoring the detective sergeant's instructions not to see her.' I see from a sideway glance that Charlotte is nodding. 'There is nothing more I can do, other than confirm in court, if I have to, that I suspect Michael killed Tom and that he definitely threatened to harm Daniella, William and Grace. Maybe Billy thought killing Michael was the only way out, and we'd all be better off without him being around. I don't know.'

'You're wrong, Richard, she didn't kill Michael. You have to trust her.'

Something niggles at me about Charlotte defending Billy so vehemently. I wonder if she is trying to convince herself too.

I don't know Charlotte that well, but I suspect she isn't sure of Billy's innocence either. I decide to play Devil's advocate. 'Well, Charlotte,' I say, 'if you're so certain, then I will try to convince myself Billy is blameless.' I don't want to play games like this, but I'm thinking about tomorrow's meeting with Bawen, Charlotte might be able to tell me something I don't already know.

It seems to work, maybe for the worse. Charlotte pulls on the handrail, so she is closer to me, and speaks quietly. 'There is something though.'

'What?'

'When I saw Billy, she said someone witnessed her arguing with Michael, she didn't know if anyone really had given this information to the police, or whether the detective had made it up to try and provoke her. But when I got back to Culmfield, I discovered it was Nala, she was the one who reported hearing them.'

I take my eyes off the road and frown at Charlotte. 'Nala heard her and Michael?'

'Yes, she was in her bedroom in The Gatehouse and she said she definitely heard raised voices outside. She recognised Michael's and she thought it was Billy with him, but she didn't check. Nala felt like Grégoire, she didn't want to get involved either.'

I can't think what to say, so I stare back at the road. My mind is buzzing.

'And Amir saw Billy too.' Charlotte coughs, clearing her throat. 'He saw her at the front gate when he drove Michael home. She didn't wave or anything. He said she just stood there, motionless like she had something on her mind.'

My stomach turns over. I wanted to believe Charlotte when she said she knew Billy hadn't murdered Michael, but instead my doubts have multiplied.

When we arrive at Culmfield, Amir is waiting to open the front gates so I can drive straight through, but I stop the vehicle by his feet, opening the door to the bus.

'Thank you, Amir,' I shout. He steps onto the bus and stands in front of me. 'I drive now if you like, Mr MarcFenn,' he says.

'Thank you. Yes please,' I reply, getting up. 'I was not looking forward to putting this back into its parking space in the coach-house.'

'All the Porsches to avoid,' he replies. 'It tricky, yes.'

I nod, feeling pleased he is taking over from me, and also pleased to see Charlotte walking back down the bus to join Jessie and the boys. I don't want to discuss Billy anymore.

'Thanks for this,' I tell Amir, sitting down again directly behind the new driver. I stare at the back of Amir's head. *Did this man see Billy, did his wife hear her? Someone must be lying?*

Amir doesn't drive directly to the coach-house, instead he parks up next to my car in front of the main house. Jessie steps off the bus immediately. I notice how she has taken it for granted that Amir will sort out the bags and climbing equipment that have been dumped on the seats.

All I want to do is jump in my car and leave. I'll go straightaway. I have Jessie's signature on all the paperwork I brought, so we can discuss anything else on the phone.

'I'm going to make a move, I need to get back to Beechwood tonight,' I tell Jessie.

She doesn't look like she's heard me, too busy telling the boys to hurry up, so they can get some food.

'Jessie, I have to go now, Freddy is on his own and I have an appointment with the police in the morning, they want to ask me some more questions.' She stops talking to Max and turns to me. 'Eat something first. I'm sorry, I messed up your day.'

'I enjoyed it,' I reply.

'Thank you for driving and helping with the kids.' Jessie smiles. 'It was fun, wasn't it?'

Charlotte nods her head at me. 'Yes, thank you, Richard,' she says. Then she turns to Jessie. 'I need to let the horses out into the field now, I'll see you in the morning.' She hurries away without saying goodbye to the children.

'Have something to eat before you go,' Jessie says again.

'I'll phone when I get back to Beechwood, so you know I got home safely,' I say, ignoring her invitation.

'Please come in.' She is at the bottom of the steps with Max by her side. 'Just twenty minutes – have some food first, then go.'

I find I am walking beside her. Inside, the smell of pepper and turmeric is enticing. Jessie has her hand on my back. I am not sure which woman is forcing me towards the kitchen, Jessie's touch or the smell of Nala's exotic cooking.

'Haytor is such a special place,' Jessie tells me, as the children take it in turns to wash their hands at the huge stainless-steel sink. I smile at her, she's like a little girl, full of excitement and contentment.

Without a single word to Nala, Jessie and the boys sit at the table, waiting for their food to be placed in front of them. It doesn't seem rude. Somehow this feels normal, they are all at ease with one another, and there is a comfortable understanding between them.

With the meal finished, the children head off to bed and Nala goes too.

'I must leave now,' I tell Jessie as I stand up.

She doesn't move.

'What's wrong, Jessie?' I ask.

'I hoped we could go together. I was looking forward to the drive to London. I wanted to get some new clothes.'

'Sorry, Jessie. I can't stay. You can get the train in the morning. I take it you have organised for Nala to look after the children. She or Charlotte can drop you at the station.'

'Yes, Nala will look after the children,' she replies. 'I'm sure someone will get me to Saint David's, don't worry.' I remember the first time I saw her after Michael died. She looks like that now, empty and sad.

'I'll ring Freddy, and see if he minds staying at Jayne's tonight, but we do have to leave early, Jessie, will that be okay with Nala?'

The human shell has life again, her cheeks flush red. 'You text Freddy, and I'll phone Nala, just to check but it'll be fine with her, I'm sure. What time, five – five-thirty?' she asks.

'Five o'clock,' I reply.

She is up in a moment, heading for the phone in the hallway, and I am left in the kitchen, texting my son, and wondering what kind of a father I am. A message comes back immediately, Freddy is staying at the neighbour's anyway.

'I'll see you in here, just before five?' Jessie's black eyes glint at me, and for a fleeting second I wonder if she was responsible for her husband's untimely death. The change in her since he died is incredible.

'I didn't kill him, Richard.'

'What?'

'Just now, that's what you were thinking. I saw it in your face. I'm glad he is dead, I am glad you're here too, but I didn't have anything to do with his death.'

I don't reply.

'*She* killed him,' Jessie says. 'I am sure she did. I know it's not what you want to hear, but I'm convinced it was her.' Jessie's certainty stings so hard that my lungs suck in. They feel glued shut, unable to refill. She is right.

She touches my shoulder. 'Don't worry, Richard, we'll get through this - *together*,' she says. Her caring words transport me back to a garden in Paris. I see an old fountain, and the still pool around it reflects my face. My mother has just died, and Billy has her arm around me. She talks softly. Kindness when I am lost. A soft caress on my mouth. Irredeemable... I open my eyes, and stare into Jessie's. I jerk my head upwards and away.

'Look, sorry, I must go, after all,' I say. 'It's been a great day. Thank you.'

'Yes,' she says, smiling as she runs her finger slowly along her bottom lip.

PART TWO

Celia Moore

Chapter 13

FOX HALT FARM

THURSDAY 14 AUGUST

BILLY

My zero hour keeps changing; originally, it was the moment when Richard left Fox Halt to go to Cornwall. When he drove away, I began counting the hours, then days since I last saw him, desperate for his return.

After that, when he went to Culmfield to help Jessie my countdown began again, but the critical moment is now, Monday the eleventh of August at seven o'clock in the evening, the time we were driven away in police cars from the Fitzclaine Mayfair Hotel, sixty miserable hours ago. Each one of these separations feels worse than the last.

Detective Sergeant Bawen said my mobile phone and our home computer might be returned today, but in a way, I would prefer it if they weren't given back. At least while the police have them, I can't check for messages every five minutes. I know there will be no texts from Richard, but it wouldn't stop me from checking, just in case.

Mary was thoughtful, she gave Mum her new smartphone, saying she didn't need it. She said if she wanted to ring her mum, she'd use our home phone. My mother never wanted anything other than her simple Nokia, so until Mary handed over her hi-tech phone, we had no means of reading our emails. The dear girl set it all up yesterday, as soon as she came in from helping me milk the cows.

'Look, it's easy, some of the girls at school have the same phone. I'll show you everything you need to know,' she said, and she did.

This morning, Mary has started the milking. It's the first time she has done it on her own, and as I walk into the milking parlour, the first thing I notice is the radio has been re-tuned to Radio One. The cows don't seem to mind the new morning DJ, and they are already familiar with Mary because she has been helping in the parlour with me or William, twice a day, nearly every day.

'How did you get on?' I ask her as she lets the last of the cows back into the field.

'Easy-peasy, the cows were adorable. They were *sooo* good.'

'Did you look at my check list?'

'Yes, but not till just now, just to make sure I hadn't missed anything?'

'Did you?'

'No, I didn't, Auntie,' she smiles – she knows I am confident in her. Mary seems to do everything carefully and correctly.

'It will be a lovely morning for a ride, it feels cooler today,' I say.

'Auntie, I need to tell you something, please?' Mary has taken off her rubber gloves. She waits for me to give her my full attention. I have an inkling she wants to tell me why she won't go home.

'We can talk for as long as you like,' I say.

'I don't want riding lessons anymore.' She speaks quickly.

'No?'

'Would you cancel them, please?'

'I don't understand, Mary. Why do you want to stop?' I ask her. 'Don't you like Annika Parkes?'

'She is cool,' she replies. 'Heaps better than the chap who used to teach Sharmarke and me. Annika has done it all, she really knows her stuff, and she explains things really, *really* clearly. She makes me laugh too. I *do* like her.'

'Why then?' I watch her eyes and think of Michael. I keep wondering how such a sincere and caring child could have such a dad, a man who walked over everybody to get his way. She looks so serious with her arms straight down by her side.

'I don't want to be a world class show jumper anymore.'

'You don't?' I frown.

'No, I want to run something like this,' she says, waving her hands around the parlour. 'Fox Halt Farm has really got to me, Auntie. I love how you're developing the business. I love the shop, and the dairy and the cows.'

I want to cry, the girl's earnest words fly straight to my heart, she feels just the way I do. My head starts to override my emotions – I realise that she is making a mistake. This is just Mary becoming infatuated with something new. Mum, I, and all the Fox Halt staff keep telling her how lovely it is to have her here, praising everything she does. It must feel very rewarding. I have to make her see sense.

'But you're so good at riding. Braveheart has so much potential too. Don't let your dreams go, Mary,' I say. 'Stick at the lessons for now and see how you feel in a month, or two.'

'That's what William said.'

A new thought charges into my head. I am wondering if she has fallen for the boy next door, and she imagines herself being on a farm with William for the rest of her life. I don't immediately dismiss this notion, deciding that if Mary likes him, then perhaps she will value his advice.

'William is right,' I tell her. 'You have to keep going, you will be a star one day, I know it.'

She doesn't reply.

'Like William said, you mustn't give up on your dreams,' I say. 'Don't have regrets later on.'

'It's not my dream,' she replies.

'But your mum said it's all you've ever wanted to do?'

'It was Sharmarke's dream, and I enjoyed being with him, competing against him, forcing him to get better all the time.' I detect a change in her as she talks about the friend she grew up with at Culmfield. It makes me think I am wrong about Mary having feelings for William.

'Do you miss Sharmarke?' I ask.

'Yes,' she replies quickly, digging her fingernails into the back of her scalp.

'Is that why you're hanging out with William, is it because you miss Sharmarke?'

'Not really. William is nothing like him. William needs me, that's all.'

'He needs you?' I say, frowning at her again.

'Yes,'

'Why?'

'William wants to make cider. There's an old orchard on his farm, and he thinks there will be a massive harvest of cider apples this year. We've been working out if he can make some money out of it. We're writing a business plan and checking out all the equipment he needs.'

'Really?' I laugh.

'What's wrong? I think it's a fab idea.'

'It's not the cider project. I just couldn't understand why William was here all the time, it's so unlike him. I thought he had a crush on you.'

'Is that so odd? I'm not unattractive, am I?' Mary asks.

'No, darling, you're beautiful, but William is usually a loner, I couldn't work it out. Our farmyard is the place where he found his dad after the accident. He doesn't normally spend any longer here than he has to.' As I say accident, I wonder how much longer before everyone learns the truth. I shiver when I think how William will feel about Mary, when he finds out her dad might have killed his. This situation feels like it's on a knife edge.

'You were thinking about Dad then, weren't you, Auntie?'

I shut my eyes thinking how like her mother she is; Jessie always knew what I was thinking, sometimes I thought we didn't need to talk at all.

'I was,' I tell her.

'You *really* loved Dad, didn't you?'

I think how this is a strange discussion to be having with Michael's daughter. *How did we move from riding lessons to my affair?* I want Mary to trust me enough to tell me why she won't go home. I hope if I'm honest with her she will open up to me.

'Mary, I didn't love your father,' I say.

'What do you mean? I don't understand.' She moves towards a stack of boxes and sits on them.

I try to speak without sounding patronising. Yes, she is only fourteen, but Mary is astute. 'I used your father, he was someone to hold me and look after me when Saffi died. Your father was kind and thoughtful. He was there for me when I needed support.'

'You didn't love him?' Mary frowns at me.

'I thought I did, once, but I think I always held something back. I knew I was sharing him with your mum, you, and your brothers. He loved you all very deeply, you know.'

'I suppose,' she nods.

'There was a short time when I thought I loved your dad very much,' I tell her.

'But…' Mary says.

'But I never loved your father the way I love Richard. I love Richard with part of my soul. I think about him all the time, and I miss him every single second we're not together.'

Mary gets up from her box and stands tall with her arms straight down by her side again. I think she might cry.

'That's how I love Sharmarke, like you love Richard, I mean.'

'Sorry?' I say, shocked because I did not expect this. I want to wrap my arms around her, but something stops me.

'Mary, if you love Sharmarke, then why are you here?' I ask. 'Were you frightened your dad would be angry if he found out? Your father is not at Culmfield anymore, you can go back, you know. Your mother will understand, I know she will.'

'I can't, Auntie.'

'Why not?'

'I'm not saying any more, I'm sorry,' she says. 'Please just cancel my riding lessons. And...' She stops.

'And what?'

'Could you speak to Mum and see if she can employ Annika to work with Sharmarke? Please ask her to get rid of our previous instructor. I am sure Annika will make such a difference to him.' Mary squeezes her eyes shut, determined not to cry.

I stare at her, unsure what to say.

'There is something else,' she says.

'What?' I ask, not wholly concentrating because my mind is still running through scenarios about what might have happened to prevent Mary from going home.

She doesn't reply.

'Did Nala or Amir know about your feelings for Sharmarke? I ask. 'Did they disapprove because you're not Muslim – or because they work for your parents?'

'No. No!' she says. 'Stop it Auntie, just leave it please.'

I mustn't upset her, I'll have to wait until she tells me some more. 'What else did you want to tell me?' I ask gently.

'I want Sharmarke to have Braveheart. It will be good for him to have two horses to ride.'

Another shock. 'Mary,' I say, as softly as I can.

'Yes.'

'I need to explain something to you.' I move closer. 'Amir and Nala won't be able to afford Annika Parkes.' I pause, reaching out to touch her hand. 'And they certainly can't stretch to keeping two horses for Sharmarke to ride.'

She jumps up. 'No,' she says, making me realise how young she is. She looks like the spoilt toddler I remember, who is about to stamp her feet because she can't have a new toy.

'They're fine,' Mary tells me. 'Amir and Nala don't pay for anything. No rent for their home, nothing. O'Rowdes' pay Sharmarke's school fees and everything for his horse – it's all part of Amir's wages.' She stares at me with wide eyes. 'Mum won't stop paying, will she?'

I don't reply.

'Mum still needs a chauffeur, and Amir is great, he's always fixing stuff. We couldn't do without him.' She sits back down on the boxes. 'And Nala, we can't do without her either – Mum can pay for two horses and Annika, she has oodles of money now.'

'How do you know about Amir's wage?' I keep my voice calm, trying to cool Mary's determination.

'Sharmarke told me. He said whatever he needed, he could have. Amir would just ask my dad, and just like me, he always has the best of everything. We called ourselves the SBs. We used to laugh about it all the time.'

'What are SBs, Sharmarke Bilehs?' I ask.

'No, Auntie, s*poilt brats*.'

'I see,' I say. 'I didn't know what Michael paid Amir, but the poor man was pretty much at your dad's beck and call twenty-four-seven. It was fair enough, I suppose. Your father could afford it.'

She shrugs. 'Will you speak to Mum about Sharmarke having Braveheart? Don't say anything about my feelings for him though. No-one else must know, not anyone.'

'Okay,' I reply.

'Will you promise?'

'I won't tell anybody.'

Mary stares at me intently. 'You have to promise. It's very important, Auntie.'

'I promise,' I tell her.

'And you'll speak to her to get Annika to teach Sharmarke?' Mary touches my hand now. 'And you mustn't tell William I told you about the cider.'

'What cider?' I frown. William's project is already at the back of my mind, while I rack my brain, trying to think how I will explain about Mary giving up riding to Jessie.

'Mary,' I say.

'What?'

'Sharmarke and you weren't planning on running away together, were you? When your mother found you packing, were you *both* going to leave Culmfield? Did Jessie mess up your plans when she discovered you?'

'No,' she replies in a voice that makes me feel this is what she would have liked to have done.

'So, you're here for good then?' I laugh, hoping to ease the building tension. 'That's great, because I love having you here.' I smile, and Mary smiles back at me. 'Thank you, Auntie,' she says.

All I can think about is how Mary is completely messed up. I have no idea how to help her. Whatever I do, I know she'll be just like I was at her age, she'll push the other way, hard against me. She believes she has all the answers, so all I can do is let her make her own mistakes and be there for her when she needs me. I feel she trusts me a little now, however I won't push her. I want her confidence in me to grow, so she might tell me later why she still won't go home.

'Did you kill my Dad?' Mary stands up, spinning around to face me.

I am stunned at her new question. 'No,' I say.

'It's okay.' She is grinning at me now. 'I know you didn't.' She seems to be treating her father's death like it's just the plot of a movie she's seen.

'But how do you know?' I ask, copying her easy tone.

'Because I know what happened.'

I try to hide my shock. 'Are you going to tell me? You should tell the police too, and I would be off the hook.'

'I need to go and ride Braveheart now,' she says, turning away from me. 'I'll be back around lunchtime.'

'Mary,' I say, feeling angry she ignored my question.

'See you later,' she says as she strides away. 'Speak to Mum,' she calls out without looking back.

Richard has told me how pleased Jessie was that I had found a riding instructor for Mary, so I am worrying how to tell Jessie that she is no longer interested in show jumping. But I promised Mary that I would deal with this, and if she is going to keep faith with me, then I have no choice.

I have to call, but I'll get the cheese started first, I need to think this through properly. Maybe I need to discuss this a bit more with Mary and get her to change her mind. I wonder how she could know for certain what happened to her father, and if her behaviour is her way of dealing with her feelings; maybe she is grieving but doesn't want to show weakness.

Too many questions.

Chapter 14

CULMFIELD

RICHARD

'I shouldn't have kissed you?' Jessie says. The smile has disappeared from her face. 'I was just trying to hurt *her*.'

I stare at the floor. I feel guilty, wondering if she kissed me, or did I kiss her?

'Look, Richard, I wanted her to know what it's like to have the man you love stolen away.' I don't say anything. 'Richard, it's so late and you're too tired to drive all the way back to Beechwood now. If you had an accident on the way, I'd never forgive myself. Please stay.'

When I look up, her eyes bore into mine. Suddenly, the kiss seems like a trivial mistake; somehow Jessie has smoothed away the awkwardness, like the click of a hypnotist's fingers, erasing all memory of it; like it never happened.

'I'll stay,' I tell her, as I start to climb the oak staircase. 'Good night, Jessie.'

'Night, Richard, sleep well,' she replies.

'If you're up a bit earlier,' I say, 'we can have toast and coffee before we set off.'

'I'll get the coffee on,' Jessie says.

I slept like a king in my magnificent four-poster bed draped in heavy gold silk, the best night's rest I have had in weeks.

It's morning now, and I am munching a thick slice of white toast loaded up with Nala's home-made spicy marmalade. Jessie sips strong coffee while writing out a note for Nala, asking her if she minds putting some washing on the line later.

'It will be good to have company,' I say. 'Having someone to chat with on the journey, Freddy just spends the time in the car texting.'

'I may fall asleep, I'm afraid,' Jessie replies, pouring herself more coffee. 'I hope this caffeine keeps me awake for a while.'

'You're not going to dribble over my car seats, are you?'

She punches me on the shoulder. 'No,' she says. 'I don't dribble, and I won't snore either,' she laughs.

I felt at ease until ten minutes ago. I am not in the least relaxed now, questioning myself. *Why did I let Jessie drive?* I wonder if my car has ever travelled this fast before. I hold on to my seat, and my knuckles are white. She is talking about her parents, but I can't listen properly because I am too scared that we will crash, or we will be stopped by the police – who will confiscate my car, making me miss my interview with Bawen.

I try to tell her about my parents. I like talking about them and I don't often get the chance to speak about them, but the speed is unnerving. 'Could we slow down a little?' I ask, keeping my voice calm.

'Of course,' Jessie says. I look across at the hand on the speedometer, hoping it will swing towards me. It moves a degree.

Jessie starts to talk about her children, while I concentrate on my breathing. Gradually, I notice how Jessie is watching everything around her too. She is like a racing driver aware of each bend – assessing every vehicle before we pass. She anticipates everything that might happen and reacts instantly. Conversation becomes easier and I start to listen to her tales of school and her time in Australia.

We discuss my old property firm – anything and everything, except for Billy and Michael – happy chatter with laughter. Even teasing each other about some of the things we say. It reminds me of time with Saffi.

Saffi and I described our meet ups as *beer and banter*, but sometimes we had meaningful and thoughtful debates. But still, time spent with him was always full of joy. I didn't realise until Saffi killed himself, how he hid his sadness and fears with laughter and jokes, and I think Jessie and I are doing the same thing, pretending. We know this isn't a heart to heart, this is a tête-à-tête. Our words are carefully chosen to avoid any discussion about the two people we really want to talk about.

We have arrived early in Berkeley Square. 'More coffee?' I ask Jessie, pointing at the wine bar.

'A cup of tea for me,' she replies, and her carefree tone reminds me how Billy and I used to be when we were together.

'Stop thinking about her,' Jessie tells me, and I raise my eyebrows, wondering what gave my thoughts away. 'Richard, I want to tell you what I want to do with the two offers for the business. I didn't sleep last night because it has suddenly come to me.'

'What?' I check, wondering why she didn't talk about this while she was driving. This is going to be a rushed conversation because I have to meet Bawen in an hour and a half.

'I'll tell you once we've ordered,' Jessie says. 'I'm paying, by the way.' She rifles in the pockets of her oversized jeans for some money and pulls out a wad of twenty-pound notes.

'Don't you have a purse?' I ask her, 'or a handbag to put that in?'

'Nope,' she replies. 'None that Michael hadn't bought me.'

As she pays, Jessie runs her fingers over the notes. I see that she is relishing giving the money away. 'Keep the change,' she says smiling broadly.

'Thank you,' the barista says. 'It will be a minute or two, I'm afraid. I haven't switched on all the machines yet. Shall I bring them to your table?' he asks.

'No, I can take them, I'll wait,' I reply.

'I'll get a table,' Jessie says. The place is empty, but she makes her way to the one in the furthest corner of the room. She moves like a ballerina. No, that's wrong, it's more ethereal somehow. Jessie fixes her eyes on something, and her body moves slowly and precisely towards it. She is mesmerising.

'So, what are you thinking?' I ask when I get to her with our drinks.

'I'll whisper it to you.' She smiles, well aware that her decision is vital to the future of the company. We do need to be careful who hears this conversation because it could seriously affect the share price, but the way Jessie says she will *whisper*, feels more than a desire to keep this secret, it is flirty, and I can feel the hair on the back of my neck stand on end.

'What?' I ask calmly, not showing how she's ruffled me.

'I know we can't do anything formal until the big shareholder meeting next Tuesday, when you'll be voted in charge, but this could be a bit tricky.'

'Go on, what do you want me to do?' I say, thinking how Jessie has all the say now. She owns a fifty-one per cent share of O'Rowdes'. We still have to go through the motions, but she should be able to call all the shots. She picks up her cup and leans forward. 'I want to sell O'Rowdes' to both of them, split the company in half,' she says.

'Right,' I reply.

'What I'm thinking, Richard,' she explains, 'is for you to map out all the outlets, and then sell every other one geographically, to each bidder. Could we do that?' I think I know what she means but I am not going to check because time is running on.

'Yes, I don't see why not,' I say.

'We can?' she checks.

'Yes – but it will affect the amount they'll each offer. The proceeds are bound to be less, and we'll have to make it clear exactly what you're selling. Seek revised bids. There is the danger too, that the potential buyers will walk away. That's my first reaction, there may be other repercussions.'

'But you'll follow this plan through for me?' Jessie asks. 'I thought the Monopolies Commission might prefer this option too. It might make the company easier and quicker to sell.'

'It's that why you want to do this, to speed things up?' I ask.

'No,' she replies quickly. 'It's more personal than that, I think it will erase the O'Rowde legacy faster. It's just how I feel, I don't expect you to understand.'

'Well, the monopolies people may like it, so the sale may be approved by them more quickly.'

'That's what I just said.'

'Yes, but you realise too, it will delay things to start with? We won't have updated offers in time for next week's meeting, and the potential lower bids are bound to upset the other shareholders.'

'Just do it please,' she says sharply, and I wonder if she thinks I'm behaving like Michael, squashing her ideas.

'I will,' I say, trying to reassure her.

'There is something else too.' Jessie fixes her eyes on me. 'I'm changing my surname back to my mother's. Mrs Stephens has sorted the paperwork for me, it came through yesterday, so can you change everything at O'Rowdes' that concerns me? Change every reference to Jessica Cambell.'

'Yes, Miss Cambell,' I reply, feeling shocked. I am not surprised she wanted to change her name, but I am shocked because she hasn't mentioned this to me before.

'I do have to go,' I say.

'Okay,' she says, her face expressionless.

I stand up, my thoughts turning to my imminent meeting with the detective. I saw Bawen on Tuesday, when he arrived at my office with an IT man, telling me that they needed to take Michael's computer away for a couple of days to interrogate the hard drive.

The detective, IT engineer and Michael's computer, all left the office together that day, so when I spoke to Jessie in the evening about signing some papers, losing access to Michael's files was a bit of an excuse to head to Culmfield when she asked.

Bawen promised the computer will be returned by the time I get back into the office this morning, just after my own interrogation with him.

I suppose I shouldn't call it an interrogation, I don't *have to* see Bawen, he said I would be *volunteering* to speak to him. It does not feel like it though, I don't feel I have a choice. My brain starts buzzing through all the questions I will face later. I think about Billy. I don't want to believe she murdered Michael, but then, she had a lot of reasons to want him dead, and she was at Culmfield that day. *No,* I argue with myself, *she didn't do it, this is all a terrible mistake. Michael's death was suicide.*

The detective has told Jessie that the second post-mortem has concluded it was definitely carbon monoxide poisoning that killed her husband, and there was no indication of any other cause of death. There were no injuries on his body either.

Michael must have killed himself. The coroner is planning to release his body next week, so that confirms it too. Bawen even said Jessie can arrange his funeral now. I am sure Billy is innocent, no-one can make someone stay in a car while it fills with gas.

'See you Saturday evening sometime,' Jessie says, as she stands up to face me. 'Thank you for letting me come with you this morning.'

'It was nice to have your company,' I tell her, but now I remember her driving.

'Sorry I drove too fast,' she smiles.

Jessie is getting into my head – I ignore her comment. 'I hope you manage to find a new look for your new name,' I say, as I follow her outside.

I ask myself if Jessie has been trying a bit too hard to convince me that Billy is a murderer? I start to wonder at her motives.

'You can send me a photo later,' I tell her. 'But make sure you label it, I may not be able to recognise you.'

'I will.' She moves to kiss me on the cheek, but I turn my head away quickly.

'I really must get going. Don't forget, send me a picture,' I say.

'I'll send it with kisses,' she laughs.

'Bye for now, Jessica Cambell. Enjoy your day.' I think for a moment how it might be fun to shop with her but then as I watch her walk away, I consider how she has completely changed since Michael died, and how she's set on eradicating him from her life.

Did Jessie kill her husband?

SATURDAY 16 AUGUST
FOX HALT FARM
BILLY

Seeing Charlotte driving a horse lorry into our farmyard makes me wince. I realise I have underestimated Mary's feelings about Sharmarke taking on her horse. I talked to her for ages about how much giving up riding would upset her mother, and I thought she had reconsidered, but she obviously hasn't changed her mind. Mary must have arranged it herself and Charlotte must be here to collect Braveheart.

Mary appears from nowhere, heading for the lorry, and I decide I ought to help her. I am upset that she has phoned Culmfield without telling me. I have let her down, when I promised to sort this out for her.

I fetch Braveheart's saddle, bridle and grooming kit. It's a lot to carry in one go but I am rushing, trying to be helpful.

With the saddle balanced on top of everything in my arms it's difficult to see immediately in front of me, and as I walk out of the tack room, I crash into someone. I stand motionless, while I take in this morning's second surprising arrival.

'Hello, Freddy,' I say. 'It's lovely to see you.' My pulse starts to race as I think Richard must be with him.

'Hi, Billy, what's happening with Mary's horse?' he asks.

'Braveheart's going back to Culmfield,' I reply.

'And Mary?'

'She's staying, I think.' I am only half concentrating on Freddy, while my eyes scan the yard for Richard, or his car. 'Where's your dad?' I ask.

'Huh,' Freddy sighs. 'Not here, I caught the train and then got a taxi from Exeter. He said he had to sort out a load of stuff at O'Rowdes'. He's going to pick me up tomorrow night, but who knows if he really will, I have hardly seen him lately.' He wipes his long blond fringe backwards. 'Mum took me to the station this morning.'

'Janette?' I check.

'Yeah, dear Mama.'

'I didn't think she was due home yet?'

'She wasn't but she said Pops wasn't looking after me properly. She cut her holiday short. I said I was fine with Jayne, but she wouldn't listen.'

'It must be nice having her home,' I say, wishing he would say no.

'Do you want me to take that?' Freddy is pointing at the saddle. 'You look a bit overloaded.'

'Please,' I say, leaning forward so he can take it.

'I have to tell you, Billy, it's nice to be here. My dear Mama hasn't left me alone since she got back, she keeps clucking around me like an old hen. Where shall I put this?'

'In the lorry, please, Charlotte will tell us where she wants it,' I reply. My brain goes back to Freddy's first question. *Is Mary going home with Charlotte?* I dump the tack on the ground at the front of the lorry, so I can speak to Mary.

'Darling, are you going back to Culmfield too,' I ask.

173

'I'm not, Auntie.'

Her words settle my churning insides. I hadn't realised how much I had come to rely on her being around. My mother is great to live with, but Mary is full of questions and energy. She's been keeping me sane, a leveller when I start to panic about everything.

Charlotte sees my relief. 'You look happy about that,' she says.

'About what?' I say, picking up the bridle.

'Mary staying here.'

I let silence hang in the air before I reply. 'Is that what you're going to report back to Jessie, that I am stopping her daughter from returning home?'

Charlotte holds out a hand, signalling for me to pass her the bridle. She looks me in the eye and walks towards the lorry ramp. I turn towards Mary. 'I'm so glad you aren't going,' I say quietly, hoping Charlotte can't hear me from inside the lorry. 'When you do go home, could you give me a bit of notice first? I will really miss you.'

Mary nods and smiles.

As Charlotte says goodbye, Mary tells her, 'Please explain to Mum that I'm not ready to come home yet. Tell her I miss her. Tell Arthur, Max and Mikey I miss them too.'

'Don't worry, Mary, I will. They all miss you like crazy,' Charlotte replies. 'No message for Sharmarke, telling him he better look after Braveheart and win every competition he enters?'

'Yes, tell him that,' she says. 'Thank you, Charlotte, for collecting him.' She turns around and starts walking to the farmhouse. Once indoors, I imagine her running upstairs to her new bedroom. I am sure she just wants to cry. I wish she'd tell me what's going on.

'Cressida's stayed in New Zealand,' Freddy tells me.

'Cressida?' I ask, frowning at him, then I remember how everyone else refers to his twin sisters as Sid and Harry, but the girls always made their much younger brother use their full names.

I think his older sisters were pretty mean to him when he was small, but he has long since forgiven them, saying they were just jealous of him getting all his parents' attention. He texts them both every day now.

'Yes, I told you how she and Mama kept meeting up with this bloke and his two daughters at different campsites. Well, Cressida is now travelling with this chap and his girls, in their campervan.'

'Is your Mum happy with Richard being in her home?'

'She only came back yesterday, and Pops is staying at Culmfield.'

'Right,' I say, not really sure what to add.

'Mama's not mad at him really, she understands he's trying to help Jessie. She didn't make him go, Pops offered. He said he's got options, like booking a hotel for a while, or staying at Mr O'Rowde's house in Richmond, but tonight he'll be at Culmfield.'

'Right,' I say again, wanting to go indoors, find Mary and hold her. I want to cry my heart out too, but I don't. 'Does Grace know you're back?' I ask Freddy.

'Yes. She's meeting me here in a moment, she didn't want her mum asking me to help Sean and William get the straw in.'

Mary comes back outside. I smile at her, quickly turning back to Freddy. 'I think Mary is quite upset about Braveheart going, could she spend the day with you and Grace?'

Freddy doesn't hesitate. 'Yeah,' he replies. Then he shouts hello to Mary as she makes her way across the yard. She comes over to us.

'Grace and I are having a picnic later,' Freddy tells her. 'We're hoping to have a swim in one of the deep pools in the stream that divides Fox Halt Farm and ours. Grace is bound to bring enough food for an army, so would you like to come with us, Mary?' Freddy is smiling.

'Sorry,' she replies. 'I'm in the shop today. I have to go in a minute.'

'Mary, I'll be in the shop all day today,' I say, 'you go with Freddy and Grace. It will take your mind off—' I pause. 'Braveheart.'

I think Freddy and Grace are being optimistic about swimming; there's been no rain since the thunderstorm the night Michael died, and I am sure the pool will only be inches deep. I don't say anything though because I think it will be fun for Mary whatever they end up doing.

'Are you sure Grace won't mind?' Mary asks Freddy.

'It was her idea, she said you have to come.' He holds up his phone, as though he has a message from Grace. 'She says it will be fun for all of us to do something together.' Freddy scratches his neck, a tell-tale gesture that I have learnt to recognise – he is lying.

I remember when I first met Richard's son, how gullible I was to his fibs. It was a while since I had spent much time with children, and at first I believed everything Freddy told me. It was Richard who pointed out his son's itchy neck, and how he presses his tongue on his bottom lip as he waits for someone to have faith in his lies.

'Alright, I'll come,' Mary says.

Chapter 15

FOX HALT FARM

MONDAY 18 AUGUST

BILLY

As I watch Mum being driven away in a police car to fetch Mary from the farm shop, I wonder how far Detective Bawen's investigation will go. He has already had our house searched from top to bottom, but surely he doesn't need to involve the children? Mum offered to be with Mary while the detective talked to her, and he drove my mother away without further explanation.

I think back to my own interview. It felt like Detective Bawen wanted me to put my hands up and confess, 'Okay, it's a fair cop, this is how and why I killed him.' After all, that is what happens in crime dramas, so maybe it does in real life too? He held up a plastic bag in front of me, and I can hear his words now… 'I am showing Billy May item zero-zero-eight. Miss May, do you recognise this earring?'

I knew it straightaway. It was so distinctive and so expensive, a half-carat diamond set in rose gold and surrounded by twenty-nine smaller diamonds. Jessie and Michael gave me the earrings for my thirtieth birthday. 'No comment,' I replied, thinking how it's partner was in my jewellery box here. I hoped I would find the missing one, tangled in a scarf, or in a jacket pocket; somewhere like that.

'Miss May, can I remind you that we can check this item for DNA. Is this yours?'

The thought of a forensic test proving positive flustered me. 'It does look like mine,' I said.

'So please tell me how it came to be in the car Mr O'Rowde was found dead in?' Detective Bawen fanned out five horrible photographs in front of me. There were two from different angles of the earring stuck in the bottom of a seat headrest, but one was of Michael's scarlet face pressed against the car window. The atrocious image has stayed in my brain ever since. I also saw the car; a special edition Porsche, a vehicle I'd never seen before, let alone been in.

'No comment,' I said again, pleased I had the option because I was so shocked and confused.

This fake *evidence*, and the lying witnesses reporting me arguing with Michael, has left me on tenterhooks, waiting for another piece of false testimony or fabricated proof to come out of nowhere. I am trying to imagine why the detective has suddenly turned up again, this time wanting to question Mary.

Grace has been standing next to me, and I notice that she's been uncommonly quiet. 'What's wrong?' I ask her.

'I'm so sorry, I was just jealous.'

'Of who?'

'Of Mary,' Grace replies. She makes me think of yesterday. 'I noticed you getting cross during our meal last night,' I say.

'What do you mean?' Grace asks.

'I saw all your sideways glances when Freddy laughed too loudly at one of Mary's jokes. Freddy was winding you up, wasn't he?'

'He was a bit.'

'But Freddy felt sorry for her. He didn't want her feeling left out, especially with William not there with us.'

'I'm fed up with my brother too, he and Mary are always hiding in corners, whispering.'

I frown, not sure what she's trying to tell me. 'So, you were angry with Freddy and William?'

'Not really, it was Mary I was jealous of. I wanted time with Freddy, I hardly see him now, but she had to tag along with us, didn't she.'

'You shouldn't be jealous, Grace,' I say. 'I know these weeks of your summer holiday are very different to the ones you thought you'd have. You expected Freddy to be here every day with you. I understand your disappointment, but you shouldn't be jealous of Mary.'

'But I *was*,' Grace says. 'That's why I rang the police when I got home.'

'You rang the police?' I check.

'Yes.'

'Why?'

'Mum drove me to the police station this morning.'

'Grace, why did you phone the police?' I ask again.

'Because Mary wasn't with me the night her father died.'

'She wasn't?' I stare at her, feeling wholly bewildered.

'That afternoon, the day before Mary's birthday we went to Trout Lake, do you remember?'

'Yes of course I do,' I reply.

'Well, we gave up fishing because it started to rain. A bit later, a taxi picked her up from the end of our lane. I didn't see Mary again until the next morning.'

'The next morning?' I ask.

'Yes, the morning she found her horse here, the morning you told her that her dad was dead.'

I think back. Mary wasn't at Fox Halt that night either. I remember when I got home with Braveheart, no-one was around, except the extended family from Birmingham who were renting two of our holiday cottages. I am not sure they were even in residence because I didn't notice any lights on.

Mum was playing Mah-jong in Okehampton, as she does every Tuesday evening, and I thought Mary was staying over with Grace watching DVDs and scoffing popcorn. I can't imagine what she was really doing. I suppose she might have been with Freddy in Richard's cottage but that seems very unlikely.

'Where's Mary?' I ask Mum, when she comes home.

'She wanted to go back to the shop,' she replies.

'Is she okay?'

'She put on a brave face, but I think she is quite upset really.'

'Was she with Sharmarke the night Michael died?' I ask. I am sure Mum was cautioned not to discuss what Mary said, but I think my pretty accurate guess regarding her whereabouts has given my mother an excuse to tell. Besides, Mum can't keep a secret.

'You knew about them?' Mum frowns.

'No, not really, it was just a lucky guess,' I say, feeling shocked that I didn't have an inkling of Mary's whereabouts. I feel hurt too that she sneaked home without telling me. I wonder how many times she has returned since.

'I think I need a cup of tea,' Mum says.

Usually, I marvel at my mother's resilience, struggling to believe her age because she is so fit, but now I notice her shoulders are rounding over. All this upset is getting to her. 'I'll make us both tea,' I say, feeling guilty that I haven't had a tighter rein on Mary.

Mum eases herself onto a chair, and within seconds both of our house cats jump onto her lap. 'What did she tell the detective?' I ask.

'Mary said she and Sharmarke spent the night together in the empty flat above the stables at Culmfield. Is that the flat where you used to live?' Mum asks.

'Yes, it was,' I reply, wondering if it has remained empty ever since I left.

'Mary kept saying that they were just holding each other. She must have said that twenty times. The little mite was crying,' Mum tells me as she gently strokes each cat in turn. Both animals close their eyes in blissful contentment, purring loudly.

'Did Mary see me?'

Mum looks at me blankly.

'At Culmfield that night?' I explain.

'The detective asked her if she saw you, but Mary said she only saw Sharmarke and her mother. It was funny...'

'What was funny?' I ask quickly.

'Oh, it's something I noticed.'

'What?'

'It was just that when Mary said she saw Jessie, the detective seemed to lose focus on her, switching his attention to her mother instead.'

'What do you mean?' I pass Mum her drink and then I sit in the easy chair next to her, cradling my mug on my knees.

'Mary said Jessie is writing a children's story, she said she has been secretly doing it for years. She said her mother goes to the chapel to write. Mary told the detective she thought her mother's make-believe world was the only place where her mum could escape from her father. I couldn't believe that Mary thought her mum was hiding from her dad. Isn't that horrible? Poor child, what a way to grow up.'

I nod at Mum. 'Did Mary say that Jessie was mistreated by Michael?' I ask.

'Yes, she did, she called him a bully.'

'So what else did she say?'

'That she reads the handwritten story when Jessie isn't there. Sorry, darling, I missed out something, she said her mother hides her manuscript in the chapel.'

'Why was Bawen interested in that?' I ask.

'I have no idea, darling, but he asked Mary the same question in different ways, it was obviously important to him to confirm that she saw her mother in the chapel that evening.'

'What did he ask her exactly, can you remember?'

My mother looks up at the ceiling. 'Well, he asked Mary if she noticed the light was on in the chapel and if she thought someone was in there.'

'What did Mary say?'

'That she had arranged to meet Sharmarke in the chapel because she expected her father to be home. Apparently, Michael always came home for his children's birthdays. He always took the day off work. Did you know that?'

'Yes,' I say, not wanting to think too much about the way I disliked him always putting his children first.

'Sharmarke had told Mary that his father was bringing Michael back to Culmfield that night, even though Mary was staying here with us.' She stops, distracted by Crinkle who has dropped a toy in between the cats on Mum's lap. My mother hands the soggy toy back to the dog. 'Not now,' she says, and Crinkle and the toy return to her basket. Mum looks up at me. 'Sorry, darling, where was I?'

'About Michael coming home.'

'Yes,' she says, 'So Mary and Sharmarke knew Jessie would not be in the chapel that night. Therefore, they arranged to meet there.'

'And?' I ask, feeling impatient.

'And when they opened the back door of the chapel, they saw Jessie. That's why they went to the flat above the stables instead. Nala, that's Sharmarke's mother, isn't it?'

I nod again, three times in quick succession, trying to show I want her to keep talking.

'Mary explained that Nala has the key to the flat because she dusts it every couple of months.' Mum has finished her tea, so she moves to get up, pushing down on the arms of the chair. 'Look, Billy, we'd better get some work done today. Are you coming over to the dairy?'

'In a minute,' I reply. 'But what else did she say?'

'I think that was about it, darling. Mary spent the night there and they only held each other. Oh, there *was* something else.'

'What?'

'She threw an old mobile phone at the policeman. Mary said it was one that Sharmarke had given her ages ago, and that's was how they communicated with each other. She said Sharmarke bought top-up credit for her. She said she hadn't used the phone since the night her dad died. She also said that was the last time she saw Sharmarke. Mary told Bawen to keep the phone, so he could check she was telling the truth.'

'That's why she took the money,' I say.

Mum sits back down. Her voice is faint. 'Sorry, Billy, what are you talking about? Did Mary steal some money from you?' I think the thought of Mary taking some money has upset my mother more than the possibility she's been sneaking off and having under-age sex; but then, perhaps my mother believes Mary's claims about the relationship being platonic, believing they really did just hold each other all night.

'I don't know for sure,' I say, 'but I do know some money was taken from the petty cash tin in the dairy when she first came to live here. I think she must have used it to pay for her taxi back to Culmfield.'

'You didn't ask her if she stole it?' Mum is clearly shocked.

'No, but I have kept a close eye and no more went missing. The till in the shop has been balancing too. I thought she just wanted to keep some money in her pocket just in case. I didn't want to say anything. Mary was welcome to it. It wasn't much and no more was taken. I didn't want to upset her. She'd only just got here.'

'But she took it without asking you.'

'Yes, it was wrong. But, Mum, I am sure if Mary needed money now, she'd just ask me.'

'I see,' Mum replies, but I can hear in her tone that she will raise the missing cash with Mary as soon as she gets back from the shop. Poor girl, she will hate letting my mother down.

Chapter 16

CULMFIELD

RICHARD

Just before twelve o'clock, the phone rings at Culmfield Court. Jessie answers it.

'Are you alright?' I ask her as she walks back into the kitchen and sits down next to me. She is frowning.

'It was Detective Bawen, he is at the front gates. He has some questions, apparently.'

'What about?'

'I don't know,' she shrugs. 'We'll find out in a moment.'

'I'll stay here, if you don't mind,' I say. 'I do really need to finish this, ready for tomorrow's meeting. Will you talk to him on your own?'

'Yes,' she says, 'of course, you can check that last sum again, those figures don't add up. I think we've misunderstood something somewhere.'

When the doorbell rings, Jessie greets the detective. I can hear their voices, and I note that the policeman has a woman with him. Jessie leads them both into the drawing room, leaving the door slightly ajar so when I move to the hallway, to a spot where I am hidden from view, I can hear their conversation clearly.

The visitors politely refuse Jessie's offer of tea or coffee and then the detective comes to the point straightaway. 'Mrs

O'Rowde,' he says. 'I need to tell you that our investigations are going in a number of directions.'

'Yes,' Jessie replies.

'You know we've been looking into the files on the computer in your husband's office.' Bawen pauses. 'Well, we have discovered some anomalies that we're digging into a bit deeper.'

'Oh, what sort of anomalies?' Jessie asks.

'It looks like someone has been copying some of the reports and possibly altering figures, that sort of thing,' the woman tells Jessie. 'We believe we know who that someone is, and we're making some more checks. That's all we can tell you at the moment...'

'Mrs O'Rowde,' Detective Bawen cuts in, 'please can I just ask you everything you remember from the moment your husband got home on the day he died – particularly *your* movements. Tell me exactly what happened and give me the times, so I can check I definitely have everything in order.'

'Yes, detective, of course I will,' Jessie replies, and I think how I have heard her addressed as Mrs O'Rowde three times now, and how she hasn't asked them to call her Miss Cambell instead.

'Sorry about this,' Bawen says, sounding friendly, 'but I just need to check something?'

'Yes, Sergeant Columbo, you have just one more question, is that it?' Jessie laughs, but I don't hear any response from the detective or his companion.

After a second or two, Jessie speaks again. 'My husband returned to Culmfield at about five o'clock in the afternoon.'

'With Amir Bileh, his chauffeur?'

'Yes, with Amir, that's right.'

'Carry on please,' the woman says.

'When they got back here, Amir rang me from the coach-house to tell me my husband had just left again, but he was driving himself this time. He had taken one of the Porsches.'

'Your husband didn't phone you himself?'

'No, he didn't.'

'Was that unusual, did he always get his chauffeur to communicate with you?'

'No, but Michael was a busy man. I often received messages from his secretary, and occasionally Amir would phone when Michael needed to be getting on with something else, or if he had to finish something, or perhaps if he was running late.'

'Right I see. So, what did Mr Bileh tell you?'

There is a pause. 'He said Michael was cross because they were later getting back than he had expected; there had been a bad accident on the M5, just after Bristol, and they'd been stuck for some time in a four-mile queue. Sorry, Mr Bawen, I've told you all this, do you really want me to tell you it all again, or is there something specific you need to ask me?'

'Everything please, everything you can remember, and in the order it all happened, if you can,' the woman says.

I think Jessie has sat down, or moved towards the window, as her voice is further away now. 'Michael asked Amir to tell me that he had to fetch something he had ordered for Mary for her birthday,' she explains. 'Amir said Michael had told him he would need him to drive the Bentley again early the following morning, so we could drop Mary's present off to her at Fox Halt Farm. You do know it was our daughter Mary's birthday the next day? That was the day Michael was found. And you do know Mary was staying at the farm, don't you?'

'Yes, we do know that, Mrs O'Rowde, thank you. Please go on,' Bawen says.

'Michael didn't tell Amir what it was he was getting for Mary, nor where he was going,' Jessie says.

'And you don't know what your husband was going to fetch, Mrs O'Rowde, Is that right?' Bawen asks her.

'I am sorry, as I told you before, detective, I don't know what his plans were, but it wasn't unusual for Michael to sort out birthday surprises,' Jessie says. 'Michael loved seeing our faces, the more extravagant the present was, the more unusual, or unexpected the better as far as he was concerned.

He often didn't tell me what he'd arranged; he liked to see the surprise on my face too. He enjoyed organising bespoke gifts. Michael always found something you would love; he was thoughtful and incredibly perceptive.' I listen, thinking how Jessie sounds like she adored her husband, acting like a grieving widow.

'And you still don't know what it was he went to pick up for your daughter that evening?' the woman asks.

'I would have told you before if I knew, but I don't, sorry.'

'Has anyone contacted you to say they have something your husband hasn't collected? There was nothing that resembled a potential gift in the car,' Bawen says.

'No, no-one has, and I assure you, I would have told you if someone did.' Jessie sounds fed up. I can understand her annoyance. It feels like they don't believe her, or the pair know something, and they are deliberately trying to trip her up.

'So, when did you get worried that your husband hadn't returned?' Bawen asks.

'About eight o'clock, I suppose. Maybe later. I wasn't really concerned until ten, when I tried to phone him. I kept trying but there was no reply. It was about an hour after that when I phoned the police to see if there had been an accident.'

There is a rustling, which I assume is the detective flicking through a notebook. He must have found the page he wanted, because now I think he is reading out loud, his tone is flat. 'And you were in the house with the children all that night? Mrs Nala Bileh cooked you all dinner and Mr Amir Bileh was in here with you, setting up a new home cinema system that your husband had ordered?'

'Yes,' Jessie replies. 'The new equipment had been delivered that morning. Amir said Michael had told him it was meant to be part of Mary's birthday present, even though Mary wasn't here, Michael wanted it set up anyway, so the boys could enjoy it.'

'Mr Bileh came into the house just after he told you that your husband had driven away?'

'Yes.'

'You were here, in this room, with Mr Bileh and your three boys whilst Mr Bileh set up this new home cinema?'

'Yes, that's right,' Jessie replies. 'There were a lot of boxes and things to unwrap, and the boys helped him. They were quite excited by it all. Amir was ages adjusting the speakers and hiding all the cables.'

'And when it was done you watched a movie, is that right?'

'Yes, *The Golden Compass*.'

'Mrs O'Rowde, I have to tell you we have new information that is contrary to what you're telling us, it would be helpful if you could provide a formal statement.'

'But you have my answers already, Mr Bawen.'

'Yes, but before, we've not needed to record them on a more formal basis, we do require a proper written statement, now – a signed statement from you –' he pauses. 'At the police station. Later today would be best. Can you give me a time that suits you?'

'Mrs O'Rowde, if you would like, we can drive you there now,' the woman offers.

Jessie sounds calm. 'Sorry, but I'm going through some important information about my husband's business at the moment,' she says. 'You probably don't know, but there is a big meeting tomorrow in London about the future of O'Rowdes'. I am the main shareholder, so there is a lot to get in order ready for the presentation that I will be making.'

'I didn't know that,' the detective replies.

'And what you've told me about the files on Michael's computer will mean extra work. I imagine if there are anomalies, then there will probably have to be an internal inquiry. Your information is going to have many implications, I suspect.'

'Yes, I can see that,' Bawen says. 'But we do need you to come to the station as soon as you can.'

'How about two o'clock this afternoon?' Jessie replies, as though she is talking to a friend who wants to meet her for a coffee. 'Where am I going? To Exeter, the police station at Middlemoor?'

'Yes, that will be fine, just ask for me.'

'Okay, I will.'

'I'll see you later then, Mrs O'Rowde.'

'Yes, you will,' Jessie says. I wonder when she is cautioned later, that the information she is providing may be used in court, whether she will be quite so calm and collected.

As soon as she closes the front door behind Bawen and his associate, Jessie makes a phone call. 'Have you or Amir spoken to the police again about the night Michael died?' I assume she is speaking to Nala. There is a pause. 'Good,' Jessie says. 'Can you both come up to the house straightaway? I need to speak to you urgently.' As I continue to listen, I understand that Amir's not with Nala.

'Nala, if the detective stops at The Gatehouse, don't answer,' Jessie says. 'I need to speak to you first. Please call Amir and tell him not to say anything either.'

She puts the phone down and sees me standing behind her. 'You heard everything?' she asks.

I nod.

'I was on my own that night,' Jessie says. 'I don't have an alibi and Amir just stepped up to the mark, saying I was with him while he set up the new cinema system.'

'So, where were you, Jessie?'

'In the chapel.'

'What, the whole evening?'

'Yes, Richard.'

'Why?' I frown.

'I was writing.'

'Writing?'

'Yes, I told you that the chapel is my place of what ifs, I have been writing a series of children's books.'

'You have a publisher?'

'No, I haven't sent anything away. No-one else has read them, I don't know if they are any good.'

'You haven't read your stories to your children then?'

'No,' Jessie replies as she turns to go back to the kitchen, but then she stops. 'It was my secret, I couldn't tell them.' Jessie rubs her eyes and makes half a smile. 'Listen,

Richard, Michael criticised everything I did, I didn't want him to take my writing away from me too. I couldn't bear him to disillusion me, which I knew he would if he found out.'

I shake my head and find I am staring into her eyes, wishing things might have been so different for her. 'So, you kept it secret from everyone.'

'Yes, I did.' For a split second, it seems as though all the energy has been sucked out of her, but then her face lights back up, and she talks with more passion in her voice than I've heard all morning. 'The chapel is such a wonderful place. I think it's been the only thing, other than my children of course, that's got me through the last couple of years. My world of make-believe was my escape. I am in control of everything that happens there.'

I nod at her.

'In my stories, I can decide the fate of all my characters. I can pretend to be the heroine, who achieves anything she wants.' She smiles. 'Wonderful and fabulous things happen, evil is conquered, and there is always a happy ending. I was able to hide from reality.'

'So, you were in the chapel, then,' I say. 'On your own?'

'Yes, I was.' She breathes in heavily. 'That night, when Amir phoned me to say Michael had left again, Nala was already in the house, so I took the opportunity to write. I didn't have any tea, I just kept scribbling. All the time though, I was listening out for the sound of Michael's car on the gravel. While he put his precious Porsche away in the coach-house, I knew I would have plenty of time to get back indoors with the boys, so long as I moved the moment, I heard the car.'

'You have no alibi, Jessie?'

'No, I don't.' She shakes her head. 'I write everything out by hand, it's not like the police can check when I was typing. There is no computer record to prove where I was.'

'And you thought you'd be the chief suspect?' I ask. 'But when he was found, you thought it was suicide?'

'I panicked, it was such a shock that he was dead. It's always the wife that murders the husband, isn't it? In the movies, I mean. I certainly had reasons to want him dead, I was at my wits' end with Mary's refusal to come home.'

'But you didn't kill him?'

'Richard, if I'd had the courage and the knowledge to get away with it, then I would have liked to have done it. I won't deny it, and I'm very grateful to *her* that she did manage it, I was questioning if Michael was the reason behind why Mary left, and I suspected too, that he was the reason she wouldn't return.'

I try to ignore her certainty about Billy, wondering if Jessie is trying to deflect my attention from her own guilt. 'Why did Amir say you were with him?' I ask her. 'Are you two having an affair?'

Jessie laughs. 'An affair? Please don't be ridiculous, Richard. When would Amir have had time to be with me? He was hardly ever with his own family, let alone with another woman. Michael always had him running around here, there and everywhere for him.'

'So why would Amir give you an alibi?'

'Loyalty, I suppose? He's a good man. He and Nala, they're good people.'

'What will you do now?' I ask.

She raises her eyebrows at me. 'I am going to tell the detective the truth too, but I want to warn Nala and Amir first. I don't want them getting into trouble.'

'What information do you think he's got? Bawen, I mean. You don't think he is bluffing?'

'Maybe he's been putting pressure on Amir. Nala said he wasn't there, when I spoke to her just now.'

'You think Amir has owned up. Said you weren't with him?'

'What do you think?' Her question makes me wonder why she didn't tell me any of this before.

'I don't know, Jessie. I really don't know,' I reply, shrugging my shoulders. 'Maybe you should speak to Nala. Get hold of Amir too, and then go and see the detective. I really can't help you out here. It's up to you what you put in your statement. You're the only one who can decide.' I move towards the front door.

'Are you going? Jessie asks.

'Yes.'

'What about the presentation, the meeting?' she asks.

'As you told the policeman, that's all a bit up in the air now, you're hardly going to be able to sell O'Rowdes' with a business investigation going on. How is any bidder going to be able to trust our figures?'

'But, Richard−'

'We'll look at that later, Jessie, just go to the police station. I need a change of scene for a while. I'm going to the Barrowculme Arms to get some lunch. I want to be on my own.' I turn the brass door handle and step outside. 'I'll see you later,' I say.

It's starting to rain. Fat water droplets splash my neck as I jump into my car. I am not heading to the pub.

Chapter 17

THE FARM SHOP, HAMSGATE

RICHARD

Thick green letters spelling out, *Fox Halt Farm, Dairy & Farm Shop* encircle the black and white cow painted on the side of Billy's van. I remember her spending hours designing the logo, and me suggesting she needed to add addresses, telephone numbers and the website details. 'No,' she said. 'Potential customers can look that up from the name alone, any extra information will reduce its impact.' As I park up next to her vehicle, I see she was right, it certainly grabs my attention.

    I watch Billy inside the farm shop talking to Herbie Harris, her manager. I know her normal routine well. Billy will be dropping off supplies of cheese, milk and yoghurt, while she checks with Herbie that everything is okay. I look at my watch and calculate she'll return to her van in seven or eight minutes to head back to the farm.

    Nineteen minutes and fifty-three seconds later, Billy opens the door of the shop and rushes to her van. It is raining hard and she doesn't realise I am parked next to her.

    'Billy,' I call out to her. Without a word, she runs around the front of my car and jumps in beside me.

    We grin at one another and my insides turn over from just being close to her. Now, I know for certain that I was right to flout the police advice not to see her.

    'Hello.' Billy smiles.

'Hello,' I say, at exactly the same time, and then we both laugh.

There is so much to say, but hello is the only word we manage to utter, maybe we are both waiting for the other to speak.

Billy stares out through the windscreen and I try to follow her gaze, but condensation and rain obscure everything outside. At first I don't see what she is looking at; but now I make out Mary. She is coming out of the shop, and is about to dash to Billy's van.

Billy lowers her window and leans out. 'Mary – over here,' she calls, beckoning the girl towards us.

The girl scrambles onto my back seat. 'Well, this is turning out to be an unusual day,' she laughs. 'Hi, Richard.'

'Hi, Mary,' I reply. 'Sorry, I came to talk to Billy, I didn't think about you being with her.'

'Would you like me to sit in the van? Can you let me have the keys, Auntie?' She pushes her hand between the front seats with her palm open.

Billy turns to face her. 'No, it's fine, darling, don't worry. You won't tell anyone Richard was here, will you?'

'Of course not,' Mary replies.

'Then stay where you are,' Billy says.

I start the engine. 'I will drive down the lane a little way,' I tell them. 'I don't really want to be seen here.' I wish Mary would offer to get out again, but I don't say so because I am frightened of upsetting her or Billy.

'Okay,' Mary says, stretching the seatbelt across her.

'The gateway to Red Acre field is open, drive in there a little way. Park up next to the hedge and no-one will be able to see your car from the lane,' Billy suggests, and that's what I do. As I stop, Mary presses her skinny body forward through the gap in the seats. 'Did you know, Richard, that I went to the police station this morning to answer questions?' she asks. 'Does that have anything to do with you being here?'

'No, I didn't know about that,' I reply, talking to the rear-view mirror.

Mary tells me everything that happened at the police station. I think she is embarrassed about being in the car with Billy and me. She keeps on talking because she feels awkward.

I am unhappy too, I want to forget about Michael dying. I want to be alone with Billy, hold her hand, stare into her eyes and work out a way to fix everything that's gone wrong between us. Stupidly, I snap a quick-fire statement at Mary, and straightaway I regret it. 'Your mum should be in Exeter police station now doing the same thing,' I say.

'Gosh! Mum is being interviewed by the police?'

Billy turns to me. 'Do they suspect Jessie now?'

'Billy, I have no idea if Jessie is actually at the station,' I reply, 'but she was supposed to meet Bawen at two o'clock. She originally told the police she was in the house all evening on the night Michael died, but she lied. Jessie doesn't have an alibi either.' I stop, glancing back at Mary, worried about her hearing all this, but Billy doesn't seem to care.

'Go on,' she says.

'Bawen came to Culmfield this morning asking more questions. He said he wanted a signed statement from her.'

'Oh no, Mum.' Mary sounds upset. 'I shouldn't have said anything.'

Billy unclips her seatbelt and kneels on her seat, so she can talk to Mary face to face,

'It will be okay, darling, don't worry,' she says. 'We all know your mother couldn't have hurt your dad. The police will sort it out, they'll get to the truth.'

'Yes, I know that,' Mary replies. 'It will be fine, I'm sure.'

I scratch the back of my ear, thinking how Mary seems unfazed, as though Billy had just turned around and asked her what she wanted for tea.

Billy rests her hand on my shoulder as she sits back in her seat. 'You know, Richard, I didn't kill Michael either, don't you?'

I want to say yes but I can't find the right words.

After a few seconds, Mary saves the situation. 'Yes, we know you didn't hurt Dad, Auntie,' she says.

Billy's hand presses hard into my collarbone. I don't think she intends to hurt me, unaware of what she is doing. 'Richard, I promise you, with all my heart, on Mum's life, I did not see Michael that night. I have no idea why someone said I was arguing with him. It is *not* true. You have to trust me, I promise you.' As Billy stares into my eyes I believe her.

'All the evidence they arrested me for is wrong, the argument with Michael and the earring that they found in that damn car, that isn't right either.'

'What earring?' I ask.

'One I lost years ago, before Michael even owned that car. I have never been anywhere near that vehicle.'

'Okay, Billy,' I say, touching her hand.

'In any case, when have you seen me wear any jewellery lately, it's hardly appropriate on the farm.' She pauses. 'And the earring they found was worth at least five thousand pounds – that's not the pair, Richard, that's just one. Not something I'd be wearing to fetch a horse, is it? I don't even wear Saffi's ring when I am working on the farm,' Billy holds out her bare hands, 'or in the dairy, or in the shop – I'm too scared I might lose it, or it could get caught in the machinery.'

'Yes, Billy, it's odd.'

'Like someone is setting me up,' she says.

'It was Nala,' I tell her.

'Nala?' Billy frowns.

'She told the police she heard you with Michael,' I say, 'but Nala wouldn't lie, would she?'

'So, you're willing to believe her but not me?'

'And Amir,' I say.

'What about him? Did he witness this argument too?'

'No, he didn't,' I reply, 'but–'

'But what, Richard?'

'Amir has informed Detective Bawen that he saw you by The Gatehouse when he drove Michael home. Amir said you were standing there as though you were waiting for someone, but Michael told him to ignore you.'

Billy's voice breaks up. 'It's all lies. Those two are lying their heads off. Yes, I went to their home. I don't know what time exactly. I needed to open the side gate, so I could load Braveheart. Nala gave me the access code, but I didn't see Michael or Amir there.'

'I don't see why they'd make things up,' I say.

Mary interrupts. 'There might be a reason,' she says.

I'd forgotten about the girl, so quiet on the back seat. 'What?' Billy and I ask at the same time, both turning to face her.

'I can't explain,' she replies.

'You have to, Mary, Auntie Billy could end up in prison if you don't,' I tell her.

'I shouldn't have said that, I am sorry,' Mary says. She looks away, seemingly staring at something in the hedge.

Billy and I continue to watch her, trying to fathom out what she might know, and why she won't tell us. There is a long silence in the car before Mary starts speaking again.

'There isn't enough evidence to convict, Auntie,' she says. 'What the police have so far would never stand up in court. That's if the case even goes to court in the first place. The Crown Prosecution Service will need to be more certain than they are, that Dad was actually murdered.'

'How do you know this, Mary?' Billy asks, frowning hard at her.

'Yes, Mary,' I say. 'How do you know?'

'From the Internet, and Mollie, my best friend at school – her mum's a barrister. Mollie told me.'

'When?' I ask, shaking my head at her.

'When Auntie was arrested. I called Mollie then. She asked her mother for me. Don't worry, I told her it was a school project William was doing, I didn't give names or anything. I was in the dairy phoning all those companies about their cheese products, no-one heard me call her. William wasn't there either.'

Billy and I shake our heads, I don't think either of us can understand her calmness as she continues to explain. 'Mollie's mum said at the end of the day, the police or the court will have to accept it was probably suicide, or they'll leave it as an unsolved case with insufficient proof.' Mary doesn't seem to care one tiny, miserable iota that her father may have been murdered.

'What do you think really happened to your dad, Mary?' Billy asks.

'If I tell... it'll only cause upset. Everyone I love will be destroyed. Leave it alone, Auntie, just let the police run around in circles for a bit longer. They'll give up in the end, I'm certain of it.' Mary opens her door.

'Where are you going?' I ask.

'I'm going to walk back to the shop. You two need to talk,' she replies.

Outside, she stands by my car window and waves her hand for me to lower it.

'Are you okay?' I ask.

'Richard, please see how much Auntie loves you.'

'Thank you,' I say and then I watch in my car mirror as Mary disappears back down the lane.

'Do you know what's going on with her?' I ask Billy.

'I don't. I can't work out why she won't go back to Culmfield. She told me a few days ago that she knows what happened to Michael, but she refuses to elaborate.'

'She seems so blasé, I don't get her at all,' I say.

Billy nods. 'Can we forget her for a moment? I'd like to talk to you…about us.'

'I want to come home to Fox Halt,' I tell her quickly.

Billy closes her eyes and keeps them shut. 'I am so sorry, Richard,' she says at last.

'It doesn't matter,' I assure her. 'When you're in love with someone, feelings don't go away. I will always love you.' I practised this sentence on the way to the farm shop, but now I've said it, it seems really corny.

'I hurt you, Richard. I took you for granted. I wish I hadn't, but I did. Can you really forgive me?' she replies.

Another cliché spills out of my mouth. 'I lie awake at night and all I do is miss you.' It's as though we have forgotten how to talk to each other, trying to explain the emotion we have bottled up inside for weeks.

'And I lie awake too, crying over you,' Billy tells me.

We both start to giggle. We are incapable of sounding real at the moment.

'I don't just want to come back to the farm. I want to ask you to marry me again,' I say. Even though it's the truth my words still feel hollow. Maybe it's just the relief after all the heartache.

'Yes, and yes!' Billy grabs my hand.

I feel like we are both drunk, as I watch tears run down Billy's cheeks. 'I want to marry you, Richard, and I want you living back at the farm, but…' Billy looks me straight in the eyes. I am suddenly sober again.

'But what?' I tremble, fearing she is going to tell me she doesn't think it will work between us after everything that has happened.

'I desperately want you back here, and I want to be your wife, but…'

'But? But what, Billy?'

'But not yet. You have to go back to Culmfield to find out what's been going on. We have to get Mary home.'

'The girl just said we had to leave it alone.'

'Richard, she is fourteen years old. What did we know when we were her age? Everything and nothing. I want us to fix things for her.'

'No, we mustn't.'

'I can't leave it, Richard,' she says. 'As things are, I don't think Mary will ever go home and I can't bear to think what it's doing to Jessie. Mary may seem grown up and self-assured, but she needs her family. Perhaps between us all, we can discover what happened. We can mend whatever it is she has run away from.'

'Alright, I'll go back to Culmfield, if you're sure that's what you want?'

'Yes, I am…' She pauses, and I sense there is something else.

'Go on, Billy, what is it?' I try to sound calm. 'What else?'

'Jessie,' she replies.

'What about her?'

'You can't leave her in the lurch at O'Rowdes'. She needs you, Richard, you have to get yourself elected in tomorrow, and stay with the business until the sale, or someone else can take your place.'

'You remembered it's the extraordinary general meeting tomorrow?' I say, wondering if I can tell Billy about the 'anomalies' the police have found. I decide I can't, this is confidential and sensitive information, so I mustn't tell her, not yet.

'The meeting is important,' Billy says. 'I do think about you all the time, imagining what you're doing. I can't stop thinking about you.'

I touch her cheek, and my lips press against hers. A kiss that makes everything right again, and it is all that matters.

I love you, Billy.

Chapter 18

CULMFIELD

RICHARD

I find Jessie in the chapel. As I approach her, she looks up. 'How was she?' she asks.

'Your daughter was fine,' I reply.

'I wasn't talking about Mary.'

I laugh. 'How did you know I went to Fox Halt Farm?' I sit down next to her in the front pew.

'The landlord at the pub said he hadn't seen you.'

'I asked her to marry me.'

'She said yes?'

'She did,' I reply.

'For your sake, I hope she stays out of prison then. I imagine it would be a long sentence if Bawen finds enough evidence to convict her.'

'Stop, Jessie, I know she is innocent. Billy is not going to jail. Someone is trying to make it look like she killed Michael, but she could never harm anyone.'

'So, you think *I* murdered him. Am I trying to frame her?'

'No,' I say, before quickly changing the subject. 'I was thinking, it would be nice to have our wedding in here. Could we?'

'I'll think about it,' she replies, not sounding keen. 'Richard, the weddings just saved my skin.' Jessie smiles.

'What?' I frown at her.

'We used to hire this place out for weddings,' she says, standing up and then spinning around with her arms outstretched.
'Go on. Explain?' I ask as she stands still again.
'Look,' she says, pointing up at the painted ceiling.
'Some sort of bird, is it a roc? Sorry, Jessie, I don't know much about the Greek myths.'
'Its eye, Richard. Look at its eye!'
I shrug.
'You can't see it, can you? It's a camera lens. I'd forgotten about them – Michael installed security cameras in the nave here, in case something was damaged or went missing. I don't think we ever needed to check anything. There are no cameras anywhere else on the estate, so I'd forgotten about them.'
I examine Grégoire's bird and I still find it hard to spot, I can see why she hadn't thought about the CCTV. She is smiling. 'Michael only had them installed to get footage of some drunken guest causing mayhem. He just wanted reasons to give up hiring this place out. Weddings usually took place at the weekends, when he was here, so he didn't like the intrusion. As usual, I gave in and stopped its use as a venue, but I did love those celebrations – seeing people admiring Grégoire's work, and all the laughter around the place. So, I'm saved. There will be proof I was here.'
'Great, Jessie,' I say.
'That's if they are still working properly,' she adds. 'The cameras work on a loop, storing only the last month's recordings. They were expensive enough and no-one has cancelled the maintenance contract, so they should be fine.' She seems to be trying to convince herself.
'That's excellent,' I say, feeling genuinely happy for her.
'What is it?' Jessie asks.
I frown, not understanding.
'There's something bothering you, I can tell.'
'We need to talk about the meeting tomorrow,' I say.
'Right.' She waits for me to speak again.

'Is Nala looking after the children? Could we go to the pub to get something to eat? We can talk there?'

'You *really* want to go to the pub?' Jessie smiles.

'Yes, I do, I haven't had anything to eat since breakfast.'

'I'll tell Nala we're going,' Jessie says as she stands up.

'Can I wait here, while you find her?' I ask.

'Of course, I'll be five minutes, tops.'

I don't wait inside the chapel, instead I follow her out and then I head to the back of the building.

The sunflowers against the headstone are almost ready to burst open, and as I read the dates under his name, I think how Saffi would have been forty-seven next week. I miss him all the time. My thoughts run on to his recruiting company, my friend would have found someone perfect to take on the leadership role at O'Rowdes'. He knew everyone, everyone loved him...

'Come on, Richard, I'll drive.' Jessie is standing behind me. 'Are the car keys still in your pocket?' she asks.

Five minutes later, we walk through to the garden of the village pub. The rain has stopped but the wooden seats are still damp.

'Shall we go back inside?' I suggest.

There's a voice behind us. 'It's a lovely evening now, that would be a shame.' It's the waitress, she must have followed us out. 'I'll get you cushions,' she says. 'Please just wait a moment.'

Later, when she brings our order to our table, I think the waitress could mistake us for happy lovers engrossed in each other, oblivious to the rest of the world. How wrong she would be, the rest of the world is closing in on us.

'I can't run O'Rowdes' for more than two months,' I tell Jessie, having skirted around the subject for at least half an hour, discussing tactics for tomorrow's meeting.

'That's fine, Richard,' she says, smiling at me. 'I'm just grateful for everything you've done.'

'I just want to be back at Fox Halt,' I explain. I can't think of anything more to say about the meeting or O'Rowdes', but there is something else on my mind.

'Amir and Nala seem to be lying about what Billy did when she came to pick up the horse, do you have any idea why?' I ask Jessie.

She shakes her head. 'No.'

'What do you know about Nala and Amir?' I ask.

'What do you mean, Richard?'

'Well, their background,' I say, unsure what I want to find out about them.

'I know.' She pauses. 'No, I *think* they are both Somalians.'

'They are both from Somalia originally?' I check, not really caring. Questioning Jessie seems futile; this was Billy's idea, not mine. Mary's warning to leave everything alone keeps running through my mind.

'Nala is Somali for sure.' Jessie's words cut across my thoughts. 'I remember her telling me about the tiny remote farm where she grew up. Nala said it was really just scrubland. Her family could barely grow enough food and they lived as an extended family, with her parents, grandparents and her siblings. But when the civil war started, her family were forced off their land.' Jessie pauses. 'Is this what you want to know, Richard?'

'Please carry on,' I say, nodding at her.

'Nala's mother, her grandparents and her baby sister were shot and killed by the guerrillas as they tried to get their things together to leave. Nala explained the different factions, but I am afraid it didn't mean much to me.' Jessie stops to drink some water. 'Her father forced Nala to marry a man she'd never met when she was just twelve, so she ran away. She said she ended up in Mogadishu for a while, which was a dangerous place for a young girl on her own. She told me about bombings, killings and beatings – she met Amir in a refugee camp in Ethiopia.'

'God, that was rough. You can't imagine it, can you? What's his history?' I ask, uncertain I want to know if it was as dreadful as Nala's early life.

'I think Amir was in the capital too, but Nala said he doesn't talk about it. She told me he lost all his close family and he witnessed some of his friends and family blown to bits in the street. He still has nightmares about it.'

'What else do you know?' I ask.

I feel ruthless that I am not commenting on what Amir went through; the truth is, I don't know what to say. 'When did they come to Britain?'

'All I can say for sure, is that Nala worked for an agency in Richmond, and she used to clean Michael's house. Michael said when he found out how little Nala was paid, he offered her a job working solely for him as his cleaner. She also cooked for him too sometimes, and after a while, Michael employed Amir as well.'

'I remember the first time I met him,' I say. 'He may have saved my life, that day.'

'Really?' Jessie asks.

'Yes, really,' I reply. 'The first thing I remember about him was sitting in the back of Michael's Rolls Royce thinking how intimidating his new driver was. I believed if Michael was ever in trouble this man would soon draw out a knife from the folds of his oversized, yet immaculate uniform. I was mesmerised by Amir's powerful hands lightly spinning the steering wheel and I thought how he easily could link his massive fingers around someone's neck and crush them.'

'What happened? Did Amir have to deal with someone who threatened you, or Michael?' Jessie asks.

'No,' I laugh. 'Amir dropped us off in Cavendish Square because we wanted to look at a property Michael had his eye on. We didn't know it, but minutes earlier an IRA bomb had gone off in Oxford Street, which had injured four or five people. We were about to go into the property when a policeman told us to leave immediately because there was another suspected bomb. News of the first attack had spread, so people were panicking. Amir appeared in seconds and drove us away. That must have been 1992, I remember the Christmas lights in Oxford Street when they showed it on the news that evening. It was November or December, I suppose.'

'Did another bomb go off?' Jessie asks.

'Yes, near where we'd been standing. I was very grateful Amir got us away so quickly.'

'Michael never told me that story,' Jessie says.

'Do you think Nala or Amir could possibly be here illegally?' I ask.

'No, Nala was granted asylum here first. Then Amir. Why?'

'It was just a thought, that's all.'

'So, is there anything else you'd like to know?'

'Are they happy?' I reply.

'Sorry, Richard, what do you mean?'

'Well, do you think they may have wanted to get rid of Michael?' I ask. 'Could he have been blackmailing them in some way? Maybe they didn't have all the right papers to be here in the UK.'

'You're barking up the wrong tree, Richard. It seems to me that all Michael has ever done is look after them, even their son has always had the best of everything. Michael really valued Amir, and in turn Amir would do anything for him.'

'And Nala, did she always get on with Michael?'

'Nala and Michael didn't spend time together, she helped me when he wasn't about, and when he was around, she would disappear to do something else in another room or head back to The Gatehouse. I don't think I ever saw her speak to him. I think it was a cultural thing, it was the way she was brought up. Or maybe, it was a general fear of men, after her forced marriage, or her time in Mogadishu.'

'So...'

Jessie cuts across me, she hasn't finished her reply. 'Nala said in rural Somalia, women and girls were expected to do all the domestic work. A sisterhood who didn't have much to do with the men. Nala wasn't allowed to go to school because she had to help with all the chores around the farm, but all of her brothers were educated for a time.'

'So, Jessie, what do you think Nala or Amir would say if you asked each of them what they thought of your husband?'

Jessie sighs. 'Nala would say only good things about him. He gave her a generous wage, he was looking after her family. I suspect that even the way he behaved towards me probably wasn't that odd to her. I expect she thought his control was quite normal.'

'What about Amir?'

'As Michael's driver, he would have known everything my husband got up to, Amir drove him nearly everywhere he went. He would have seen who he was meeting. But I believe Amir, just like his wife, was pragmatic. He is loyal, works hard, and gets rewarded well. I'm not saying he liked Michael, but he certainly wouldn't have had any reason to kill him.'

'What about Billy, do they have some kind of grudge against her, is that why they are trying to make the police think she is involved in Michael's death?'

'No, why would they?'

The waitress returns and asks if we want to see the dessert menu.

'Yes please,' Jessie replies.

'I'll get the blackboard, you can choose off that,' the young woman says, before she disappears again. I turn to Jessie. 'There is something you ought to know.'

'What?'

'It was Mary who told the police you weren't in the house the night Michael died.'

Jessie frowns and shakes her head, 'But Mary was at Fox Halt Farm, so how would she know that?'

'Sorry, Jessie,' I say. 'Mary came back to Culmfield. She wanted to see Sharmarke. She was here all night with him; they were together in the flat above the stables.'

Jessie's shivers. 'Are you sure about this?'

'Yes. She told the police she was with him that night.'

There is a long silence between us now, which lasts until the waitress has taken Jessie's order for strawberries and cream.

Once we are on our own, Jessie asks, 'Has my daughter been sneaking back to Culmfield all the time she's been away?'

'I don't think so, Mary told the police it was just that night. She said she wanted to say goodbye to her friend.' Jessie gets up quickly. 'Can we get the bill please? We need to go.'

'What about your dessert?'

'I'll pay for it, but I don't want it now. I've got to talk to Nala – I thought she was hiding something.'

'What do you mean?' I check.

'Ever since Mary left, she's avoided me, but I thought she felt sorry for me because she knew how much I was missing my daughter, and she just didn't know what to say.'

Back at Culmfield, Jessie wastes no time finding Nala, sitting her down at the kitchen table.

'How long have Mary and Sharmarke been sleeping together, Nala?' Jessie asks.

Nala's heavily made up eyes become black and green saucers. 'They not,' she replies.

'Nala, they were; maybe they're *still* having a relationship?' Jessie pauses. 'Your son and my daughter were together the night Michael died. I don't know if Mary has been here again since then. Has Sharmarke seen her?'

'No, she not, I warn her,' Nala says.

'What do you mean, did you catch them and try to stop them?'

Nala shakes her head.

'Did you say they were too young, and it was illegal?'

'No.'

'What then? Did you warn Mary, telling her she mustn't get pregnant?'

Nala stares at the table but doesn't reply.

Jessie tries again softly. 'Please, Nala, tell me.'

Nala keeps her head bent. I lean forward and look up at her face. 'Please, Nala, we just want to get Mary to come home, we need to know what upset her. Look, I'll go,' I say, 'so you can talk to Jessie; mothers, face to face.'

'No, Mr MarcFenn,' Nala replies. 'I tell you too. Jessie, she needs you.' Nala looks up, her eyes still wide open. 'Please, Jessie – not be angry with me – not my fault.'

Jessie tries to put her arm around Nala, but she pulls away. 'I won't be angry,' Jessie says.

Nala licks her bottom lip, keeping her stare focused on Jessie.

'Sharmarke and Mary, I hear them talk. I worry. I talk with Mary. I worry for long time – she and Sharmarke always close. Must stop. Mary not listen – Mary, she says she love my son. I scared, not think. I sorry.'

'What were you scared of Nala? Were you frightened of Michael finding out? Or Amir? Is it because Mary is not a Muslim?'

'Yes,' Nala nods, 'I scared.'

'Please, Nala, what happened?' Jessie has her arms tight across her body. 'Why did Mary want to run away? Why won't she come home? Did you threaten her?'

'I not threaten. I should not tell Mary. I sorry, Jessie.'

'What did you tell her?' I jump in, anxious to understand.

'Mr O'Rowde, I sorry, Jessie, he bad. He, he hurt me.'

'What do you mean? Did he hit you?' I ask.

'No,' Nala replies; she blinks hard, sniffs and then tears start running down her cheek. Jessie puts her arm around her.

'Nala, tell me. Tell me what he did.'

'He...rape me.'

'No,' Jessie gasps. 'He raped you? No! He wouldn't. Never.'

'He *rape* me, Jessie. I knew you not believe me...He rape... ' Nala's sobs make it almost impossible to hear her. 'I...sorry.'

Jessie puts both arms around Nala. 'What do you have to be sorry about, it wasn't your fault.'

'Sharmarke – he...Mary's brother. I tell her this, I tell her truth. I sorry.'

Jessie lets go of Nala. It's as though she has been kicked in the stomach. She hugs her knees.

I don't know who to help first, they are sitting on opposite sides of the kitchen table. Jessie with her head bent over, and Nala sitting staring at the ceiling.

'Mr O'Rowde want me get rid of my baby,' Nala says, her eyes still looking up at the ceiling.

'Why didn't you?' I ask.

'But I cannot – it wrong.' She turns to face me now. 'I say to Mr O'Rowde, no. I say to him, I will go to police tell how he rape me. I say police tests show his baby and then Mr O'Rowde, he changed mind. He say he take care of the baby.'

I nod at her, and she starts to tell me some more. 'He keep his word all time,' she says. 'Sharmarke in Somali language, it mean protect from evil. Mr O'Rowde, he try keep Sharmarke safe.'

'So, you told Mary she mustn't have sex with Sharmarke because he was her half-brother. You told her about Michael raping you?' I ask.

'Yes,' she replies. 'I not know how to stop them. She say they love each other. I try other reasons before, reasons like Jessie say, but Mary, she not listen. I had to stop them. When I tell Mary, I say Sharmarke must not know Mr O'Rowde his father, so Mary say to Sharmarke her feeling change for him, she not love him anymore.'

'I see,' I tell her. 'I understand, it must have been so difficult for you, Nala, you must have been desperately worried.'

My sympathy starts her tears again. 'But I should have spoken to Jessie, not Mary, I wrong, all my fault.'

I guess the assault must have happened a few months before Michael and Jessie were married. I wonder if Jessie was in Australia at the time. Questions charge through my brain, about how Michael concealed what he did, and how he kept his secret son at Culmfield.

Jessie must have questions to ask but she seems paralysed in shock, I need to know something else. 'Nala, did you definitely hear Michael and Billy arguing?' I ask.

'He argue with woman, I think Billy,' she replies. I detect a difference in Nala's tone. The woman's eyes shoot quickly towards me and then back to Jessie. I believe her about Sharmarke, but this answer doesn't feel the same, she is lying.

Nala catches hold of Jessie's hand. 'I sorry I not tell you.'

Jessie moves her fingers, but she doesn't say anything.

I intervene again. 'Jessie and I have an important meeting about the company in the morning. I think she needs some time to take this all in. Maybe Jessie can talk to you and Amir on Wednesday, when she is back from London, after our meeting?

'Yes, we talk on Wednesday,' she replies.

'Does Amir know Sharmarke is not his son?' I ask Nala.

Nala nods. 'He know,' she says, standing up. As she reaches the door, she turns back to face Jessie. 'You and Billy go to Wales,' Nala says. 'And Mr O'Rowde, he very angry. He say he get tickets for new film opening, he going surprise you. He bought you beautiful dress, but you go climb. You don't go Leicester Square. Mr O'Rowde telephone me, he say he want me cook for him. When I walk in, he rape me. Mr O'Rowde very angry with you. You hurt him, Jessie, so he hurt me.'

Chapter 19

FOX HALT FARM

TUESDAY 19 AUGUST

BILLY

A noise wakes me up. I check my alarm clock – half-past-five in the morning – and decide I was dreaming. I close my eyes again, kicking at the duvet so it covers my feet. But now, something hits my window so hard, I'm scared it may have cracked the glass. I am out of bed in a second, pulling back the curtains.

The almost full moon casts a shadow across the yard, and I see the silhouette of a person, it's Richard waving up at me. I wave back, before rushing downstairs to talk to him.

I expect Mary or Mum to open their bedroom doors, thinking they must have heard the gravel being thrown up against the window, but when neither follow me, I decide they haven't.

As I open the front door I see Jessie too, and I wonder if the guests in the holiday cottages were woken by the heavy purr of her Ferrari. I don't want our voices to be overheard, so I signal Richard and Jessie to follow me into the dairy.

'What's going on?' I ask as soon as we are all inside.

'I couldn't call you,' Richard tells me. 'The police might check your phone records.'

'What have you found out?' I rub my eyes trying to wake up properly. Standing in my pyjamas next to Jessie and Richard in their smart business suits feels surreal.

Jessie speaks first. 'Nala says Michael raped her, and Sharmarke is his son.' Her voice sounds empty of emotion.

'No!' I say.

'He did,' Richard confirms. 'When you and Jessie went climbing together. He was so furious about it, he raped Nala as soon as she came into his house.'

My body starts sweating, but I'm cold. I lower myself to the floor, determined not to black out, trying to push away a memory replaying in my brain. *Poor Nala, so helpless*, I think.

Jessie crouches next to me.

'You must believe Nala,' I tell her.

'We do.'

It seems minutes pass.

'The floor's wet, Billy, sit on here instead,' Richard tells me. He has fetched a chair and waves his hands towards the seat.

'Yes.' I nod, and he helps me. Straightaway, I feel faint again.

Jessie must see my face change. 'Put your head on your knees,' she says quickly, and I do as she suggests.

'Sorry,' I murmur.

'It's okay.' Jessie places her hand on my shoulder. Her reassuring touch makes me feel better but as she kneels on the floor in front of me, all I can think of is that her trousers will be ruined. I can see wet patches already. 'Look,' I say, pointing at her knees.'

'It's only water, it'll dry out. Are you okay? That's all that matters,' she replies.

'Yes, Jessie – you hit a nerve. It brought things–'

'I know,' she says, her voice gentle. 'Will you be alright? We should get going in a minute or two.' I look up, staring into her eyes. I don't want to have false hope, but suddenly I am feeling close to her again. 'Billy, will you tell Mary that I know about Sharmarke?'

'Yes, of course.'

'I think she'll feel less pressured to come home if you were the one to tell her. Make her see there is no longer any reason for her to stay away.' Jessie is shaking.

I put my arms around her. 'I can't believe Michael kept this secret,' I say.

'Nor me.' She rubs her forehead.

I suddenly remember her interview with the police. 'What happened yesterday? Did you see the detective, give him your statement?' I ask.

Jessie frowns at me.

'Richard told me about it,' I explain.

'Yes, I saw Bawen. Luckily, there are cameras in the chapel, they should have recorded where I was,' she says, holding out both hands with fingers crossed.

'It will be fine, I'm sure,' I say. 'Jessie...' I stop, uncertain how to say what I need to tell her.

'What, Billy?' she asks.

I stare at her for a few seconds, before I eventually speak. 'I'll tell Mary that you know about Sharmarke, but I really don't know what's going on in her head, it may take a little while to persuade her to go back to Culmfield.'

'You're trying though, I know you sent Richard back to me to find out what's going on. If we all work together, I'm sure Mary will come home.'

'We need to leave now, Billy, or we'll be late.' Richard moves towards us. I stand up and he wraps his arms around me. 'I love you,' he says.

O'ROWDES' HEAD OFFICE, BERKELEY SQUARE

RICHARD

Arriving in the office, I feel shaky. I have decided I will never be a passenger with Jessie again. Riding in the Ferrari was terrifying. I will return to Culmfield by train tonight.

'No Sarah?' I check as Matthias comes in to talk to me. 'Another migraine?'

'No Sarah,' he confirms, 'not a migraine though, no Sarah Lancaster full stop. Look at this,' he says, handing me a folder. 'It's her personnel file, I called it up for the detective.'

I open the folder and then I look at Matthias. 'There is nothing in here,' I say, frowning.

Matthias nods. 'Exactly – I couldn't find anything about her at all to give to the police.'

I sit down at the desk. 'Give me five minutes, will you?' I ask, unable to discuss my suspicions that the absent employee was the one tampering with Michael's files. The big meeting starts in forty minutes, and I'll announce the irregularities the police have found then. I wait for Matthias to leave but he doesn't. 'Five minutes please,' I tell him again.

'But there is a police detective here to see you,' he replies.

'Detective Bawen?' I ask, putting my head in my hands and massaging my forehead. *This is all I need.*

'No, *her* name is Moss, Detective Inspector Moss.' It isn't Matthias speaking, it's the woman I saw yesterday at Culmfield with Bawen.

I stand up to welcome her, holding my hand out.

'You have your big meeting in a minute, Mr MarcFenn?' she says. I am unsure if this is a question or a statement.

'Yes,' I say, gesturing for her to sit down.

'Right, Mr MarcFenn, I'll be quick, I came here to bring you up to speed with what our people found when they looked at Mr O'Rowde's computer.'

I stop her. 'Please, call me Richard,' I say.

She nods. 'Richard,' she says and smiles, 'we've looked at all Mr O'Rowde's computers, including the one at his house and the one he had in his Richmond home. We've checked his laptop and his phones too. Our computer forensics team have found she has messed around with quite a few high-level reports–'

I cut in. 'Detective Insp-'

'Call me Carol, it's easier,' she says.

'You said *she*, did you mean-?'

'Her personnel file is on the desk in front of you, I thought you'd guessed.'

'Yes, I had,' I say, picking up the folder again. 'Carol, I know this sounds stupid, but I think she may have bugged this office. I dismissed it before, but do you mind if we move to a different office, and then maybe your people, or someone from O'Rowdes' can check this room over for any surveillance equipment.'

'We can, but Miss Lancaster seems to have vanished and I expect if there were cameras or listening devices, she has probably removed them. She seems pretty good at covering her tracks.' The detective stands up. 'Where would you like to move to?' she asks.

I point to an empty office. 'That one is usually free,' I say.

As soon as we sit down again, Carol continues to tell me about Sarah. 'She was clever, and it took a little while to see, but she had left some minute signs of her interference on the computer drives. Our findings suggest that she could have been gathering quite sensitive information for a competitor, or it may have been sabotage. Maybe both. We don't really know.'

I look at my watch. 'I'm sorry, but I only have a few more minutes.'

'I put this together for you.' The detective hands me a sheet of paper. 'A summary of our findings, items which you may want to report in your meeting. Bullet points but it should be helpful.'

'Thank you,' I say.

'We've been looking for a few days now, but it's as though Miss Lancaster was never employed by O'Rowdes'. Any reference to her seems to have been deleted. We're drawing a blank so far, but we'll find her soon enough, I'm sure. I'll keep you informed, Richard.'

'Thank you for this,' I say, waving the page of information she has just handed to me.

As the inspector leaves, I think how clever Sarah must be. She convinced Michael to trust her for a start. Jessie is checking the meeting room, making sure everything is ready. She'll be here in a second. I guess it will be a short extraordinary meeting now, because we can't discuss the future of the business without knowing if our facts and figures are accurate.

I rustle around in my drawer. When I took over this desk, the contents were immaculate, with every item laid out in straight lines. Since I've been here, I have thrown things in any old how. The clear desk policy – where paperwork has to be locked away at night so the cleaners can't have access to anything confidential – is a nightmare for me. I just don't work like that.

I find what I need, and I try to pull it, but Sarah's plastic swipe card is attached to a neck cord, which has caught up in something at the back of the drawer. I manage to untangle it as Jessie walks in.

'Look,' I tell her. 'Sarah Lancaster lent this to me on the first day I arrived here.' I pass Jessie the identity card. 'By the time I remembered to return it to her, she told me not to worry, because she'd organised a new one for herself.'

Jessie frowns at me. 'And?' she asks, glancing at the photo. 'This is the person who I think has messed with Michael's files,' I explain. 'Do you recognise her? I wondered if you'd met her, she was Michael's assistant.'

'No.' Jessie shakes her head. 'I'll show this picture in the meeting, it will be nice for everyone to see the face of the person who is going to cause a fair bit of disruption for a while.' A thought flashes across my mind. 'Jessie,' I say. 'The major setbacks in Asia. I wonder if Sarah harmed the negotiations?'

'Michael would never have allowed anyone to do that, surely?' Jessie replies.

FOX HALT FARM
BILLY

Five long hours have dawdled by since Jessie and Richard left me in the dairy, but I still haven't managed to say anything to Mary. We milked the cows and had breakfast together, and now I have suggested we take Crinkle for a walk.

I think Mary knew something was up as soon as I said she wasn't needed in the farm shop this morning. I believe she only agreed to the trip to my favourite place on Dartmoor because she was curious about what I might be up to.

My intrigued passenger sits the Border terrier on her lap, so the dog can look out through the windscreen. Crinkle is already excited, and I haven't even turned the engine on yet.

'So, what's this favourite place of yours?' Mary asks.

'Tavy Cleave, it's near Tavistock. It will take us thirty minutes, I guess, to get to the carpark where the trail starts, and then the walk will take another two hours.'

'Are you planning for us to have lunch somewhere too?'

'We could,' I reply. 'There's a good pub in Mary Tavy, which Crinkle will be allowed in.'

'Cool,' Mary says. Her words don't match her tone, she is far too astute to think I have suddenly decided to start showing her the delights of Devon.

I have virtually ignored this poor girl since she came to Fox Halt, too preoccupied to worry about her, or even keep a proper track of her movements. As I drive us out of the farmyard, she turns to me. 'So, Auntie, what do you need to talk to me about?' she asks. 'Sorry I took the money for the taxi.'

I laugh. 'Mary, please forget it. It doesn't matter. I'm sure my mother has scolded you enough about that. Simply promise me, if you ever want anything else, you'll just ask.'

'I will, I promise. You know that I didn't go back again to Culmfield, don't you?'

'Yes,' I reply. This is my opportunity to tell her there is something else I need to say, but I don't. Instead, I decide to wait until we are walking. It will be better if I can concentrate fully on Mary; not half my attention on her, and half on the road.

I try to remember the exact route through the lanes to the remote start of the walk. As I drive, neither of us talk for the first few miles, the only noise is Crinkle's panting.

'You know about the Culmfield Cuckoo, don't you, Auntie?' Mary says suddenly.

I turn to her. 'You mean *you* living here at the farm?' I reply. 'You leaving the luxury of the Culmfield nest to live with me and Nan Dan. You said you were like a cuckoo.'

'No,' she shakes her head slowly. 'No, not me.'

'Right,' I say, unsure where this is leading.

You know,' Mary says, 'that a cuckoo lays its egg in another bird species' nest.'

'I think everyone knows that,' I reply.

'But did you know that the cuckoo's egg hatches before the unsuspecting host's eggs, and that the cuckoo chick will grow faster too?'

'No,' I tell her.

'Well, the alien chick pushes out the others, so it ends up being the only baby in the nest, pretty mean, isn't it?'

'Yes,' I say, nodding. 'I didn't know that, I imagined all the chicks would grow up together, and when they fledged, the young cuckoo would just go its separate way.'

'Do you think that's what Dad imagined too?'

'Sorry, Mary, what are you talking about?'

'The Culmfield Cuckoo,' she replies, frowning.

'You've lost me.' I frown back at her.

'It's my new name for Sharmarke. I was pushed out of my family's nest because of him, and he's grown up amongst us with a different father than we thought. He's the Culmfield Cuckoo,' she explains. 'You're taking me away from the farm today, to tell me Mum knows about him, aren't you?'

'Yes,' I confess.

'I still love Sharmarke, not like a brother, not like I love Arthur, Max and Mikey. My love for him is like the way you feel about Richard. It's like the sky, all-encompassing; it's endless. Auntie, I am not going back.'
'But–'
'But nothing. I couldn't bear to be near Sharmarke, knowing that all our dreams for a future together can never happen. Don't tell me everything will be okay. It isn't, and it will never, ever be okay,' she says. 'I have to stay at Fox Halt Farm. Besides, I love it there.'
'Mary–'
'No, no, no.' She puts her hands over her ears.
We arrive at the start of the walk. 'I followed you downstairs this morning,' Mary says, 'I heard you through the dairy window.'
'So, you heard everything?' I check.
'Yep. Sorry, Auntie, your idea of bringing me here to tell me that Mum knows about Sharmarke, was a waste of time.'
'Do you still want to walk?'
'Yes.'
'You do?'
'Yes. It will be nice to do something together, and Crinkle will be disappointed if we don't.' It's as though the dog knows what we are discussing because she looks from Mary to me. Her black eyes glint, seemingly begging us not to cancel our walk.

We follow an old leat, which was constructed to feed a long-abandoned copper mine. The ancient water channel is so well maintained that a deep stream still rushes along it. With no cows or sheep in sight, Crinkle runs free along the narrow track, nose down, tail up, hunting some small unsuspecting moorland mammal.

When she is a hundred yards in front of us, she sits, and waits for us to catch up. Impatient with our slow progress, she huffs.

'It *was* suicide,' Mary says.

'Sorry?' I ask, feeling suddenly disappointed – I hoped we'd talk about something other than Michael, it's a lovely day and I thought we could chat about the beauty of the hills or the history of the place.

'Dad committed suicide.'

'But Grégoire saw someone with your father that night, and that someone, probably killed him – that's what the police believe.'

'Maybe there *was* someone with him, but the police haven't come up with an explanation about how they managed to keep my father in his car while they filled it with poisonous gas. It's just not possible, you can't kill someone like that, they'd get out.' She pauses. 'Unless this person restrained Dad in some way, but there were no ligature marks on his body,' she says.

'Right,' I reply, unable to find an argument against what's she is saying.

'Look, if my father was choking, he would have got out of the car. Auntie, Dad killed himself.'

'How can you talk so calmly about this?' I ask. 'Aren't you upset?'

'No,' she replies quickly. 'I'm not. Dad has destroyed my life. What he did to Nala was bad enough, but allowing Sharmarke to grow up with our family is unforgiveable. We spent every hour we could together. Since he was ten years old, Dad insisted that he join us on our holidays, skiing in Klosters, on the yacht, just about everywhere we went. My father made it seem like he was being benevolent, but as usual, he had selfish reasons for his charity.'

Mary sits down on a rock next to the stream, and Crinkle lies at her feet. I stand still, not saying anything.

'I hate my dad,' she says, leaning down to stroke Crinkle. 'I will never forgive him.'

'Mary…'

'No, Auntie, don't defend him,' she says quickly.

'I wasn't going to,' I say. I wait for her to speak again. She stares back at me. Several seconds tick by.

'Sharmarke has been there all my life,' Mary says eventually. 'And my father could see how deeply I felt about him. He should have sent Sharmarke away a long time ago.' She looks up at me, and I can see there are tears in her eyes. 'Dad could have paid off Nala and Amir before Sharmarke was born, bought them a new home and created distance between us. But no, Dad couldn't do that, could he? He had to have all his children at home, no thought for anyone else but–'

'You know what happened to your dad's parents, don't you?' I ask, believing I should put some perspective on her father's behaviour. Mary doesn't reply. 'Do you know about your dad's childhood?' I ask again.

Her cheeks turn scarlet. 'He was a poor orphan, is that what you mean? Dad was brought up by his gran. Yes, I know. What's that got to do with anything?'

Having raised the subject, I change my mind. All morning I have been using Michael's childhood to defend his actions. Raping Nala is horrific, I can never forgive that, but Michael would never have allowed Sharmarke to grow up with an uncertain future, feeling duty bound to look after his child. Now though, I reconsider; we are all a victim of circumstance, but that doesn't mean we are not responsible for our choices. There is no justification for how Michael behaved. 'You're right,' I tell her. 'How your father grew up doesn't matter.'

'Yes,' she says. 'I am right; my dad was a 's' 'h' 'one' 't'.' Mary starts walking again with Crinkle up against her ankles. I think the little animal picks up on Mary's misery and wants to be near her, intent on cheering her up.

We arrive at the point where the River Tavy feeds the leat, and we start to follow the river upstream. The path has widened so Mary and Crinkle fall back to walk next to me. I think how the U-shaped valley here could be mistaken as glacial, but the last Ice Age never came this far south. I have been here so many times but the drama of the high-sided hills and the continuous waterfalls as the river drops hundreds of feet are still awe-inspiring to me.

'If I was Dad, I would have killed myself too.'

'What?' I ask, not understanding what Mary is trying to tell me. She is dealing with so much, and I am frightened she could break down. I snapped my response to her just then, and now I feel terrible about the way I spoke. I smile. 'What do you want to say, Mary?' I ask, hoping I sound like someone she can trust.

'When Dad came to pick Mum and me up from the farm, I told him I knew his sordid little secret, and I said I would never come home while Sharmarke lived at Culmfield. I told Dad I loved Sharmarke, and I lied to my father, telling him we'd been sleeping together. I said it was over, but I couldn't bear to see Sharmarke ever again. I threatened to tell Mum everything if he didn't let me stay with you.'

'I see,' I say, picturing her and her father in the car at the farm.

'Auntie, I backed him into a corner, his life was about to crash into tiny little pieces. Don't you see why he killed himself?'

'Okay,' I say, not wanting to argue with her.

'Dad only knew how to win. He was King Manipulator, but I had called checkmate on his despicable games. He couldn't face losing. He couldn't face up to all the stuff that would happen if the truth about him was revealed. I know he bullied Mum, but I'm sure if she had found out about Sharmarke, she'd have found the strength to divorce him. He could have lost his children and everything. His whole world would have been destroyed. He loved Mum in his own sick way, I know he did. He couldn't bear the thought of losing his marriage and his picture postcard life.'

'So, that's why you are so sure he killed himself?' I ask.

'I know he did, and I know who was in the car that night.'

'Who?'

'Nala.'

'How do you know it was her?'

'Because she told me,' Mary replies.

'Sorry, when did she tell you this?' I ask.

223

'When she drove me back to Culmfield in the morning. She discovered Sharmarke was missing. She found us in the flat. Nala said she tried to talk to Dad about how they could stop Mum discovering the truth, but he saw no way out. No way to keep Mum in the dark, but still making me come home.'

'So, you think your dad killed himself after he spoke to Nala?'

'Yep. End of story. *Kapow,*' she says, throwing her arm out in front of her.

'So, why did Nala and Amir lie?' I shake my head, disturbed by her attitude. 'Why did they try and frame me?' I ask.

'I expect they were scared. I imagine they were trying to deflect the police away from Nala being in the car, wanting to keep the truth about Sharmarke quiet. You were probably an easy sacrifice. You had a motive, an opportunity too, and you didn't have an alibi. Auntie, you were an outsider, someone who Amir and Nala didn't really care about.'

'What about my earring, how did they get that?'

'I don't know anything about an earring,' she says.

I wonder if maybe Amir found my lost jewellery years ago, when I was with Michael one evening. Maybe he kept it as something he could use against his boss? Or he planned to sell it if times got tough for him and his family?

'Auntie? Do you believe me now?' Mary asks. 'Do you believe Dad committed suicide?'

'Yes,' I nod. 'So, this is what we need to explain to the police,' I tell her.

Mary stops walking. 'No, we don't. Like I said before, we have to let the inquiry run dry. The police have virtually nothing. It's all circum...' She stops.

'Circumstantial?' I say.

'Yes, that's right, the information the detective has isn't strong enough to convict you, or anyone else for that matter. No-one wants the truth about why Nala was with Dad in the car that evening uncovered.'

I don't know what to say, maybe she has a point. 'Could we talk about something else, please?' I ask. 'Tell me about your friend at school. Tell me about Mollie. Maybe she'd like to come over to see you at Fox Halt?'

Chapter 20

RICHARD

The extraordinary general meeting is done and dusted in ninety minutes, and I am voted in as the new director of O'Rowdes'. Sarah Lancaster and the future of the company were discussed at length, and a new meeting scheduled in seven weeks for a progress report.

Jessie and I are driving back to Culmfield. We are both exhausted from lack of sleep and dealing with the vehement disbelief in the meeting that Michael was duped by his own personal assistant.

The objections to the possible future sale of the business, and Jessie's proposal to sell it in a way that will no doubt reduce the potential proceeds, was a tame and reasonable debate compared to the shock over Sarah.

My phone rings, and I answer it quickly. Jessie is driving too fast so I'm finding it hard to concentrate. I'm thinking how I should have kept my resolve and caught a train back, but Jessie persuaded me she would drive like her old grandmother. She has only just confessed that her gran won at the Brooklands motor racing circuit in 1939, just before all racing stopped there. I think if her grandmother drove like Jessie is right now, then she must have lapped her fellow competitors.

'Billy,' I say to both the phone and Jessie.

'Richard, can I give you an update about Mary?' she asks…

The boys are in bed when we get back, so Jessie quickly asks Nala to go home. We both follow her to the front door.

'Thank you, Nala. You're an angel,' Jessie says.

Nala looks Jessie in the eyes, nods at her once, smiles, and steps outside.

Jessie and I stand in the doorway, allowing the light from the entrance hall to illuminate Nala's silhouette as she walks quickly up the drive to The Gatehouse. We keep watching until the door to her home opens and closes, and she disappears inside.

Another figure immediately appears in the courtyard. Billy was hidden by one of the large, conifer sentinels along the forecourt. The tree's triangular foliage reaches the floor, so it provided perfect cover. Our late-night visitor has, as we agreed, parked her car by the side gate and walked across from the stables. She dashes up the steps towards Jessie, and as soon as she's across the threshold, I shut the door quietly behind her.

'Sorry,' Billy says as she walks into the kitchen.

'Don't worry,' I tell her, watching her sit down. Billy seems comfortable, but I suppose she did live at Culmfield for a long time, I imagine her sharing many cups of tea with Jessie across the table here.

'What's so urgent then?' Jessie asks her. 'Please excuse us if we don't seem super happy to see you, it's been a long day.'

'I'm sorry, I just don't know what to do,' Billy says. 'As you know I've just come from Charlotte and Grégoire's, and Grégoire told me he is sure the person he saw in the car with Michael was not Nala. They were too tall, more my size, he said.'

'So, you doubt what Mary told you this morning,' I say.

'I do,' Billy replies quickly, 'because when Grégoire started thinking it through, he decided it was Amir not Nala. Before he thought Michael's companion had long hair, but now he thinks they were almost certainly wearing a hood.'

'Amir is about your height,' Jessie says.

'Yes,' Billy agrees, 'my build too, except for those enormous hands and feet of his.' She looks worried.

'What's wrong?' I ask her.

'The trouble is Grégoire is now so convinced it was Amir, that Charlotte wanted to ring Bawen to tell him straightaway.'

'They've called Detective Bawen, is that why you're here?' Jessie asks. 'You wanted to warn us that the world is about to discover what a detestable Svengali Michael O'Rowde really was?'

'No,' Billy replies. 'I asked them not to call the police. Begged them to wait until I'd spoken to you.' She pauses. 'I want to know what you think we should do, I'm so confused. Like you say, Jessie, if they go to the police then, the whole scandal about Sharmarke is bound to be exposed, and I don't think that is a good thing for your family or Amir's.'

'Did you explain to them why you thought Nala might have been in the car?' I ask.

'No, I didn't. Again, I was thinking about Sharmarke, I didn't want anyone else to know about him being Michael's child,' Billy replies.

Jessie stands up. 'So, what you want to know, Billy, is should we go to the police with this new information?' she asks. 'Truth is, I don't know either.'

She closes her hand into a fist and holds it still in front of her. Jessie looks strong. I noticed her regained strength earlier, when she was addressing the meeting. Her returned confidence brought back memories of her before she married Michael; the day she came to London, stood in my boardroom and told Michael about Culmfield. I had known Michael a long time before that, and I had never seen him pay over the odds for anything before, but Jessie bowled him over. 'Do you think your boys will remember if Amir was in the house all evening, setting up your new cinema screen?' I ask her.

'Why?' she replies.

'We could check Amir had time to be with Michael,' I reply.

'They might, Arthur might, we'll ask them in the morning,' Jessie says as she props her back against the sink. I feel I need to clarify something. 'Sorry, I'm on information overload at the moment,' I say. 'If it *was* Amir in the car, did he kill Michael, or did Michael kill himself?'

'No,' Billy replies, at the same time as Jessie says, 'Yes.'

Jessie looks at me. 'Richard, I think if Amir was in the car it's possible that Michael and he were working out a future plan. Maybe Michael offered him money to leave Culmfield and to keep quiet about the rape. Maybe Amir refused to accept his terms, we don't know, I don't expect we'll ever discover what they were talking about.'

'Afterwards,' Billy cuts in, 'after discussing things with Amir, Michael could still have killed himself. Everything was pretty much falling apart for him, and he hated it when he couldn't keep control.'

I nod at Billy. 'Perhaps he loved Sharmarke too, he'd watched him grow up,' I say. 'Maybe he couldn't bear the thought of sending him away. I know I couldn't cope if I could never see Freddy again.'

'Like I said before,' Jessie says, 'we'll never know, but last night, when I found out about him raping Nala, I wished Michael had committed suicide. I hoped he couldn't live with himself – imagine losing your mother like Michael did, at the hands of a person who abused her – only to become an abuser yourself.'

'Yes,' I agree. 'Michael certainly had a lot of things to deal with. Don't forget, he might have discovered what his personal assistant had been up to. Or perhaps Sarah Lancaster was blackmailing him over something she'd unearthed on his computer?'

Billy frowns at me. 'Richard, I told you, you were imagining that, she isn't a spy.'

I shake my head. 'Sorry, I couldn't tell you before, but it seems she was, she *has* tampered with the files at O'Rowdes'. The police had Michael's computer checked out, and they discovered what she'd done.'

'Have they arrested her?' Billy asks.

'No, because she's vanished into thin air.'

'Gosh, sorry I doubted you, Richard,' she says. 'However, I can't believe Michael killed himself. It's not sitting well with me. He believed for years that his mother committed suicide. He was haunted by his memories. For years, he didn't know his mother was pushed off the balcony, and he believed his mum had jumped intentionally, abandoning him. I'm sorry but he wouldn't have chosen to leave his family. I think we're missing something. This still feels wrong to me.'

'What if Amir argued with Michael about Sharmarke's future?' Jessie suggests. 'What if Michael pushed Amir too far, and Amir killed him in a fight?'

My brain is tired, I don't think I can do more questions and answers without sleep. 'Look,' I say, 'we're not getting anywhere with this now. Let Jessie talk to her boys in the morning. She can talk to Amir and Nala tomorrow, like we planned, and then I can ring you, Billy, to fill you in on what we learn.'

'You're right,' Billy says, turning to Jessie. 'Will you talk to Charlotte and Grégoire too?'

Jessie nods.

'Something else too, it's about Mary,' Billy says.

'What?' Jessie asks.

'Mary knows that you know about Sharmarke being her brother but...' She pauses.

'But what, Billy?' Jessie says.

Billy talks quickly. 'But she is determined at the moment that she won't *ever* return to Culmfield. She can't bear to be near Sharmarke. I'm sure she will change her mind, but you need to be patient. It could be weeks – not days, or hours before she comes home.'

'Yes, Billy, you told Richard all that on the phone earlier, don't you remember?'

'But you were driving, Jessie, I wanted to tell you face to face, to make sure you realised what was happening.'

It is as though Jessie hasn't heard. 'Yes, I'll talk to Charlotte and Grégoire,' Jessie replies. 'I really don't want the detective stirring anything else up.' She steps towards Billy. 'Can you go now, please?' Jessie asks her.

Billy looks at me. 'Richard, will you walk me to the door?' she asks.

I get up and grab her hand. Jessie snatches at her shoulder. 'Give me a hug,' she says. Billy spins towards her, pressing her body into her friend. 'I'm sorry,' Billy says with eyes full of tears.

Jessie replies – but her voice is muffled in Billy's neck, I think she says, 'I know you are…I know you are.'

BILLY

Richard kisses my forehead. 'I will be back with you at Fox Halt soon. I promise, darling.' I want to kiss him, but instead I hold my breath. Jessie is with us, so I feel I can't let kissing Richard overshadow my embrace with her. 'Love you, forever,' I reply, my statement directed at both of them.

As I walk towards the stables and my car, I suddenly change direction, heading for The Gatehouse instead.

Three or four minutes later, I am hammering on the door but there is no reply. Not surprising, it is late – but every light is on inside, and I can hear voices.

It was the way that Nala and Amir's home was lit up that drew me here. I agreed with Richard, Jessie, and Mary not to go to the police, but I didn't say I wouldn't confront the people who have fabricated evidence and used me as their scapegoat. Rage wells up inside me as I continue to knock.

When Nala eventually opens the door, she steps outside. I move forward to meet her, standing so close that a piece of paper wouldn't slide between our bodies. 'Right,' I say. 'I've come for some answers.'

I tower over her so my proximity and my height, must be intimidating. I don't feel comfortable either, so I move back a little. I can see past Nala now, into the house.

Sharmarke is running down the stairs, two steps at a time, moving in a way that makes me think of a gazelle, his feet don't seem to touch the steps. The deer is soon next to his mother with an arm around her shoulder.

'Miss May,' he says lightly.

He must be shocked to see me, but if he is, his broad smile doesn't give him away. I haven't seen Sharmarke since he was seven years old, more than half his lifetime ago. The boy is striking, his soft black waves crown his symmetrical face. I remember him as Mary's young friend who lived in The Gatehouse and hung around the ponies and horses all the time. The little lad who always fell in with whatever Mary wanted. He was shy, and I wished he had more confidence in his own ability, but now it seems that my wish has come true. The boy before me stands tall – a foot taller than me at least – with broad shoulders and penetrating eyes.

'Sharmarke,' I reply, trying to sound as nonchalant about seeing him again as he did, having found me outside his home.

'To what do we owe this pleasure?' he asks, but I am not thinking about his question, more mulling over the pitch and tone of his voice – *how nicely he speaks* – obviously influenced by his posh school. 'Miss May, it's late. Why are you here?' I study his face trying to see if he has any of Michael's physical characteristics. I decide no; no-one would guess he wasn't Amir's son. Suddenly, my attention switches to five leather suitcases lined up at the bottom of the stairs. Something tells me they are full.

The smile on Sharmarke's face slides off as his eyes follow my stare.

'Are you going somewhere?' I ask.

'A holiday in Cornwall,' he replies quickly.

'Oh,' I say, 'that will be nice.'

'Amir, he get car,' Nala says. 'We just about leave.'

On cue, I hear someone behind me, and I assume it is Amir but I don't check. Nala stares past me, frowning slightly.

'What Mary tell you?' It is Amir, I recognise his voice.

'Everything,' I say, keeping my eyes on Nala and her son. I suspect Mary has not been wholly honest with me, but I hope my one-word reply will instigate a response from one of them.

My answer does set off a reaction – Amir grabs both my hands, pushing them up my back.

'What Mary say?' My assailant's cheek brushes my face, his bristles scratching my skin. I feel his chest beating and my heart pulses rapidly. 'Tell me?' he hisses into my ear, as he forces my arms further up my back. I want to scream but I don't think it will help. His breath is heavy; the warm expelled air on my bare neck makes me shiver.

'*Dad!* Let her go.' Sharmarke moves towards me, but Amir manhandles me past Nala and him, into the house. The door slams behind us, as he kicks it shut. He spins me around, shoving my back against it. Sharmarke beats the other side. 'Dad, don't! Dad, don't!' he yells over and over again.

'She tell you everything?' Amir stares into my eyes. 'Mary tell how I kill Michael, is that what she tell you?' A flash of light – *the reflection from a blade?* I feel it held tight against my throat. There is moisture on my neck. *Blood!* But maybe it's sweat?

'Mary said it was suicide,' I whimper, too terrified to move.

'She know. She tell you, Billy May,' he says, refusing to believe me.

'No, Amir, she said her father killed himself.'

'You kneel,' he instructs, moving the knife so I can see it. 'Down,' he says, his wild eyes glaring at the floor. I suddenly realise what he wants me to do. Evil ritual killings I have seen on the television news run through my head. I feel sick. I want to wipe my forehead...

...My hips crash onto something sharp as my back smacks into the ground. I try to gasp for air but my lips won't separate. I suck in hard through my nose, trying to work out what's happening. It is dark, but I make out the outline of Amir's face looking down at me. 'I take Nala and Sharmarke to safe place.' His voice is raspy. 'Then deal with you, Billy May. Need time to think.'

My eyes grow accustomed to the blackness. I see his fingers tapping on the side of his head. 'We make police see you kill Mr O'Rowde. We make more proof. Need think more. Was mistake not to kill Mary too. Sharmarke, he should not tell girl what he see.' Amir sucks slowly through a thin gap in his bottom teeth. 'Mistake,' he says, shaking his head. '*Mistake.*'

He presses hard on my shoulders forcing me into a Z shape, before something slowly lowers onto me. I can't lift my arms to stop it. I try to kick my feet, but my legs won't move either.

Darkness.

Voices.

Silence. Then an engine starts up – confirming my thoughts that I am in the boot of a car. I attempt to wet my lips with my tongue, but I can't because my mouth is taped shut. I must not cry; my tears could choke me.

A heavy suitcase thumps into my chest. I jar my neck. There are other things too, sharp and bruising. The only sound is the road noise under the tyres. The only taste is the sourness, like vinegar from the stale air. The only smell; the plastic of the tape, tight across my lips – and the only colour – black. Aching and hurting.

Hours go by with never-ending thoughts about what is going to happen. *Will I die tonight?* Thrown off some cliff somewhere? Will my body ever be found? Starved, suffocated, stabbed... what is my fate? Could Amir really conjure more evidence to brand me as a hateful murderer?

Mary, be safe. He mustn't harm you too. I think about my mother, poor Mum. How will she deal with the news? *Mum, and Richard too, please believe in me, I am innocent. I love you. I will always love you, Richard.*

In my dark prison, the note from the wheels deepens. There is more vibration. The car stops, and Amir must be turning the vehicle around.

I hold my breath.

There are voices again and now silence.

My overriding fear is that I will die of dehydration. I can't remember the last time I drank anything, my mind keeps wavering, but now my every thought comes back to my thirst. If only I could wet my lips but the tape won't let me.

The car engine starts again.

Thirsty...

I wake up to a purring sound as the lid of my jail rises evenly and smoothly upwards, revealing the exact same shade of blackness as before. The air is colder and sweeter. I work out there is a thick canopy of trees above me. No stars and no moon, but I smell damp earth. A car door opens, and I imagine Amir climbing out as the car rocks.

A flickering light highlights branches and I see the outline of leaves moving gently in the breeze.

Only whiteness now as a torch is directed at my face. I am blind until the light is jerked away, so I don't see the knife until it's right in front of me. I wait to feel the sting as the blade is speared into my chest. I hear tearing, but instead of pain, my legs release. Now my arms are set free.

'Get out,' Amir orders, but I can't move. I have been stuck in the same position for hours. '*Get out*,' he repeats. If I could see his eyes, they would be slits.

'*Move*,' he says.

Adrenalin rises through my body, numbing the soreness. I stretch out a little. I kick my legs and push on my hands until I fall out of the boot onto the ground. I am like a newly hatched chick, exhausted from its final effort to release itself from its shell. Gravel cuts into my face.

My hips are lower than the rest of me, and my jeans start to feel wet. I guess I am on the edge of a track, partly in a culvert.

I bring my legs together and I feel tender on the inside of my kneecaps, soreness everywhere. I think I may have a cracked rib. Pain in my stomach and chest. Hunger, thirst, and tiredness swamp me.

Amir flicks his torch off and slumps down against one of the wheels of the car. 'You lucky,' he whispers. 'Miss Billy May, you lucky lady.'

Fortunate is *not* how I would describe my current situation, staring up at him paralysed with fear. *Perhaps he plans to kill me painlessly and quickly; maybe that's why I am lucky?*

The blackness is lifting, it must be near sunrise. I think to check my watch, but then I exhale, a sort of faint whining noise. A new overriding thought has come. *What does the time matter anymore?*

I think how the coroner will want to find out that information if my body, or various dismembered parts of it, are ever discovered. Why? Where? How? Why and When? There will be so many questions for them to answer. My mind is in turmoil about the imminent ending of my life. I can't stop trembling.

'You want to know why you lucky, Billy May?' Amir asks. My mind has shut down. I am waiting to die. 'You lucky,' he tells me again, 'Sharmarke, he keep on say you tell truth. Sharmarke keep on say Mary tell you Mr O'Rowde, he kill himself.'

Amir claps his hands together, four or five times in quick succession, and my body jumps each time his palms come together. I cannot work out what he is doing, or what he might do next. All I can do is stare.

He shines the torch in my eyes and as I squeeze them shut against the light, a scorching pain wipes across my face. Amir is wrenching the tape from my mouth. '*Talk*,' he hisses. 'You tell exactly what she say to you. *Tell*.'

I open my mouth but no sound comes out. I can make out Amir's black shape, but I can't see his features, as he kneels beside me. 'Tell me exact – girl's exact words.' His voice is menacing, making me think he is condemning me before I even reply.

His torch is still switched on, lying on the ground beside him, and it illuminates his knife as he picks it up and starts to twirl it in the air. It sparkles. I cough.

'Exact, tell me exact.'

I recount everything I remember Mary said about the businessman, her father, the rapist and the liar. Adding every reason why I think he couldn't live with himself; why he had no choice but to take his own life. I wish Amir would shine the torch on my face, so he can see my sincerity as I give my account. I don't move. My legs are in a stream of water, so my jeans are completely soaked. My lower body is numb with the wet coldness. If I could move, I would remain still, desperate not to distract Amir from my narrative. I have to convince him.

When Amir sets the point of the knife in the ground to lever himself to his feet, I stop talking.

'Always remember, Michael O'Rowde, he kill *himself*,' he says, moving to the boot of the car.

For the first time I see the Rolls Royce badge. I remember how my dad loved driving this car. 'Dad, my last journey, and I travelled in style,' I sort of laugh and cry at the same time.

Pins and needles begin in my arms from lying in the same place too long. The deep pain may be from the surge of blood caused by the release of my tight bindings. My legs could be aching too, but I can't feel them because they are freezing.

Amir stares at me; he has fetched something from the boot, which he is concealing behind his back.

He steps over me but I am still too scared to move.

– a blunt force to the back of my head…

And then nothing.

Chapter 21

O'ROWDES' HEAD OFFICE, BERKELEY SQUARE

WEDNESDAY 20 AUGUST

RICHARD

It feels like a circle has been completed in a way, because I am now hauled up in the very first office I had at MarcFenns, the one I used when my father was still running the company.

I have arranged to meet up with Father next week, so I'm considering asking if I can borrow the desk that now fills most of his study, for here. It's the desk that used to be in this room before we moved MarcFenns to Canary Warf. It will make me feel more comfortable about working at O'Rowdes' for the next few weeks. I can picture the old desk clearly – its inlaid green leather top with its heat rings. I can almost smell the wood polish, it would be nice to sit behind it again. The phone rings, it's Matthias.

'Miss Cambell is on the phone for you,' he says.

'Please put her through,' I reply, and as the phone clicks, 'Jessie,' I say.

'They've gone,' she tells me straightaway.

'That's good, isn't it?' I check. 'That's what you wanted; Amir, Nala and Sharmarke out of your life.'

'Yes, Richard.'

'After Billy spoke to me yesterday morning, on the phone – on our way back to Culmfield – you said we had to do something to make them leave.'

'But I didn't think they'd disappear overnight, they didn't even say goodbye. It's going to be so weird without them. Nala and Amir have lived here since Michael and I moved in.'

'Yes, I thought they'd want a day or two to organise themselves,' I say.

'The Gatehouse is a bit of a mess, they must have picked up everything they wanted and then run out the door.'

'You weren't expecting Nala to give it a spring clean, were you? I ask, lightly.

'Have we done the right thing? Paying them to go, I mean?' She pauses. 'I'm going to struggle without them. Nala has been helping me out for years. She was always here when I needed her.'

'You want Mary back at Culmfield, don't you?' I ask.

'Yes, of course I do, but–'

'No second thoughts, Jessie. You'll be fine, and the Bilehs will be fine too. They are survivors and we have given them access to a heck of a lot of money.'

'They took the Rolls,' Jessie says.

'Yes, and I'll register them as the new owners. It's not a problem,' I assure her. 'Jessie, you said Amir could have the car. You do remember?'

'Yes, I know, but I didn't really think he'd follow through. What's he going to do with it?'

'I don't care. You don't need the damn car. It'll cost a fortune to keep on the road. He's welcome to it as far as I see it. It's old, and worth twenty thousand pounds max, that's nothing in the scheme of things. Hell, Jessie, there is a new Rolls Royce due in the next few weeks, the one Michael had just ordered, and you still have the Bentley.'

'That's what I thought, until just now.'

'Why?'

'Because of Detective Inspector Bawen…'

'What about him?'

'He's just left – he told me the CCTV from the chapel has confirmed I was in there all evening – but he also said that Amir lying for me had made him suspicious.'

'And,' I prompt her.

'He said he wanted to know why my husband's chauffeur had so readily provided me with an alibi.'

'Right? So, what's that got to do with giving Amir the car?'

'Bawen asked me to confirm what happened again the day Michael died.'

'Surely not, he has your statement now.'

'Yes, but all he wanted to know was the bit about when Amir spoke to me on the phone, when he arrived back from London with Michael. He said I had stated that they came home in the Bentley, before Michael left again. Bawen told me that Amir had given him the same story.'

I don't see where Jessie is going with this. I have a lot of research to do and people to employ, to unravel Sarah Lancaster's meddling. Jessie was happy when I left this morning. She was looking forward to telling Mary that Sharmarke was leaving Culmfield for good, and she was planning on collecting her from Fox Halt Farm as soon as possible. 'Right, so what exactly is the problem?' I ask, hoping she will get to the point.

'Richard, the policeman was here early, and I couldn't think of an excuse not to let him in. He explained to me that they've now checked various camera footage on the route that Michael and Amir would have taken that afternoon from London to Culmfield. He said they have CCTV footage in London, and they have also found some from the M4 services at Swindon. Apparently, he's discovered that they were in the Rolls Royce, not the Bentley. Bawen asked me if I was sure about what Amir had told me that night. I said I thought so, but I was upset so which car Michael came home in wasn't important to me, and I could have remembered it wrongly – I asked Bawen if he'd checked with Amir. The detective said he wanted to speak to him, but no-one was answering at The Gatehouse, and his mobile had been on voicemail since yesterday morning.' She stops.

I think she is waiting for me to comment, but I don't know what to say. There is a pause before she tells me, 'He asked me where I thought Amir was.'

'Did you say?'

'Yes and no.'

'Sorry, Jessie. Did you tell him about the flat Michael let Amir use in Richmond, that's where you suggested the family could go for now, didn't you?'

'Sort of.'

'Jessie, you can't lie to the police.'

'But I didn't want to tell him about Sharmarke being Michael's child. I couldn't explain why they'd suddenly left.'

'So, what did you say?'

'I said, somewhere in London. That they'd gone to visit Nala's very sick aunt, and they must have left just after we got back last night.'

'Jessie, I don't believe you, how could you make that up?'

'What would you have done? We just allowed them access to over four million pounds from some dodgy looking offshore fund, which Michael obviously set up for his illegitimate son. What do imagine Bawen would make of that, when he found out?'

'Okay,' I say. 'Look, give me a minute to think this through.'

'There is something else.'

'Christ, what?'

'Arthur said it took Amir no more than thirty minutes to set up the new cinema system. He wasn't in the house with my kids for long.' I hear her doorbell ring.

'Richard, hang on, Bawen must be back. He can't have left, I haven't let anyone else in the front gate, and the entrance buzzer is diverted here now that The Gatehouse is empty. I'll leave the phone off the hook, you should be able to hear what he wants. He must have forgotten something.'

She speaks loudly. 'Hello again, detective,' she says.

'Would it be okay for me to look at the Rolls Royce? It's kept in the coach-house with the other cars, isn't it?'

'Yes, it is kept there.'

'So, will you show me, I imagine that building is locked and alarmed to the hilt – with all those valuable vehicles in your late husband's collection?'

'I can't, sorry, not today.'
'You can't?'
'No, the Rolls Royce is not in there, Detective Bawen.'
'It's not?'
'No, I lent it to the Bilehs.'
'You lent it to them?'
'Yes, Amir is insured to drive it, if that's what you're worried about?'
'No, Mrs O'Rowde, I'm surprised you would lend such a valuable car to a member of your staff,' he tells Jessie.
'The Bilehs' car is pretty unreliable, so Amir asked if he could borrow the Rolls. I didn't mind.'
'Could I still look in the garage?'
'Of course, but there is an entry code. I'll come with you.'

I hear the door close and then nothing, so I hang up, thinking Jessie will ring me back when she can. I have got to get some work done. But as soon as I put the receiver down, the phone rings again. It's Matthias again, and this time he tells me Mrs May is on the phone, and she has been waiting for some time.

'Hello, Daniella, what's wrong?'

'Richard, I can't get hold of Billy. She's not answering her phone. I thought she might be with you?'

'No, she's not here.'

'I know that, your assistant told me, but can you think where she could be?'

'No,' I reply.

'I'm worried, Richard. She didn't come home last night, and she didn't organise for anyone to do the cows this morning. I've been trying your mobile too, but you weren't answering either. That's why I'm ringing the office.'

I pull my phone out of my pocket, and see I have a missed call from Jessie, as well as four from Daniella. None from Billy.

I click the switch on the side, taking it off silent mode. 'Billy left Culmfield about ten o'clock last night,' I tell Daniella. 'I thought she was heading back to the farm.'

'I'll check with the police,' Daniella says, 'and the hospitals, to see if she has had an accident. Gosh, Richard, there are so many places between Culmfield and here where her car could leave the road and not be found. She might be lying in a ditch somewhere.'

'Look, I'll leave here right away,' I say.

'You'll come to Fox Halt?'

'I'll go to Culmfield first, I can get there in three hours. Jessie and I will start there, and then we'll check the routes Billy might have driven home last night.'

'Alright.'

'If Billy hasn't been admitted to hospital, then please see if you can persuade the police to check the roads too. Or if you can think of anyone else, get them to drive around as well. We'll find her, don't worry.'

'Okay, Richard.'

'Daniella,' I say, stopping her from hanging up.

'Yes.'

'My mobile was accidently on silent before, but you can ring me on it now, it's working again. Keep me posted.'

'Yes, alright,' Daniella replies, but I can hear she is not thinking about me, she is working out where to find the numbers for the hospitals; which hospitals? Did Billy have anything on her to identify her?

'There's a family crisis. I'll be back as soon as I can,' I tell Matthias.

Billy

I scan my surroundings but nothing registers. I shiver as I rub the back of my head, where there is a sore lump. I close my eyes.

Flashes of consciousness, until I can focus on the silvery branches of the giant beech trees above me, so close together that I can only make out tiny triangles of blue sky.

I'm alive! Joy floods my veins, but now terror, trepidation – worrying if Amir is still around. I check one way and then the other, but see no sign of him or the car. Everything is quiet.

I notice a green tartan rug covering my legs and I realise too, that I am no longer lying partly in the culvert. Something presses into my hip, it's my mobile phone in the pocket of my jeans. I hurriedly extract the lifesaver, but as soon as I have the phone in my hand, I see it is soaked and useless. Desperate, I push it back into my jeans.

Lifting my body gently, I try to stand up but it's too fast and I collapse back onto my knees. From this slightly higher viewpoint, I see an O'Rowdes' carrier bag by my feet. I crawl towards it.

Inside the bag, I find a small bottle of water and a sandwich wrapped in cellophane; like the ones you get in petrol stations. I quickly break open the water, dribbling it into my mouth. The best drink I have ever had.

I am up again. A small step. Another. I will get out of here, *wherever here may be*.

RICHARD

'Mr MarcFenn, stop!' I look back, and Matthias slows to a walk.

'What is it?' I ask him.

'There's a man on the phone. He says, he has to talk to you urgently.' Matthias circles me but I don't want to be herded back, nothing is more pressing than finding Billy.

'Who is he?' I ask, not wanting to return to the office to answer this call.

'Not sure, he said it's about Janette. She needs your help.'

I frown hard, trying to work out why my ex-wife needs me, and who the man is. A doctor perhaps? I wonder why everyone is ringing the office and not my mobile. I check my phone; it's fine. Now I worry if it might be about Freddy, or our daughters.

'Did he give a name?' I ask, hurrying back towards my office.

My assistant follows. 'I can't remember sorry. Sounds Scottish. Does that help?'

'No, just put him through, please.' My hand hovers over the telephone.

'Hello, Mr MarcFenn,' the caller says.

'Hello,' I reply, not recognising his voice.

'I'm Jamie Robertson,' he tells me. 'I'm on speakerphone, Janette is with me–'

'Hello, Richard,' a female cuts in, 'it's Janette, Jamie is driving me to the train station.'

'Okay, Janette,' I say even though I feel certain the voice doesn't belong to my ex-wife, it's Billy.

'Sorry to land this on you, Richard, but Alistair is convinced I'm having an affair. He threw me out last night. I need to see you, today, if that's alright?' I'm certain now this is Billy, but I don't know how to reply. I can't understand why she is calling herself Janette. For heaven's sake, I don't know anyone called Alistair. This strange call has to be related to Billy's sudden disappearance. At least, I know she is still alive. Maybe she is suffering from concussion and is delusional.

'Jamie is taking me to Carlisle train station. We'll be there soon, so I should be at Berkeley Square by two,' Billy says. 'I need to talk to you face to face. I've got myself in a bit of a pickle, and I hope you'll be able to help me.'

'Of course,' I say, keeping my voice calm, when I feel far from it. I am wondering if she really is in Carlisle, and why she might be there? 'I'll see you in the office about two then,' I tell her, playing along.

'Richard.'

'Yes.'

'I haven't got my phone.'

'Do you want to explain why?' I ask, still trying to sound like I am not panicking.

'Not really, it's a long story. Jamie's been my saviour this morning. He has really taken care of me.'

'Thank you, Jamie,' I say.

'Just pleased to help,' he replies.

Suddenly, I wonder if Billy is being held by this man against her will. The stranger could be a kidnapper. I panic, thinking he might have made her speak to me. I can't reason why he should do this, but none of this is making sense. I wonder if Billy is hiding her identity from him.

'Janette, I just need to check something,' I say.

'What is it?'

'You're not bringing that cat with you, Piggy isn't coming?'

She replies quickly. 'Her name is Crinkle, and she's a dog. Don't call her Piggy, it's mean.'

I feel reassured. 'Do you want my mobile number?' I ask.

'Good thought,' she replies. 'Yes please.'

Jamie tells her there is a pen and pad in the glove box. A catch opens. There is rustling.

'Ready,' she says, and I give her the number. 'Can't wait to see you, it's been so long.'

'Yes, looking forward to it,' I reply. 'Keep safe. Thank you again, Jamie.'

'No worries,' he replies, 'the station is on my way, it is not a problem – sorry, mate, have to go now, we are here.'

'Thanks again,' I say quickly, before the phone goes dead.

I sink into my chair, realising my trip back to Devon is postponed. I have to be here when Billy arrives.

After a minute or two, I pick up the phone again and start to dial, ready to try and explain to Billy's mother about the odd call. At least, I can tell Daniella that her daughter is safe.

Just before two o'clock, my office door flies open. 'My taxi is still waiting outside. Can you pay my fare for me?' Billy asks.

'Sorry, Mr MarcFenn, I couldn't stop her,' Matthias says, as he follows her into my room.

'No worries,' I reply. 'Matthias, could you pay the cab, please?'

'How much?' I ask Billy, taking some notes out of my wallet.

'Thirty pounds including a bit of a tip.' She shrugs.

I give my assistant fifty. 'Please let the driver have the lot, he's had to hang around.'

'Okay,' he says as he leaves. I turn to Billy. 'My God, I've been out of my mind, are you alright?' I ask, putting my arms around her. I don't give her a chance to reply. 'Look at the state of you. You look terrible. Sit down. I spoke to Jessie earlier, she says your car is still parked on Wall End Lane. What the hell were you doing in Carlisle? What happened to you?'

'Oh, Richard, it's horrible.'

'Sit down, Billy,' I say again, releasing my hold on her so she can collapse into the chair. 'When Matthias gets back, I'll ask him to get you a drink.'

'Thank you, and something to eat too, if that's alright?' Billy says quietly, staring up at me.

I nod at her, I am desperate to know what she has been doing, but first Daniella needs to know she is here. As I dial, I can't take my eyes off Billy. She continues to stare back, but it seems like her eyes aren't registering anything. Every muscle in her body is set still, whilst I talk to her mother.

When Matthias returns, I send him straight back out again for food and drink. I want to shake Billy's shoulders, demanding an explanation, but she looks so fragile and in shock, so I need to treat her gently. Kneeling on the floor in front of her, I take her hands in mine. 'Carlisle?' I say, hoping she realises it's a question.

Billy blinks at me. I run my fingers over hers.

'I'm sorry,' she says at last.

'What for?'

'For the worry I caused, I didn't mean to...' She stops. I wait for her to continue, looking into her eyes.

'I want to explain everything...' She stops again and just stares back at me.

'Just tell me when you're ready, don't worry,' I say.

'The trouble is, I really need to talk to Mary,' she replies. 'I was desperate to see you, Richard, but I wasn't thinking clearly before.'

'I can take you to Fox Halt right this minute,' I offer.

'I kept running it all through on the train. I must speak to her urgently – face to face.'

'I'll drive you home now,' I repeat.

'But–'

'No buts, Billy,' I say. 'O'Rowdes' doesn't matter. If needs be, I can come back here on Friday, work all this weekend, if I have to, but let's get you sorted first. You are all that matters. You can sleep in the car. Explain what's happened when we get back to the farm. If you feel you can tell me.'

'I want to, Richard, but can we talk in the car?' She sounds brighter.

'I'll tell Matthias I'm off, and grab your drink and food then we'll go.' I shut the folder on my desk, scooping it into my arms, not bothering to stow it in my briefcase, or lock it in a drawer. That would delay things. 'Come on,' I say, touching her elbow.

Billy finishes her cheese rolls and orange juice, by the time I have manoeuvred out of my car space.

She sleeps all the way, and at six o'clock, we arrive at the farm. 'Billy, wake up,' I whisper. She turns to me and opens one eye. 'Richard MarcFenn, how do you put up with me?' A smile spreads across her face.

I lean over and kiss her on the cheek. 'Because I love you,' I say.

Billy moves her fingers to the place I kissed. 'Will you stay tonight?' She leans forward and kisses my mouth. I close my eyes, savouring this precious moment.

'Yes.'

Daniella approaches the car, clutching a wriggling hairy creature. The dog's tongue smears my window in greasy circles.

'Hello, Crinkle,' I say, as I get out of the car.

'Dinner is ready.' Daniella drops the dog at my feet and rushes to hug Billy.

'Mum, I'm really sorry how I worried you,' she says before she snuggles her face into her mother's neck.

'You're home, darling,' Daniella replies as she puts her arm around her. 'You're home.'

Billy lets go of her mother. 'Where's Mary?' she asks.

'In the kitchen,' her mum replies. As Billy turns towards the house, Daniella pulls her daughter back into her arms. 'I'm so glad you're alright,' she says.

Chapter 22

FOX HALT FARM

BILLY

The kitchen is bursting with an appetising aroma, and I am suddenly famished. Crinkle runs through my legs making me wonder if she is expecting to share the meal too. *It's so good to be home.*

Mary has found a white linen tablecloth and laid out the best cutlery. There is even a vase with yellow roses and contrasting blue cornflowers set in the middle of the table.

'I wanted to make it nice for you, especially with Richard being here,' Mary says.

'Thank you, and thanks for doing all the milking today,' I tell her.

'I enjoy doing it, you know that,' she replies.

As Mary puts the casserole she has made on the table, I start to cry.

'It's alright, darling.' Richard puts his arm around me but his sympathy doesn't stop my tears.

'Thank you, everyone, for caring so much about me,' I sob as I sit down at the table.

Slowly, while we eat, I explain everything up until I started to walk away from where Amir had left me. When I get to this point, I turn to Mary. 'You have to tell us what you know,' I say.

'I have, Auntie,' Mary replies quickly.

'I don't believe you,' I say. 'What happened last night and this morning, makes me certain that Amir killed your dad. I'm also convinced that Sharmarke told you what his father had done.'

Mary shakes her head.

'Mary, listen,' I say to her. 'I think we all want the police to believe your dad committed suicide. Nonetheless, I think that after having a knife at my throat, and spending hours in the boot of a car expecting to be murdered, I deserve the truth. I want answers from you.'

'Where were you left?' Mary asks.

'I'll only tell you the rest of what happened to me, if straightaway afterwards, you'll give me some answers,' I bargain.

She nods at me, 'Okay,' she says. 'Now please tell us, Auntie.'

'Well, when I started to walk, I had no idea where I was but, in a few steps, I came to a track and just a little way along that, I saw a lake less than a hundred feet below me. The still water was so peaceful after the horror of what I'd been through. I simply stood and stared at the scene for ages. I wondered if I was in North Wales, Cumbria or the Scottish Highlands. I'd been in the boot for hours, so all were possibilities.

'I made my way down to the shore so I could refill the water bottle. Washing my face in the cold lake helped me to think clearly. I had to get home, but I had no money, no phone and no idea where I was. I decided to hitch a lift to the nearest train or coach station and find someone to pay my fare back. I didn't want anyone to be suspicious, so I tried to make up a plausible explanation about why I looked a wreck, and why I was lost without my mobile or cash. I didn't want to ring alarm bells because I had made up my mind by then it was best for everyone, especially you, Mary, if Michael's death is written off as a straight forward suicide.'

'Why the hell not?' Richard pushes his chair back and stands up. 'Amir should be punished for what he did to you.'

'But he just wanted to get away,' I tell him softly. 'Get his family to a safe place. He didn't kill me, he just knocked me out. Amir covered me up with a blanket and left me food and water. And before he left me, he dragged me out of the stream. I might have died from hypothermia otherwise. Don't you see?'

Richard raises his eyebrows. 'Okay, but no-one in their right mind should ever let a kidnapper get away with it.'

'Look, Richard, please sit down. Yes, I've been knocked over the head, but still I have thought this through carefully. I think it's best to keep quiet, I really do.'

'Go on, Billy,' Mum says, leaning across the table to hold my hand. Richard sits back down as I continue. 'I stood on the beach, while I made up a story to explain my situation without giving reason to call the police. I took my SIM card out of my phone and slipped it into my pocket, before I threw my useless mobile into the water.

'I climbed up to a road that I had crossed to get to the lake, and tidied myself up as best I could. I was dithering around in the middle of the road when Jamie came along.

'I told him a pack of well-thought-out lies, saying my name was Janette. I said I had a controlling boyfriend who I had been with for ten years and I explained how this man, I called Alistair, had pushed me out of his house the night before. Alistair wrongly suspected I was seeing someone else, and that was why he'd shoved me out into the night with nothing, refusing to let me back in. After an hour, I decided to go and stay the night with my friend, Fiona, but I had become disorientated and lost in the dark, and nearly died of exposure. All I wanted to do was go to London to see my first true love because I knew he would take care of me. So that's how I got home, I told a complete stranger a love story, and luckily Jamie took pity on me. He wouldn't even give me his address so I could send him a cheque when I got to London. He gave me money for some breakfast too.'

'There you are, you know the rest,' I say, looking at Mary now, so she can tell us what she knows about Amir and how her father really died.

'Not a whole pack of lies,' Richard cuts in.

I frown. 'What do you mean?'

'Well, you *are* sorry, and we *will* be getting married.'

I am smiling now. 'Soon?' I ask.

'A Christmas wedding, what do you think?' Richard looks happy.

My heart thuds. 'Yes, at Christmas, that would be incredible,' I reply.

'Grace and I will be bridesmaids.' Mary claps her hands.

'Another brilliant idea,' I say, but immediately, I have a reservation because I'm unable to imagine Grace wearing a dress.

'What's wrong?' Richard has noted my concerned expression.

'It's nothing,' I tell him. I turn to Mary. 'We had a deal,' I remind her. 'How did Amir kill your dad and fake the suicide? And why did he do it?'

Mary's face loses its colour.

'Darling, please.' Mum gives Mary a look which I instantly recognise. Mum's stare says, *'confess or else'*, but it also says, *'I won't be mad at you, just tell me.'* I wonder how my mother manages to convey so much with a subtle frown.

Mary obviously reads the silent message too, because she takes a deep breath, before diving into her account.

'Dad was already dead by the time Amir got back to Culmfield,' she says, and I gasp, not really believing she is going to tell the truth at last. Mary flashes her eyes at me, but she still continues. 'Amir set up the Rolls so that the exhaust was running into the back compartment; the rear seats are sealed off from the driver once the electric window is up between the passengers and the chauffeur. He disconnected the power to the windows and locked the doors so Dad couldn't get out.

'My father had no idea what was happening as Amir drove him home, he just fell asleep as the oxygen level reduced. The windows at the back of the Rolls Royce are blacked out, so nobody could see him. I am glad he didn't suffer, no-one deserves that.' She stops.

253

We are all staring at her. I am sure none of us can believe her lack of emotion. Mary looks at us all in turn but we don't speak, we just keep our eyes fixed on her. She goes on.

'When Amir got back to Culmfield, he transferred my father's dead body to the Porsche, and he drove him to where it was found later, setting up everything to make it look like Dad drove there and killed himself. And then Amir walked away.' She stops again.

'But why did he want to murder your father?' Mum's voice is firm but still coaxing.

'It was because of me, I made him do it.' My mother gets up and touches Mary's shoulder. Mary looks up at her, gazing into Mum's eyes. 'Amir thought killing my dad was his only choice. My ultimatum to my father that I wouldn't return to Culmfield whilst Sharmarke was there kicked everything off.'

'How?' Richard shakes his head.

'Dad was terrified that Mum would find out about Sharmarke, and I think he was worried the discovery might give Mum enough strength to divorce him. He loved us all, he didn't want to lose his children. We were his world, I'm sure of that.'

Mary wipes underneath her eye, but I see no sign of a tear. 'I think you all know my father, how he controlled people, and how he always found a way to make others do just what he wanted. This time, he thought money would make the problem of his secret son disappear. He calculated raping Nala could be erased with cash.

'I only know what Sharmarke told me, but Dad offered Amir millions from an account he set up for him when he was born. My father transferred thousands of pounds each year into this hidden account, and he offered all of it to Amir if his family left Culmfield for good, never to be in touch again.'

'They wouldn't take it?' Richard asks.

Mary shakes her head. 'No,' she replies.

'Why not?' Richard probes some more.

Mary explains, 'Sharmarke's life was centred around Culmfield. Nala's too. She'd lived in Barrowculme for a long time – knew the mums from school. Nala and Amir didn't want to move Sharmarke away from the only place he had ever known. They didn't want to take him away from his school and his friends.'

I have found my voice again. 'Sharmarke had all he needed for his show jumping too: the top-quality horse, the stables, ménage and everything,' I add.

'Yes, Amir was working for the man who raped his wife, but Dad had done his best to make amends, he had set up a good life for Amir and his family, which they did not want to give up. Dad kept upping his offer, but Amir wouldn't take his money.

'Amir said they were willing to say Nala had made up the rape. At this stage, only four people knew the truth: Nala, Dad, Amir and me. Amir offered to guarantee that it would stay that way. But Dad knew I'd never come home if Sharmarke was there. He knew too, I was ready to make a great big fuss, and therefore he felt he had to get the Bilehs to leave.

'Next Dad used intimidation. He dug into Nala and Amir's past, and with all my father's connections, he soon discovered Amir had used forged papers to get into Britain, coming to this country illegally. Dad said he'd be deported back to Somalia. My father even threatened him, by saying he could easily make it look like Nala had no right to be here either.

'Sharmarke would be torn away from the only life he ever knew, he'd have to go with his parents back to Somalia, or be adopted by a new family in the UK. That was enough for Amir, Dad was set on destroying him and everything he had, so Amir killed my dad to save his family.'

Richard stands up again, moving to sit back down next to Mary. He speaks softly to her. 'Sharmarke and his parents left Culmfield for good last night.'

Mary stares blankly back at him.

Richard touches her hand. 'Your mum gave them all the money from the account your father set up, it had a bogus business name called ProtectFE. Your father had been depositing large amounts on Sharmarke's birthday each year. I had no idea about its significance, until Nala explained what Sharmarke meant in Somali.'

'They took the money?' Mary asks.

Richard pauses for a second. 'They must have agreed to accept it this time because they knew the police want to question Amir. Detective Bawen has suspicions about the Rolls. That's why they took the old car, I think Amir must have been worried a forensic search would confirm where and how your father really died.'

Still Mary shows no real emotion. 'That's it then,' she says, sliding her chair backwards to get up.

Richard blocks her, moving so she can't stand up without pushing him away.

'Your mum needs you back home, Mary, can Billy take you tomorrow, even if it's just for the day? She would love to see you. Billy can bring you back the next morning. Stay here for the rest of the holidays, but please think about going home.'

'Not yet, I'd prefer to stay a few more days,' Mary replies, looking at me. 'Then I'll go.'

'You're not going to like this,' Richard says.

'What?' Mary does look a little concerned now.

'Your father's funeral. Your mum has to make some plans for it. I know it will be horrible for you all, but could you give her a bit of support with organising it?'

'Alright, you win, but just for tomorrow,' she says. Mary stands up and heads straight over to my mother. She puts her arms around my mum's shoulders and squeezes her tightly, resting her head on her arms. 'When I do go home, I'll come back all the time. I love you, Nan Dan,' she says.

My mother whispers in her ear, but loud enough that we can all hear. 'Love you too, Mary. We all do. Come back whenever you want, I'll pay your taxi fare every time.'

My eyes sting with tears.

I know Mary has to go back to Jessie, but I also know how she fitted into Fox Halt life. She feels like my daughter. How I wish she was. But there is still something I don't understand. 'Mary, how do you know all this about your father and Amir?' I ask.

'Sharmarke told me.'

'He told you?' I repeat, still unable to understand. 'But why did he tell you? When was that?'

She pushes her back against the rail of the Rayburn. 'The day my dad died,' she explains, 'that was the day before my birthday, and Sharmarke had bought me a present. He had texted me at Fox Halt Farm, and said he had something for me. He begged me to come back to Culmfield so he could give me his gift in person. Just an hour, that's all he asked for.'

'That's why you went to Culmfield that day?' I ask

'Yes, he gave me these silver earrings in the shape of horseshoes.' She flicks her hair back. 'You've probably noticed that I wear them all the time?'

I had spotted them on her birthday, and I asked her then if they were a present, but she hadn't replied, so I hadn't mention them again. 'Mary, they're lovely,' I say.

'Thank you.' She nods at me. 'I messaged Sharmarke back, arranging to meet up in the chapel the night before my birthday. Sharmarke watched out for Amir that afternoon. He wanted to be sure that my dad was home, and that Mum wouldn't be in the chapel. My father usually gave Sharmarke a twenty-pound note whenever he saw him, so Sharmarke was also keen to see him. He thought some extra money would help with my taxi fare back to Fox Halt.

'When Sharmarke saw Amir drive through the front gates, he followed on foot, down the drive to the coach-house. He planned to have a chat with my dad, and get his usual pocket money, but Sharmarke walked into the coach-house just as Amir opened the back door of the Rolls. At first, Sharmarke thought my dad was very drunk and had passed out. But when he saw Amir's face, he quickly realised that something was very wrong.

'When Amir told him to leave, Sharmarke was really frightened for him, and he insisted on helping, so there'd be no signs my father had been dragged into one of the older Porsches, one without a catalytic converter, so it still produced carbon monoxide from the exhaust. Amir told Sharmarke everything; that he wasn't his dad, and why he had no choice but to kill his real father. Sharmarke watched Amir drive my dad away and tried to forget what he'd seen. Amir promised him no-one would ever know that it wasn't suicide.

'As you can imagine, Sharmarke was shaken up when I met him, about an hour later. I didn't believe him when he said he was upset because I'd dumped him, and I had left Culmfield. I could see it was far more than that. I have grown up with him, and he has always confided in me. Eventually, he did tell me what had happened. He was in shock; discovering he was my brother and seeing his real father dead.'

Richard and Mum are shaking their heads; like me, they are struggling to take this all in but Mary keeps talking.

'All that night I held him, telling him over and over that everything would be okay. I said Amir had done us all a massive favour; that my dad was a tyrant and we were better off without him. But Sharmarke was scared that Amir would be found out, he was terrified Amir would be sent to prison, or deported and he'd never see him again.'

Mary looks up at me, and I smile at her.

'I still believe we're better off without him,' Mary says. 'If only Grégoire hadn't seen Amir in the Porsche, if only he'd been a few minutes later, and if only Charlotte hadn't phoned the police. Everything would have settled down. I could have stayed at Fox Halt, and Sharmarke could have lived at Culmfield. Everything would have been fine.'

'But Grégoire and Charlotte did contact the police,' I say, 'and that's why Nala and Amir tried to point the finger of suspicion at me. They were trying to push any guilt away from Amir.'

Mary nods.

'We need to speak to your mother, Charlotte and Grégoire,' I say. 'We have to work together to keep Bawen from finding out the truth, make this murder investigation fade out through lack of hard evidence, no motive and no suspects. That's how it's needs to stay. What do you think, Richard?' I ask.

'What about your earring, they found in the car?'

'The police know Michael and I had an affair, if they question me again I will say I lost it years ago, while I was with him.'

'You said he didn't have that Porsche back then.'

'I don't believe he did, I'm sure Amir must have found it and put it there, but the police can't prove that my earring didn't get caught up in Michael's clothing – he might have transferred it to that vehicle, who knows?' I say. 'One lost piece of jewellery is never going to be enough to build any sort of murder case on, is it?'

He shrugs at me, which I take to mean he agrees. Now I turn to my mother. 'And, Mum, what do you think?'

Mary cuts in, 'Yes, no evidence, no motive and no suspects.'

I cross my fingers and hold them up to her. 'Let's just hope it stays that way,' I say.

Mum stands up. 'A Christmas wedding. Well, I'm going to get myself a white coat with a white faux fur collar, I'll feel like a movie star,' she says, making it feel like the subject of Michael's death is done and dusted.

Richard laughs. 'Remember please, Daniella, you mustn't outshine your daughter.'

It's just after nine o'clock, when I say I have to go to bed. I can hardly keep my eyes open. 'I will be up shortly,' Richard tells me, 'but I've left my briefcase and a folder in my car, and I'd be happier if they were in the house.'

'Okay,' I say, as I kiss Mum good night. I turn to Mary. 'I will definitely be doing the milking in the morning, darling, and I'll take you straight over to Culmfield afterwards.'

'I'm helping you with the cows,' she argues back. 'I'll see you first thing, Auntie.'

'And I'll ring your mum now, to tell her you will be home at ten.' The fact that Mary is leaving hits me in the chest. I feel like I am about to cry. 'Can I have a hug please, Mary?'

We are still holding each other when Richard comes back in. Crinkle charges towards him like he is a new visitor she hasn't met before, running almost sideways and wagging her tail so much that it slows her progress. As Richard bends down to smooth her head, the contents of the folder he is carrying spills onto the floor.

I let go of Mary, so I can help him gather everything up before Crinkle thinks he has presented her with a new toy. I pick up some of the papers and a security pass. The pass instantly catches my eye. I assumed it would be Richard's, but I see that the photograph is of a woman. I hand everything to Richard. 'Hope you didn't have those in a particular order,' I say.

'No, it's just a few bits I was working on this morning, a hotchpotch of different tasks.'

Curiosity bites. 'Why do you have someone else's security pass?' I ask.

'It's Sarah Lancaster's. This morning I was organising an internal fraud investigation and her pass seems to be the only photo we have of her. Everything suggests she wasn't using her real name. All her qualifications and security information she provided when she joined O'Rowdes' are fake.'

'Can I see?' I ask.

Richard opens the folder and fishes out the plastic card. 'Here,' he says.

The card has faded a little but still, I feel the woman's face is familiar. I stare at it for a minute.

'Billy,' Richard says. 'Come on, you were going to bed. We've both got early starts again tomorrow.'

I look up. 'Yes,' I say, as I remember Ed's funeral. I hadn't met his sister Sarah before, and I haven't seen her since. But on that awful day, it felt like we were vital to each other.

I told Sarah Mackintosh how fabulous her brother always made me feel, about the fun we'd had, and how I thought for a little while, that we might have got together permanently. I told her too, how I hated what had happened to her dear brother when Michael split us up; making it clear he must never see me again, how Ed started taking the drugs, which slowly destroyed him.

Sarah told me all about their childhood, and growing up with Ed. She talked about their family and other things I'd never known about him. All we discussed that day was how amazing Ed was, and how we'd miss him. Sarah was in no doubt about who had been responsible for her brother's demise. I picture her standing by his coffin, wringing her hands together, vowing to me that Michael O'Rowde would pay for what he'd done.

As I hand the pass back to Richard, I take a last look into Sarah's eyes. Once again, I'm struck by how many lives were affected by Michael and the heartache he caused.

'Billy, do you recognise her?' Richard asks.

I shake my head. 'I'm going upstairs,' I say.

Chapter 23

CULMFIELD
WEDNESDAY 24 DECEMBER
RICHARD

Not everyone invites their ex to their wedding, but Janette and I remain friends and she has come with Martin, the chap she met on the motorhome trip. We seem to get on, and the man obviously makes Janette happy. Our daughter, Harry, and her husband arrived from New Zealand yesterday morning, so it is nice that her mother can enjoy her being in the UK too.

I am not sure how much we will see of the New Zealanders for a while, because Harry announced last night at a pre-wedding family dinner that we are to expect our first grandchild in May. I had tears in my eyes, thinking about my mother – if she was alive, she would have arranged to move to New Zealand straightaway, so her little great-grandchild could be the centre of her universe, just like my twin girls were.

Father welled up at the news too, while Sid declared that she would be with her twin sister for the birth, whether Harry's husband liked it or not.

The prospective Uncle Freddy just cringed at the thought, reminding everyone we were supposed to be celebrating my last night of freedom.

Jessie loved entertaining us all, accommodating all the family with their respective partners at Culmfield. She even let me invite our mutual friends Jayne and Jock, the couple who live next door to Beechwood.

The meal last night was cooked by Mary. Our chef made me laugh when she told me she expected less crying over her food than the last time she cooked for me. Jessie's daughter left after dinner by taxi, so she could stay with Billy and her Nan Dan at Fox Halt. I imagine them all there now having breakfast. Mary and Grace will be so excited. I can't wait to see them, and of course I can't wait to see Billy. I keep trying to imagine her standing in the doorway of the chapel.

Our wedding venue looks incredible – Jessie hasn't spared a penny bedecking it with flowers. But no matter how magnificent the floral displays are, Grégoire's mythical animals and spirit birds outshine them. The stunning flowers and the murals will make it hard for our guests to keep their eyes on the bride as she walks down the aisle, but nothing will be more stunning than Billy today, in my eyes.

Fox Halt Farm
Billy

Sixteen years may seem a long time to keep a dress, but it feels like only yesterday that I packed this garment in the softest tissue paper that I could lay my hands on, wondering if there would ever be a time when I'd wear it again. I gaze at the pale-blue dress, made of the finest silk and smothered in intricate lace. As I stare, my mind drifts to the wonderful afternoon when Saffi bought it for me. We were in Paris and he spent a fortune on my 'out of this world' outfit for the opera that night – such a special date with Richard, that Saffi insisted I had to look amazing.

What a man darling Saffi was; kind and fun and loving, the truest friend Richard and I ever had. I recall the top hat he wore when we visited the Champs-Elysées and all the swankiest boutiques in our search for the dress. All that afternoon, just like on many occasions later, Saffi referred to me as his beautiful wife. He was never in love with me though, our dear friend had a secret love that none of us realised, until it was all too late. I twist the ring he gave me around my finger and think how magnificent it still looks. Even more special since Richard let me use it as our engagement ring. I think of Saffi each time I see it. He got us the best seats at the Palais Garnier, and his half-sister joined us on that special night at the opera. I met lots of his friends too; the performers and all the theatre crew. This was the last time I wore this dress; a night I'll never forget, just like I'm never going to forget today.

Mum looks amazing as she walks into my room; the hairdresser has worked a magic spell on her, Grace, Mary and me. Our different hairstyles are all entwined with flowers.

'Come on, Billy, you'd better finish getting dressed,' Mum says, and I wonder how many times she has instructed me to do this in my life. 'Yes, Mum,' I say.

As she zips up the back of my dress, I hear a snuffle. 'Were you wishing Dad was here?' I ask.

'I was.'

'He is here,' I tell her, pointing to an indent in the duvet on my bed, where I sat earlier. 'Look, you can see where he is sitting.'

'Yes, darling, he is,' she says, and then she sits down next to the dip in the bed cover. She turns her head. 'Hey, Jack. I'm sure you're as proud of our little girl as me.'

I am in tears as Mum holds out a small box. 'This is from us both,' she says. 'It's a replica of the necklace your dad gave me on our wedding day. Sorry I couldn't let you have the original, I still need mine.' She taps her fingers on the heart-shaped locket outlined in little diamonds on the chain around her neck.

'You look beautiful, Mum. Dad would have been so proud of you too.' I hold up my present. 'Will you help me with the clasp, please?'

'Yes, but then we must go, Herbie's been waiting outside fifteen minutes already. Grace and Mary are with him, and Grace is being merciless, teasing him about his outfit, despite her looking as out of place as him, all dressed up to the nines.'

I look at Mum and then glance to the side of her. 'Thank you, both, for everything,' I say.

The ceremony was a blur. I fixed my eyes on Richard and kept them there. I repeated words the vicar instructed me to repeat, and I put a gold ring on Richard's finger. He gave me his mother's wedding ring, and we kissed.

Mrs MarcFenn. No, not Mrs MarcFenn, because Richard did the same thing my dad did, he took my surname. He made a short speech, just like Dad, about how Fox Halt Farm had been in the May family for years, and that's how it was going to stay. I haven't asked him how he plans that to continue for the next generation. He knows we will never have children. It's just not a subject I can talk about, but there you are, the May name lives on for another generation. My parents, and grandparents before them, would not have foreseen how that could have happened either.

Before we leave the chapel, I place my bouquet on Saffi's grave. My husband runs his finger under his name. 'We wouldn't be together now if it wasn't for you, Saffi,' he says. Richard traces the date. 'Billy, eight years without him.' I squeeze his hand. 'We have each other though,' I say. 'And Saffi would be so happy we are married at last.'

Richard

I get the last word. I didn't think I would because while Jessie drove us to Gatwick, Billy wouldn't stop talking about our day. I kept on reminding her that I was there too, but she just wouldn't shut up.

She talked about the Battenberg wedding cake that her mum made for us, and how Grace looked so beautiful that my son couldn't keep his eyes off her.

She told me my father and her mother talked all afternoon and long into the evening. The two of them have decided to go to New Zealand as soon as Harry's baby is born, and when Daniella said she'd never been abroad before, Father said he'd make sure she was fine on the long flight.

Billy laughed about how drunk Herbie had got and how kind it was of Jessie to make a detour to take him home.

She cried over William and Mary leaving early so they could get back to Fox Halt Farm to milk the cows. And she cried some more when she saw her old flat-mate from university, Simon, and his wife. The couple invited us to stay with them in the South of France, telling us how their daughter is planning a degree course at Exeter University. On and on, laughing and happy with every little detail until she fell asleep on my shoulder.

Jessie stops the car at the terminal's carpark. 'Enjoy Paros,' she tells us.

'Thank you,' Billy says. 'Thank you for being my friend again.'

Jessie smiles, showing her dimples as her phone beeps. 'It's Herbie Harris,' she says, 'he's left his house keys at Culmfield, so he got a taxi back to the estate. He says Arthur has sorted one of the master bedrooms for him to stay in tonight. The cheeky man suggests we have breakfast together and is asking if I would pick up some bacon and some eggs too.' Her car engine roars into life. 'I'll tell you what I replied to Mr Harris when you get back.' Jessie laughs.

Many hours later, I see our honeymoon hotel perched high on a cliff overlooking the sea – the beginning of our future.

Epilogue

MONDAY 7 DECEMBER 2015

A woman newsreader talks over live pictures. 'Flood-water has swept away the one-hundred-and-fifty-year-old Pooley Bridge. This is a very important crossing for residents and tourists alike.

'Not only has the historic bridge been washed away, but the lake has over-spilled its banks. Ullswater Steamers Pier is drowned. Properties are swamped, and sheep are stranded on a thin island that was a wide field only yesterday.'

Her report continues. 'The River Eamont has caused widespread devastation. This waterway flows into the River Eden and parts of Carlisle are flooded badly too. Many roads are impassable with land slips, flooding and fallen trees.'

For the third time, I replay the sequence; there is an isolated stone building with its front wall missing. Its rafters torn apart by a fallen beech tree. Half inside the remaining structure is a Rolls Royce Silver Spur II Touring Limousine. The nose of the car is partly submerged but I can still identify the special model. The image isn't very clear, but it is possible that upper half of the number plate reads. 'ROWD'.

I am certain this is the car that Amir Bileh drove away seven years ago. The vehicle has not been seen since. I frown hard…

–o–o–

Can I Ask for Your Help, Please?

I hope you enjoyed this book. If you did, please post a short review on Amazon and/or on Goodreads. Reviews make a huge difference in helping others discover my books. They help a good deal with the success of my novels too.

Your review doesn't need to be long, just a couple of lines would be great. I assure you each and every one will be read and is greatly appreciated!

Please recommend my books to your friends.

Acknowledgements

So many people have helped me to create my books – I have to thank the following: my husband Paul, my mother, my daughter Kate, and Tracey Lee, Emz Whaling, Heather Legge, Jane Burrows, Carol Noble-Smith, Rachel Gilbey, Curworthy Cheese, Elaine Morgan & Rachel Stephens.

Thank you to everyone else who helped with advice and encouragement along the way, especially Anne Williams.

I painted the picture on the front cover but the amazing Harrison Pidgeon put the design together.

Thank you to my editor, Amanda Horan, who is totally brilliant at what she does, opening my eyes to so many better ways to get my story across. Without her extraordinary help and knowledge, I could never have felt the delight I have for my books. Thank you too, Julia Gibbs, for proof reading and finding all the mistakes I would never have seen.

And finally, thank you for reading my book. Without you, I couldn't have the joy of sharing my passion for telling my stories.

Celia Moore

Fox Halt Farm
Fields of Dreams
Acres of Secrets

A sweeping story of love, families, betrayal and heartbreak
ANNE WILLIAMS – TOP 1000 AMAZON VINE REVIEWER

Celia Moore

A Hare's Footprint
Grasping at Dreams
Part 3 of the Fox Halt Farm Trilogy

Celia Moore

Other Books by Celia Moore

Culmfield Cuckoo is the sequel to Fox Halt Farm and the final part in this trilogy is *A Hare's Footprint*.

If you would like to know when more books will be available, or have questions about the author's writing or her talks about writing her novels, please contact Celia: she would love to hear from you.

Website Celiascosmos.com
Facebook Celia Moore Books

cMb

Printed in Great Britain
by Amazon